Amber Raven carries ~~~~~~~~~~~~~~~~~~~~~~~~~~~~~ nd whilst her bones agre~~~~~~~~~~~~~~~~~~~~~~~~~~ her husband, three adult c~~~~~~~~~~~~~~~~~~~~~~~~~~ ght have other thoughts on the matter!

Born on Hallowe'en, her fascination with anything Wiccan-related spans nigh on fifty-five years. During her later years, Amber turned her attention to reading more about the white witch and their magick. She has waited many years to release her fantasy childhood friend Myrtle into the real world as a fictional character, Myrtle Netherwell – a witch with the knowledge and skills to turn weeds and herbs into medicine.

A visit to Weybourne in Norfolk, England triggered the urge to write, and *The Weybourne Witches* began its journey from head to paper.

When not writing, Amber enjoys relaxing with Reiki and Sound Bath sessions. She attempts exercise with minimal success, reads, walks a lively Cockapoo and loves coffee breaks with girlfriends.

www.amberravenauthor.com

instagram.com/amberraven_author
facebook.com/amberravenauthor

THE WEYBOURNE WITCHES

AMBER RAVEN

One More Chapter
a division of HarperCollins*Publishers* Ltd
1 London Bridge Street
London SE1 9GF
www.harpercollins.co.uk
HarperCollins*Publishers*
Macken House, 39/40 Mayor Street Upper,
Dublin 1, D01 C9W8, Ireland

This paperback edition 2025
1
First published in Great Britain in ebook format
by HarperCollins*Publishers* 2025
Copyright © Amber Raven 2025
Amber Raven asserts the moral right to
be identified as the author of this work

ISBN: 978-0-00-870758-3

Printed and bound in the UK using 100% Renewable Electricity
by CPI Group (UK) Ltd

To my husband and best friend, Peter.

The man who supports me and my work, who respects and understands my spiritual journey without question or concern.

Here's to the day we met and fifty years of friendship and love – thank you.

The real me
xxx

Kelling Heath

Plumtree Cottage

Beach

Weybourne Village

Shop

The Ship Inn

When Mother calls, sisters — heed her word,
Tend to her roots,
Feed and nourish.

When a Sister shines,
See her light,
Praise and encourage.
Unity in both will uplift the world.

Amber Raven

The Tree of Life

I am the eternal sentinel, a bridge between the realms of the living and the dead. I am the custodian of secrets whispered on the winds and echoed through the ages.

The combined energies of the Netherwell sisterhood at life's end nurture me. I am their tree alone. No other can hear the words I channel from the depths of my roots.

My gnarled bark holds the echoes of forgotten centuries, and my leaves shimmer with the essence of countless souls. In the hushed twilight, beneath the moon's silvery glow, or on a summer's morn, I release the haunting memories of bygone eras through the voice of a soul reaching out.

Each tale of triumph and tribulation woven intricately into the fabric of time becomes a beacon of light for those who sit with open hearts and wait in anticipation beneath my outstretched boughs and listen. As the constellations weave their cosmic patterns, I reveal the ancient spells and wise magic gifted by their foremothers to the living.

Ragnis

For generations, my family have watched over the Netherwell women.

I am devoted to Myrtle and live to serve the Netherwell witches of Weybourne.

Their pain is my pain, and their joy is my joy. Their fear of the past trembles on the wind, and the darkness that seeks them out grows stronger.

Chapter One

1841

Camomile and buttercups surround me as I open my legs to allow my child into the world beneath the Tree of Life.

I am not a devil's whore, nor a seducer of men, as cruel Mistress Longe would have folk believe; I had been her scullery maid.

I am Hazel, the daughter of a white witch.

I hear voices in the wind, see faces in the clouds, and shadows crouch with cat-like eyes in the corner of our home – waiting to pounce and take my child from me – but I accepted my place within the sisterhood and learned the skills of banishment.

I hear the heartbeats of my ancestors within the walls of our cottage. They offer hope against the threat of the Longe family, whose aim is to ensure we wither and die – and a

Netherwell woman will never heal or nurture the planet ever again.

Our witch bloodline is torn in two: light and dark.

As I gripped the ground in pain, I felt the power of a woman giving birth, and when I looked at my daughter, she was as delicate as the flowers in the Weybourne meadow and as beautiful. I named her Daisy Mystia, and I hope she has not inherited the dark side of her father, a distant relative of a grandfather many times removed.

The trickery of the dark mind is to be feared.

Myrtle Netherwell

Myrtle Netherwell sat exhausted at her desk, unable to read any more.

She looked around her home; fragrant herbs hung, drying from nails hammered into the low ceiling beams by women over hundreds of years. Brickwork dipped with decades of scrubbing, and the fireplace stained black with smoke burned a large fire as it had done from the day the cottage was habitable. Heirlooms and tools valuable to witchcraft sat proudly on the tops of wooden furniture made by independent women learning to survive in a world filled with people intent on hurling accusations their way.

On her desk in front of Myrtle was an oversized old leather book engraved, *The Netherwell Book of Voices*. A tremor of nervous emotion shimmied throughout her body as she stroked the cover. Myrtle could feel the tingle of anticipation of the book, waiting to be read and to hear a new voice.

Her ancestors had sat and carried out the task for hundreds of years in the same home, and now it was her turn to record her personal life story.

Candles – one white and one orange – representing creativity and calm flickered on her altar, and the incense burner wafted out a fragrance, Herbal Dream. Casting her eye around the room to ensure no unwelcome shadows still lurked amongst the colourful furnishings, Myrtle took a moment to ponder the words she wanted to record about her history up to its final victory.

Three large logs on the fire crackled and shared their warmth around her sitting room in Plumtree Cottage. The home mentioned in the words she had just read.

Like so many other Netherwell women, Hazel's story was one Myrtle related to the most.

She had also given birth in the woods.

Lying her arms with palms face down across the book, Myrtle closed her eyes and inhaled all the room offered her. The incense, the wood burning and the smell of old leather stimulated a stillness and a sense of serenity inside her. She touched the rose quartz crystal that hung around her neck, a family heirloom smooth and glistening thanks to the many hands that had handled it when seeking a moment of peace for themselves.

'Bless my home and the spirits who keep me company. Grant me the emotional courage to record my journey past and present. I thank the Mother of all nature for giving me another day to enjoy her offerings – the beauty of the planet and beyond. Today is a good day, and may tomorrow be the same. May my writing be clear and without error. As I wish it, so mote it be.'

Lifting a new sheet of cream parchment paper, she began writing, her fountain pen making a satisfactory scratching sound as she wrote.

Merry Meet, Ancestral Voices.

My name is Myrtle Netherwell, and today, I am writing my story for The Netherwell Book of Voices.

Two months have passed since my twin sister passed over. It was a natural death, and I nursed her until the end. I witnessed the moment her spirit joined our mother's and other ancestors living beyond the veil of this universe, but I will write down the memory another day. Marigold and I are the only recorded set of twins born to a Netherwell witch of such long descent, and it was a phenomenon the sisterhood was unprepared for, to the point they considered leaving me, the second born, to die. We were born May 1st 1963.

As I understand it, this was to ensure they watched over only one child and to teach her to challenge the Longe family – our enemy. The argument went against those in the sisterhood who wished me dead, and I survived. I do not resent those who feared protecting the two of us; my mother fought for me, and that is all I can ask for in a woman who sometimes struggled in life.

I became the Netherwell with light in her veins. Marigold

was the opposite of me. I am short; she was tall and willowy. If I laughed, you could guarantee Marigold would be scowling. Yin and Yang. We had one thing in common besides our mother: our red hair. Rich, fox red. In the stories within the book, each woman writes they have red hair – our trademark as Netherwell women.

Marigold was a loner. I like being alone, but I am happy to socialise. Mari – and she did not like me calling her by that name – did not like people. Animals, plants and dark magick were her style. She inherited a magick she could not control. Again, within my story, I will attempt to describe how this affected us.

With Marigold dead, the ancestors had to suppress my twin's power in the afterlife to prevent our enemy from increasing their power tenfold. Marigold's magick was to harm, to bring fear to those she met. It was the cause of her troubled mind, from childhood until the age of sixty. Mine was and is to regain control.

What we call The Longe Bloodline seeks revenge for what it sees as crimes against them. Yet it is created from generations of deceptive men issuing accusations or physical violence against the women in my family. According to the book, they committed more crimes than they received.

In her first entry in the book, in 1670, Willow Netherwell tells a family story about the possible beginnings of how the dark evil entered our family line. Before the Iron Age, a male witch, Wolfstone Longe, leaned heavily towards the dark occult. He overpowered his cousin, a Netherwell white witch who led a life as a midwife and healer, and she conceived his child. *The woman tried to hide her son from the cousin she hated, but failed. As the boy grew, she lost control of her son to his father, and it became apparent that his inquisitive nature towards the occult and the developing powers were more potent than his father's. She became a subservient prisoner, giving birth to many more children. Daughters were removed from the home, but any male born was encouraged to follow the dark side, and their demonic genes were released into the world. The white witch, proving she was no longer a threat to the cousin, was left to her own devices, and she formed a coven, encouraging her daughters to become healers and escape the confines of the village. They met and worked on spells and magick to protect themselves.*

Their kindly blood mix merged with others over generations, but one Longe male son noticed that only the combination of the Netherwell and Longe blood appeared to host magickal power. He realised this was an advantage for increasing their control over the Netherwell white witches and commanded the Longe males to seek out and bed only the women of the Netherwell bloodline. Their mission was to absorb the dark power the women suppressed.

A dark demonic clan of Druid males formed in the Otherworld and found a way to mingle amongst the living, hunting down the witches. They perfected the art of manifesting evil intent and weakened Netherwell women to lie with them.

According to word of mouth and Willow's simple handwritten rendition. During the medieval period, it became apparent a Netherwell white witch had a powerful magick, and her female ancestors gave Theda Netherwell a mission. She was to kill a Viking, Ingulf Longe.

Theda achieved her goal. Sadly, she was already with child, and his death inflamed the Longe bloodline further. When she gave birth to a daughter, it became clear that no Netherwell woman was safe from that day on. The clan had already chosen a mate for her, and in her thirteenth year, when her magick arrived, the chosen one was to bed her and increase the clan.

Another recording by Willow was that of her mother's death. Brigid Netherwell settled a curse on the man who attacked her – Willow's father – as she burned at the stake. His death and the demise of his son strengthened the desire for revenge and added power to the dark demon, creating his army in the afterlife.

According to Willow, she was born with the gift of shapeshifting, an error in Longe's bloodline's choice of a male to lie with her. She suggests she was a powerful witch, but I think the white witch blood was not strong enough over the years, as only three Netherwell women are left in our bloodline.

During the night, the last of the dark demons were banished from the cottage for all time. The last one turned, its amber eyes glowing, then faded into nothing. I felt it disappear; leaving my raging body cold on the inside and, for a brief second, lifeless.

My twin has finally been defeated.

Turning back time was not within my power, but ensuring a peaceful future is, and as I wish it, so mote it be...

Born Myrtle Netherwell, daughter of Moonstone Netherwell, High Priestess of The Weybourne Coven. Written in her 61st year.

Myrtle laid down her pen and read through what she had written.

'It reads like a story, like fiction,' she muttered, closing the book.

Her hand stroked the cat, now purring on her lap. His wild cries had alerted her to the invasion of shadows.

'And here I am, a witch with a black cat asleep on my lap; how cliché can you get, Nightshade?'

The cat responded with a deep purr.

A tap on the window made Myrtle look up from her feline friend and smile.

'Ragnis. On time as always.' The iridescent blue-black of the raven's wings shone as the winter sunshine settled on the window ledge.

'Off you jump, Nightshade. We have visitors,' Myrtle said, looking at the clock and waiting for it to chime ten o'clock. Her daughter and granddaughter were never late.

As two shadows moved across the frozen grass, she walked to the front door and waited for the tap-tap before pulling it open.

'Blessings, Gai, Summer, come in, kettle's on.'

Her daughter kissed her cheek. 'You do not have to let us in every time, Mum. Welcoming us across the threshold is not necessary. And something smells good,' Gaia added, sniffing the air.

Myrtle touched her cheek where her daughter's warm lips had left their precious greeting.

'Ah, but had you hesitated, I would know my black salt and protection pouches have caught out an unwelcome soul in disguise,' she replied, laughing.

Her granddaughter, Summer, moved towards her, and Myrtle hugged her closely.

'Are you expecting unwelcome souls, Gran?' Summer asked, a seriousness edging her words.

Myrtle smiled. 'No, darling. I've cleansed the cottage to the rooftops today – banished them forever. I just love greeting you two at the door.'

Nightshade wound himself around their legs, purring for attention.

'Hello, puss,' Summer said, bending down to scratch his ears, then picking him up.

They moved into the sitting room, and Gaia walked over to the dresser where Myrtle had laid the family book and pen when they arrived.

'Are you writing Marigold's story?' she asked softly, one finger stroking the book's cover.

Myrtle, now at the large cauldron over the fire, stirred vegetables in the old pot, which was nearly a hundred years old. Myrtle loved to cook using the traditional methods her mother had taught her.

'After last night's cleansing, I started writing my memories in the book, adding fragments of our story. I've read the ones already written many years ago, but I am reconnecting with them again. One day, you and Summer will do it and so on.' Myrtle shrugged. 'Marigold's death made me realise how fragile life is and how important some traditions are for families like ours.'

Putting Nightshade down on the floor and encouraging him towards his food bowl, Summer gave a soft tut. 'Well, I hope I don't have to read your story for years!' she said, smiling at her grandmother.

'It might be wise to read it while I'm still alive. I can answer questions better than I can when writing things down. By the way, I love your new hairstyle – bouncy curls – gorgeous,' Myrtle replied.

Myrtle marvelled at how alike the three of them looked – each a golden redhead – the Netherwell female trait. Gaia's hair was a softer shade, sandier in colour; still, she was her mother's daughter in mind and spirit, more serious than Summer, not so random as Marigold – her twin, who had been the complete opposite of Myrtle, with a wild temper and a dark soul. Marigold's death had brought calm and peace to the home, but her presence was missed, especially in the garden, where her skills were unbeaten.

'Well, I, for one, want to read the book. I did start a few years ago, but then life and business got in the way. Let me know when you've finished, and I'll take a peek; just imagine hundreds of years' worth of words waiting for us to read, Summer,' Gaia said, pouring each of them a hibiscus and pea flower tea.

'When I've finished that, I will add to the recipe book for the business,' Myrtle said.

'I realised it all needs to come out of here before I join

the ancestors'—she tapped the side of her head, giving a light laugh—'and I've had an idea about a new face-care product for Naturally Netherwell's spring collection, "The Marigold Range".'

Both Gaia and Summer clapped their hands.

'Wonderful. What a lovely way to remember your sister. I'll get onto the printer once Mum has designed the brand. I take it you have already worked out a recipe?' Summer said, with the excited enthusiasm of a puppy.

Myrtle laughed. 'Slow down; I only had the idea this morning. My brain is good, but it doesn't work at your speed. We'll go over it another day. Now eat your carrot cake,' she instructed, cutting a generous slice and pushing it towards Summer.

'I thought about the first pot of rose face cream I made in the eighties. When I collected the rosehips and petals, I never thought it would lead to a worldwide selling brand,' said Myrtle.

Gaia smiled at her. 'You worked hard, Mum, and deserve the success. Without you, Aunt Marigold would have ended up in care at seventeen. We're very proud of you, and I'm sure she was, in her way.'

Now that two of the most important people in her life had returned home, and were fed and watered, Myrtle settled down to think about what her ancestors had asked of her. She decided the best route was to write down more memories, and remind herself of the times she did have the strength to endure whatever life threw her way.

Chapter Two

1968

'Girls!' Myrtle and Marigold's mother called out from the doorway of their cottage.

'I have fed the chickens already; leave them. Come here, it is an exciting day!'

'Quick, Mari, Mummy wants us now,' Myrtle told her sister, who was still throwing corn into the chicken coop. 'She has fed them.'

'But I haven't, and I love feeding the chickens,' Marigold retorted, still throwing the corn.

'Girls!' Their mother's voice echoed out again.

'Coming!' Myrtle called back and grabbed Marigold's arm.

'Stop, Marigold. It must be important.'

Rushing through the garden, Myrtle tugged at a stem of

lavender and handed it to Marigold. 'It smells beautiful,' she said, sliding her fingers along a stem. She crushed the flowers between her palms and rubbed the oily residue in her hair and around her neck. Marigold copied.

'There you are. Come inside. I have something to tell you,' she said and turned away from them.

Marigold made a face at Myrtle. 'I want to stay outside. It is sunny, and we can play in the woods,' she said.

Myrtle shook her head. 'Later, Mummy needs us for something. Let's do as she says, and we can play later.' She nudged Marigold inside.

On the table was a brightly coloured bag and a pile of towels.

'Get your bathing suits on. We're going to the beach for a picnic. It's Mummy's birthday!' their mother said, clapping her hands.

Myrtle joined in the clapping.

'Happy birthday, Mummy.' She rushed forward to hug her, but her mother's face remained focused on Marigold.

'Marigold, aren't you excited about a day at the beach?' she asked, and Myrtle turned to look at her sister. Marigold's face revealed that she was far from excited. She was in a sulky mood. She wanted to stay at home and feed the chickens.

'We can collect shells,' Myrtle said, hoping to inspire her sister's collecting habit.

'Go and change. Your swimsuits and sundresses are on your beds.'

Marigold sighed.

'A dress? I want to wear shorts.' She scowled. 'I *hate* dresses.'

'Do not make this day difficult, Marigold. Go and change,' their mother scolded.

Not wanting to miss out on their day together, Myrtle ran upstairs, changing her clothes as fast as possible. Her pretty dress was lemon, and she knew their mother would have made one in green for Marigold. She always made their clothes in their favourite colours.

'There's my favourite girls. Both of you are as pretty as a picture. It's time to go and have fun.'

Their mother picked up her bag and handed them both a towel. As she turned her back to them, Marigold poked out her tongue. Myrtle frowned at her.

They walked through the narrow lane and onto the street across from the church. The post office was busy with people queuing and chatting outside, and Myrtle skipped to the end of the road, waiting patiently for her mother to allow her to cross.

Dragging her heels and moaning, Marigold took her time, and Myrtle could see their mother becoming flustered, so she ran back to Marigold.

'Come on, Mari, let's see if we can find a crab today. You like crabs.'

She reached out and took her twin's hand, leading her to the end of the road, where their mother gave the all-clear for traffic. Once on the other side of the road, Marigold let go of Myrtle's hand.

'I don't want to go!' she shouted, and stomped her foot.

All eyes were on them, and Myrtle knew her mother would be embarrassed.

'Well, I want to go. It is my birthday, and we will have fun. Now off you run,' her mother said to Marigold, who rushed ahead towards the long hedge-lined lane leading to the beach.

'Not too far, Marigold,' their mother called out, and sighed.

'Myrtle, make sure she doesn't go in the water yet. It is far too deep for her. You can paddle in the rock pools when I get there,' she said, taking Myrtle's towel from her so that she could run after her sister.

As soon as Marigold realised Myrtle was chasing after her, she screamed for her to go away, but Myrtle persisted.

'Stop screaming,' she called out. 'Mummy's not happy, this is supposed to be a special day for her.'

Marigold turned to her and snatched at Myrtle's lengthy pigtail.

'I want a birthday. I want a birthday!' she said, pulling Myrtle's hair so hard that she squealed out in pain.

Their mother left the basket on the ground and rushed to Myrtle.

'What on earth is going on with you, Marigold?' she demanded, leaning down to check the back of Myrtle's head. 'No harm done. Now stop grizzling – what in goodness is she up to now?' she muttered, as Marigold was busy throwing their lunch from the basket into the small brook.

'Marigold, stop!' she called out, but Marigold ignored

her, still intent on unwrapping the food and throwing it into the water.

'The fish are hungry. I want to go home!' she declared, then returned to where they had come. Their mother ran after her.

'Grab my basket and follow us home, Myrtle!' she shouted over her shoulder.

Despite her arms aching from carrying the basket and flask home, Myrtle had kept quiet. Grumbling at Marigold for ruining the day would not help their mother, who now sat on the back porch, singing to herself in the rocking chair, which was said to be more than a hundred years old.

Myrtle need not have been there, but it was evident to her that a sadness weighed heavily on her mother's heart, and she chose to sit quietly at her feet.

Her mother looked at her, and her stare puzzled Myrtle.

'I'm sorry we made your birthday unhappy, Mummy,' she said softly, hoping her mother would remember they still needed to eat.

Her mother stroked Myrtle's head, turned away and continued sipping her drink.

The following day, Myrtle rose early. She checked on her sister, who still slept, and then tiptoed downstairs. She had not heard their mother come to her room during the night and suspected she had fallen asleep on the sofa.

Instead, she found her writing in a large book at the table.

'What are you writing, Mummy?' she asked.

'Witch magick,' her mother replied, glancing at Myrtle with tired eyes before returning to her book.

'Magick?' Myrtle was fascinated. 'Are you a witch?' she asked in a hushed voice.

'We all are,' her mother replied matter-of-factly, and Myrtle giggled.

'I am not a witch. I do not have a black cat or a broomstick,' she protested.

At this, her mother laid down her pen and looked at her with a gentle smile.

'No, but you have Ragnis and the besom outside the door. When you hear me sing, it is my chant work, spells to protect us. But it would be best if you don't tell anyone, Myrtle. No one, not even Marigold. She is not very good at keeping secrets. People are scared of witches, and they will tell you horrid things about them.'

Myrtle stared at her mother, alarmed, until her mother laughed.

'I am having fun with you. This is my recipe book,' she said swiftly, but Myrtle saw the same blush to her mother's cheeks that Marigold had when she told lies.

'It was a funny joke, Mummy,' she replied, but something stirred inside her, a notion about her mother, who she thought always told the truth.

'Now, I want you both to play in the woods today while I make jam and chutney for the market. Let Marigold be the hero today – no squabbling over dragons,' her mother said, tweaking Myrtle's nose.

'She can be the hunter; she always wants to be the hunter. I am going to be a witch – just like you,' Myrtle replied, drawing her hands into claw shapes, and snarling.

Her mother gave the loudest laugh and startled Myrtle.

'Darling girl, you will make the best witch ever and one day, you can join my friends and me in making spells.'

Myrtle squealed in delight, just as Marigold walked through the door, bleary-eyed and hungry, as always.

'You are so noisy,' she declared grumpily and sat down at the breakfast table.

Automatically, Myrtle did the same, and their mother laid down her pen.

'I will make you some sandwiches to take into the woods once you have finished feeding the animals,' she said, and without a word, Marigold turned to Myrtle.

There were days when they rarely spoke but knew what one another wanted. They did not read minds but sensed emotions. Their first day at school was strange, but they clung together arm in arm, not needing anyone else for friendship.

Myrtle felt her twin relax, and she smiled. Marigold smiled back, and they ran out into the garden. Once they had finished their chores, they grabbed the small paper bag containing jam sandwiches and an apple each. They filled an empty glass juice bottle with cool water from the well near the oak tree.

Myrtle and Marigold had fun without arguing while playing in the woods together. Both relaxed into their roles of imaginary fearless knights, magical fairies and witches. Marigold battled dragons and saved Myrtle from wicked elves.

'What do you want to be when you grow up, Mari?' Myrtle asked her sister as they sat eating their apples, the sandwiches long gone.

'A gardener,' Marigold replied, taking a bite of her apple.

Myrtle nodded. Marigold's love of gardening and her knowledge at such a young age did not surprise her; Myrtle and their mother often discussed it.

'I want to be a witch,' Myrtle said. 'I want to make potions and spells, then fly on my broomstick at night. I want to fly with Ragnis.' She pointed to the raven sitting in the tree, looking down at them.

'Witches aren't real. They are magic, and not just anyone can be one, silly,' Marigold said pompously.

'Not true!' Myrtle said, thinking but careful not to mention what their mother had told her earlier. Her mother might have laughed, but something in her face had suggested she was completely serious.

During the summer of their eighth year, the sisters stumbled across a vixen and her cubs and quietly lay amongst the grasses, watching them tumble and play. Soon, Marigold became bored of them and headed into the woods, searching for dragons.

Myrtle and Ragnis watched the little family and stared in awe when the vixen stopped and looked at them. Myrtle felt a sense of having met the fox before, and when the fox dipped its head, she swore she saw a smile play across its lips.

'Hello. Don't be afraid. Ragnis trusts me; you can trust me too,' Myrtle whispered, holding out her hand. The fox walked closer, eventually placing its head beneath Myrtle's hand. A tingling warmth ran up Myrtle's arm, just as, suddenly, Ragnis flew up into the treetops and Marigold rushed into the clearing.

Marigold stopped and stared at the fox.

'I want to stroke it!' she demanded, and her voice broke the moment. Myrtle saw a sudden change in the fox's eyes, a fear, and it backed away with its tail between its legs as Marigold reached out; it gave a swift glance of panic at Myrtle before running to its cubs and urging them back into the safety of the woods.

'Come back!' Marigold shouted and reached down, picking up a stone. She threw it towards the retreating fox.

'Stop that, it's cruel!' Myrtle cried. 'Why did you have to shout? You could have stroked her if you had been quiet.' She was disappointed that her time with the fox had been cut short because her sister had frightened it away. 'You always have to spoil things!'

Marigold stomped off and left Myrtle wishing she had other friends to play with. Then, she felt guilty and rushed after her twin.

'Let's paddle in the beck, Mari!' she called out, not wanting to fall foul of her sister's temper for the rest of the day.

That evening, they climbed into bed, exhausted from playing in the river, bug hunting and eating blackberries.

The happy Marigold was the sister Myrtle loved the most. She invented the best games, tested out the scary corners of the woods first, and gave Myrtle victory hugs. In those moments, Myrtle felt the love between them.

As the years progressed, Myrtle and Marigold shared adventures, playing imaginary games in the woods. The fox only returned when Myrtle was alone – when she sat shelling peas or stripping dried herbs from their stems. The vixen would wait for an invitation to sit at her feet, and each time it did, Myrtle felt a connection, as if it were human. The fox cubs were now adults, and sometimes they brought their own families to meet her; Myrtle treasured the moments, keeping them secret from her sister for fear of them running away.

As she neared her teenage years, Myrtle started to think about life without Marigold always at her side. As much as she loved her sister, she wanted to experience fun times with others her age.

Their mother tried her best to keep the peace between them, but tension and division grew between her daughters, so she learned to walk away and let them both work it out for themselves. Myrtle often found her mother asleep beside a part-empty bottle of honey mead and knew the following day that she would have to fend for herself and remind Marigold to eat or drink before dusk.

Chapter Three

'Morning, Nightshade,' Myrtle said between yawns.

She pulled back the green-checked curtains at the kitchen window and noted that the ground was damp with dew and not as frosty as the previous day. She broke apart a suet and mealworm loaf and crumbled it onto a plate. At the back door, she tapped the dish with a spoon.

'Morning, Ragnis,' she called out, and just as Nightshade bounded out into the garden, the raven flew to his feeding spot by the door.

Having enjoyed the best sleep she had managed for weeks, Myrtle felt energised and alert.

She turned on the radio, something her sister used to object to when she sat at the breakfast table. Now, it was part of Myrtle's new routine. She avoided the news. The world was in a state of unrest, and she refused to allow it into her life. She focused on Harry, the love of her life, and her daughter and granddaughter, her smallholding, skincare creations, and walks in the woods. Nature soothed her soul.

As she spooned fresh honey over her porridge, she listened to the opening beats of a song, and suddenly, she was transported back to the early 1970s and her thirteenth birthday, and her best friend Eve.

'I think "Breathe in The Air" is my favourite,' Myrtle said to her best friend from school, Evelyn Blakeney, 'but I quite like "The Great Gig in the Sky".'

Eve shook her shoulders, 'No, that one is about dying. I prefer "Breathe",' she said as she lifted her vinyl record from its player.

Myrtle sighed happily, leaning back on Eve's bed. 'I'm having the best birthday,' she said. 'Thank you, Eve, for introducing me to Pink Floyd – and your new record player. I'm jealous!'

'Dad got fed up with me using his every time you came over,' Eve replied. 'He decided I was ready to have my own.'

'You are so lucky,' Myrtle said. 'Mum doesn't have that kind of money to spend on us, and Marigold is not great at sharing.'

Eve looked wistful.

'You're the lucky one; having a sister,' she said. 'Try being an only child!'

With a shake of her head, Myrtle kept silent. The words

inside her head were not to be said out loud. Life with Marigold was becoming ever more difficult, and their mother just ignored her sister's tantrums now. When Myrtle objected to Marigold's tyrannical behaviour, her mother simply shushed her and said they had to help Marigold control her temper.

Marigold's hotheaded ways put her mother in many difficult positions, and Myrtle struggled to understand how they had turned out so differently as twins.

'Marigold gets meaner every day, and Mum lets her get away with it. She has trouble fitting in with people, but I'm her twin. She should like me, and I should like her, but some days ... I really don't!' Myrtle allowed her pent-up frustration with her sister to fly free.

'Finished?' Eve asked, and they both burst into giggles.

'You're such a good friend; I don't know what I'd do without you,' Myrtle said.

'I feel the same; you are my closest friend; you understand my mum, and I understand yours,' Eve replied.

Myrtle laughed. 'If you understand my mum, perhaps you can explain her to me. She is drinking more, and we hardly ever laugh these days. I sometimes miss our days of hunting fairies or chasing dragons with her in the woods. The mum I know is disappearing.'

'We're teenagers,' Eve retorted. 'Well, you are now you're thirteen. It's like my mum says. We've grown out of childish stuff now.'

Myrtle nodded but kept her thoughts to herself. Despite being a hedgewitch, Eve's mother, was more traditional than hers. Moonstone drank more every day. The empty bottles at home waiting to become candleholders were proof of that.

———————

Nothing changed on the morning of their thirteenth birthday; chores were carried out, their usual porridge breakfast was eaten, and Marigold squabbled with their mother about buying another goat.

'We have four; that is quite enough. I don't want to hear another word about it, Marigold,' her mother said and moved to the sink. Concentrate on those we do have. And today, you girls will stick together. No arguments, no sulking. Understand?'

Myrtle nodded, though she resented being made to spend the day with Marigold.

Later, as they cleaned out the goat shed, Marigold began to whistle.

'You're happy,' Myrtle said with a half-hearted smile.

'Of course I am; it's my birthday,' Marigold replied, 'the day when everyone wanted me to live and not you.'

Myrtle stopped and stared at her sister.

'How cruel can you get? What a bitch you are, Marigold Netherwell. What on earth made you say that? One day your words will bite you on the arse!' she growled, stomping out of the barn and into the woods.

'It's the truth, and I'm telling Mum you swore at me,' Marigold shouted after her, and her laughter rang in

Myrtle's ears until she felt the calming effect of the woods soothe her.

Ragnis flew to her side.

'Oh, Ragnis.' Myrtle shook her head. 'Marigold said horrible things about me when we were born. I hate her!'

'Hush now. Hate is a strong word to use.'

It was a female voice, and startled, Myrtle looked around her, confused, but could see no one there.

'Who are you?' she demanded, spooked that someone had heard her talking to Ragnis.

'I am everywhere,' the voice replied. 'Today, I am a small bird; yesterday, I was a rabbit, but mostly, I am the fox who has been at your side for years. I am Willow, your spirit guide. Take yourself to the great tree, listen to the music of the breeze and know that the ancestors love you. Those who voiced against you regret their words.'

Myrtle spun around full circle, trying to see who she was talking to. 'Voiced against me? What ... on earth are you on about? Marigold said something horrid and weird like that this morning. It's my birthday, leave me alone!' she said, agitated.

But then, suddenly, an overwhelming urge to sit beneath the Tree of Life took hold, and although Myrtle tried hard to ignore it, she eventually caved in and made her way to the clearing. From her pocket, she lifted a crystal.

'Greetings, wise tree. I bring you the gift of quartz for energy and my thanks for the air I breathe,' she said, at once realising, with amazement, that she had just heard the spirit of her ancestor, someone who had been alive hundreds of years before.

Her mother had always told them that death was not to be feared, and spirits would guide them through both good and bad times. Remembering this, Myrtle relaxed, a comforting peace washing over her, enveloping her like a warm embrace. The gentle rush of a breeze danced through the trees; she imagined them whispering secrets of ancient roots and dreams. The soft tweet of the little bird wove through the air, a delicate note of joy, while the vibrant buzz of a bee flitted by, a reminder of nature's busy magic.

Sunlight filtered through the leaves, casting playful patterns on the ground as if the forest was painting a masterpiece just for her. In this enchanted moment, time felt suspended, and Myrtle breathed in the fragrant earthiness of moss and wildflowers, feeling her upset dissolve like morning mist. Here, in this serene sanctuary, the world outside faded away, leaving only the harmony of nature and the gentle rhythm of her heart.

Although the day had started like any other, and she had envied friends who had parties and cakes to celebrate their entry into their teens, Myrtle changed her mind. What had just happened was her secret; it was too special to spoil.

Outside the cottage, Myrtle found her mother sitting quietly reading, and she sat beside her on the floor.

'Where's Mari?'

'In the barn, sulking,' said her mother, looking up from her book. 'She tried to talk to a fox, but it ran away from her, so she got herself all heated up over it.'

She peered down at Myrtle.

'I thought I asked you two to play together for the day,' she said.

'We were together right up to the moment she decided to be spiteful,' Myrtle replied. 'Everyone wanted her to live and not me when we were born, apparently!'

Her mother looked at her, eyes wide, and a horrified look filtered across her face.

'Is that all she said?' she asked, a little anxiously, Myrtle thought.

'You mean, that wasn't enough?' Myrtle couldn't help the sarcasm, hurt that her mother was not as angry as her over Marigold's choice of words.

Her mother simply waited, as if for an explanation.

'I decided not to give Mari the birthday card I made for her,' said Myrtle, 'and I went into the woods. I told her that her cruel words would come and bite her on the bum one day – well, I said "arse" actually,' she added, trying to get a rise out of her mother.

Her mother shifted, narrowing her eyes at Myrtle.

'Have you noticed any changes – not with Marigold, with yourself, inside your body, your mind since you, well, you know … got your monthlies?' her mother asked, putting down her book and taking a sip of what Myrtle assumed was mead – her mother's favourite tipple.

'No. Why?' Myrtle asked, waiting while her mother drank and poured another glassful.

'Marigold said she feels angrier and has strange dreams since she got her monthlies,' her mother said.

Myrtle gave herself a moment not to react angrily.

'Marigold is *always* angry about something. She has a nasty mouth – not like Eve. Eve makes me smile. Why can't I be with *her* today?' She was fed up with every conversation leading to Marigold and her moods.

'Right!' Her mother made her jump when she leaped to her feet. 'I need to speak with you both,' she said urgently. 'It is time.'

'Time for what?' Myrtle asked dryly. 'Birthday cake?'

But her mother was already by the door, calling Marigold indoors and Myrtle reluctantly followed. She was resentful that her beautiful moment in the woods had been overshadowed by what was bound to be another unwelcome drama.

In the sitting room, Moonstone rushed around in an agitated state, lighting candles, smudging the room with sage and lavender smoke, and setting fresh crystals and black salt on the altar. Then she began chanting.

'Protection, calm and kindness. Bring harmony into our home. Protection, calm and kindness.'

She remained chanting until Marigold barged through the door.

'What's going on?' she demanded and slumped into a chair, heeling off her garden boots.

'I don't know,' Myrtle said and sat in an armchair away from her sister.

Moonstone looked at them both, and Myrtle noticed a seriousness about her. This was not a birthday-cake moment.

Moonstone sighed softly, 'I have a story to tell – it is my story – and I need you both to listen without interruption. It isn't easy to hear, but I would rather you hear it from me, especially you, Myrtle.'

Myrtle and Marigold exchanged glances before each shrugging their okay to their mother.

All three sat around the fire, and candles flickered on the altar.

'Your grandmother taught me all I know about witchcraft; she had not enjoyed an easy life during the Second World War – in fact, she gave birth to me during an air raid. And she raised me alone. I never knew my father.

'Anyway, I studied hard under her guidance, wanting to please her, but we soon realised I had limited powers. My skills lay in foraging and cooking. I know I was a disappointment to her, but even so, when I became pregnant myself, she stood by me, supported me when I ... gave birth to you both.'

Moonstone paused to take in a breath.

'Your father, Jack, was very charming at first – when he wooed me one summer in Cromer. He travelled with the circus – a gypsy with no settled roots – and he promised me a life of seeing the world. After he had seduced me into loving him, he showed me another side, his dark heart, and I saw that he was an unkind man, a man full of demonic thoughts. Towards the end of that summer, he abandoned me. I'm sure my mother had something to do with his disappearance, though she appeared indifferent to him leaving. It was soon after that, that I realised I was pregnant.'

'With us?' Myrtle whispered.

Moonstone nodded.

'From that moment, I focused on the coven who comforted and guided me. My journey as a witch was no longer challenging; it was my way of life. The day you two were born, the weather was perfect for the Beltane ceremony, and I felt free. I danced, just letting myself enjoy the moment despite my heavy belly. When I went into labour later that evening, I chose to give birth outside to allow my body to feel the ground beneath it and to breathe in the fragrance of May blossom.' She smiled. 'In the early hours, Marigold was born on moss, and you, Myrtle, arrived four minutes later, just as the clouds parted and the moon shone down on you both. Everyone gasped when you came out. Giving birth to twins was not something I had expected and left me in shock. It also brought about a time of disquiet amongst our ancestors. I remember Ragnis flapped and cried as each voice shared an opinion – each of them loud and disorderly.'

Moonstone paused again, staring into the fire for a moment, before she continued.

'Some said I should have left you to die, Myrtle. You see, to have twins meant a split of a powerful witch bloodline.

But others said it would strengthen the protection we needed against the Longe family. Anyway ... the argument grew stronger in favour of me making the sacrifice, but I told them, you were my child, that I loved you and that leaving you to the elements on a hillside was simply not an option. You were created for a reason, so I went against some within the sisterhood for you.' A beaming smile lit up her face. 'Your grandmother supported me, she adored you both.'

The room fell silent. Myrtle was struck dumb by her mother's words and glanced at Marigold, who sat with a satisfied grin across her face, her arms folded as if she had just won an argument. At once, a pain, of sadness and disappointment, coursed through Myrtle when she realised her sister was gloating, and she dipped her head to avoid looking at them both.

'Myrtle ... look at me.' Her mother's voice was soft and loaded with concern.

But Myrtle kept her head down and shook it sadly. Her tears falling into her lap; an emotion she had never experienced before gripped her heart, squeezing the truth through every vessel. She ached with words crawling inside her head: *you were not wanted; you were not wanted.*

'She's upset because everyone wanted me but not her. Some wanted her dead; they've already told me!' Marigold trilled triumphantly.

At that moment, Myrtle wanted to slap her face.

'Shut up!' she shouted, looking over at her mother for reassurance that what she had just heard was fantasy, a fairy tale. But she saw in her mother's eyes that it was the truth. Fact. Some of the ancestors had openly suggested she was to be left to the elements, a sacrifice to appease those scared of the change of a woman having twins.

'No one wanted me dead; they wanted evil dead. Maybe they should have left *you* on the hill!' Myrtle spat out the words to Marigold, glaring at her sibling.

In that brief moment, she knew their relationship had changed irrevocably. How could she come back from the cruelty of what Marigold had said?

'Girls, stop fighting. The ancestors were scared; they did not mean to be thoughtless; they just reacted at the moment. You both lived and here you are on the cusp of receiving your inherited powers. From this day on, your status as natural-born witches becomes fact.'

Both girls turned away from one another and concentrated on their mother.

'From today, you will address me not as Mum, but as Moonstone. I am your guide of all things connected to witchcraft.'

Myrtle looked at her as if she was deranged.

'Moonstone? Mother, are you drunk?'

'Respect! Show me respect,' Moonstone said as she rose to her feet and walked from the room.

Myrtle pointed to the bottle of mead and the empty glass beside her mother's book.

'How many glasses has she had – what does she mean by telling us to call her Moonstone?'

Marigold walked up to the bottle.

'Enough that she won't miss a drop. Here's to you and your walks around the hillside – a poor, unwanted soul,' Marigold said, lifting the bottle to her mouth and taking several swigs as Myrtle stood looking at her in horror.

The sarcasm and spite in Marigold's last few words were evident. It was the last straw for Myrtle.

'You're a cruel bitch. Nasty mouth.' She flung back at her and turned to leave the room. Just as she went to walk away, their mother walked in armed with two highly decorated besoms, and Myrtle stopped in her tracks, her thoughts rolling around and colliding with one another.

Calm down, Myrtle. She's drunk. The story she told wasn't true. It was just a fantasy meant to make Marigold feel special.

Nonsense, she thought a second later, Mum would not make something like that up, drunk or not. Then she regarded her mother, saw the triumph and excitement in her face, and frowned. What the heck was she doing now? Myrtle's mind could not take anymore.

'What are you doing with those?' She gestured at the besoms.

'I made them, they are your presents,' said her mother. 'One each to mark your thirteenth year and your entry into the sisterhood. Use them to sweep away troubles, cleanse your path and yes, use them around the Tree of Life. I've decorated them with a flower each, representing your names, so you will know which belongs to you.' She handed over each one to the girls, and as she received hers, Myrtle felt her hands tingle. The broom appeared to be melding into her hands.

'It … feels alive,' she whispered in awe.

'That is you, Myrtle; you are giving life to the broom, bonding with it as it is personal to you,' her mother said with excitement in her voice. 'And tomorrow you can have them blessed at the Beltane ceremony.'

Myrtle would have preferred nail varnish or a pair of loon pants – better still a record player – as a gift to mark the arrival of her teenage years, but she also knew it was an honour to receive her first besom handmade by her mother.

Then she felt a pang of guilt as she had moments when she doubted she wanted to be marked as different amongst the teenagers in the village. And now she wondered if she wanted to practise witchcraft to follow the path set out by her ancestors when it was obvious some of them had denied her right to exist.

And yet, a part of her could not imagine life away from Plumtree Cottage.

'It's lovely, Mum, thank you,' she said, looking at the besom again.

'You can fly it around the village with your silly friends,' Marigold muttered.

Myrtle was well and truly fed up with her sister.

'Marigold, stop this nonsense. And a thank you from you would be nice,' her mother admonished her.

'Thank you, *Moonstone*.' Marigold emphasised their mother's name.

Myrtle felt her face flush with embarrassment at her mother's request to call her by her name. Mum had wild ideas sometimes, and this one did not sit right with Myrtle, though she felt obliged to go along with it. To score points against her sister if nothing else.

'Yes, thank you, Moonstone, and eternal blessings to you,' she said.

'Creep,' Marigold hissed.

Myrtle saw a flash of annoyance in her mother's eyes.

'Marigold. We live as witches with kind hearts in this house. Tolerance and patience, girls.'

Myrtle felt a flare of anger rise.

'If there's a spell for that, then use it on Marigold!' she snapped back and stomped from the room.

Thanks to Marigold, another birthday had been ruined.

The day always ended in a lecture and tears, but today ended with a story she would never get out of her head. Some of her ancestors had not wanted her to live. It felt so profound a rejection. A shock? Would the pain of knowing stay with her forever? Myrtle climbed into bed, officially a witch. Perhaps it was time to find out whatever that meant to her, and to her future.

Myrtle finished writing about her memory of that day, lay down her pen and closed the book. Reflecting upon her past birthdays, as hard as she tried, she could not remember a single good one before Harry and Gaia had come into her life.

'Memories, they can make a day special or melancholy, Ragnis,' she told the bird as he perched on the kitchen tap.

She turned off the radio. 'I still expect to see her, Marigold, stomping around the garden pulling carrots and moaning about the lack of rain or something like that. But she's gone, and I have to live with this feeling of only being half of what I once was – of course, it's not true; I am me, a whole person, but sometimes...'

Picking up a small wooden box housing tarot cards, Myrtle lifted out the cards, shuffled them and laid one face down on the table. She always stood calm before turning to see what was in store for her.

'Please bring me good news and a brighter day.'

Sitting in front of the cards, Myrtle focused on positivity and turned the card to face her. The artwork on the cards was beautiful. The card was The Death card – it represented change.

'As if I have not endured enough change! Oh well, I must face more, positive or negative, and they must be received and dealt with. Ragnis, I think it's time to walk the woods and shake off this mood. Let's refresh the coven altar. Green cloak today, I think; it is warmer.'

Myrtle hugged her green winter cloak around her and immediately felt the chill of the outdoors ease. She smelled the lavender in its storage box within the cloth. Her grandmother had earned the cloak the day she became high priestess; it was one of Myrtle's favourites. She owned four cloaks: a purple, violet-trimmed, representing the crown chakra – the spiritual chakra, it was her high priestess ceremonial cloak; her pale blue cloak, which was kept for Beltane, spring, and summer; a teal one – a work in progress – would be used for special occasions when finished. Myrtle loved adding embroidery to her capes whenever inspired by her walks by the shore or in the woods.

The walk was brisk and just what she needed to improve her mood.

Later, when the evening darkened, and her oil lamp glowed, she took another walk. Connecting with nature, no matter what time of day or night, always made her feel privileged to have led such a natural life. She blessed and tidied around the roots of the Tree of Life. As she did so, she was reminded of how it came to be and of how her ancestor, Theda Netherwell, grew a sapling which became the focus for all Netherwell females and how its energy communicated with the families.

'Time to head back, Ragnis, to settle down and read at home. Time is too precious to waste worrying about what lies ahead. What will be, will be. I need to draw on some of the brave stories, and trust I have hidden powerful genes which will guide me in the right direction to help our family.'

Back in the warmth of her home, Myrtle made herself a drink and lit a memorial candle for Marigold. Her sister's annoying and demanding presence was missed during the evenings, and now Gaia and Summer had moved into their own homes again, Myrtle sometimes felt lonely. Her good friends Eve and Harry were busy with their own lives, and although she appreciated that they wanted to give her space to grieve her twin, she missed them dropping by for a chat.

Though Harry's daytime visits were increasing, and his smile always made the world a brighter place.

'Tomorrow, Nightshade, I will pay them both a visit. It is time to start living my life my way. Now that will be a first!' she said with a laugh that resonated around the room.

Lifting down the heavy book, she turned to an ancestor's page, eager to read the story about the girl who had grown and nurtured the Tree of Life. This was Theda Netherwell's story.

Chapter Four

Theda Netherwell

Horsford Woods, East Angles, the Year 1017

When darkness entered the village and warm air carried the perfume of the forest into the room, Theda lay listening to the owl hooting its way from tree to tree and a fox screeching out its hunter's call. It was a night like any other.

Her lavender pouch wavered in the window, and when Ragnis, her tamed raven, flew onto the ledge, he bruised the pouch, releasing the fragrance.

'You bring a sleep fragrance in with you, Ragnis. The night is hot,' she said, sniffing the air as Ragnis flew to the end of her bed.

He dropped a small white pebble onto the bed and

nibbled at the piece of bread Theda offered him in return for his gift before sitting facing her, his eyes looking into hers.

'Sleep well tonight, Theda. Your dream is of great importance,' a female voice whispered around the room.

Ragnis and the Tree of Life were the vessels through which her spirit family communicated; Theda's mother had told her it would happen to her one day, but still, the voice took Theda by surprise. Hairs tingled along her arms, and her body stiffened beneath her blanket.

'Greetings, Grandmother. You are missed,' she said.

'As are you, child. Relax and listen.'

Theda immediately felt the comfort of her grandmother's love surrounding her. She missed her daily lessons; it had been a year since her death.

'This will be difficult for you to hear, but hear it you must.'

Blood pounded in her ears, and Theda sniffed the air – sage smoke. Yet the room had not been cleansed against negative energy for several days. Her ancestors were cleansing and protecting their portal. In a moment of silence, Theda understood she was about to experience something new or take instructions on a witch's mission.

She waited, her breath heavy in her chest.

'Your parents have a thread of evil blood in their veins from an enemy intent on destroying the Netherwell bloodline. A white witch who had lain with her cousin, a false witch, a devil worshipper. His heart was cold, and his blood was tainted with a magick set on destruction. Your mother's bloodline is connected to ours through this child.'

Theda shuddered. She knew her mother was not a kind woman, but the thought that she belonged to a family with dark intent made her shudder. Many hands touched her arms and head, offering comfort, and she settled back on her trestle bed, still troubled by her grandmother's news.

'We have no time to waste. Your mother must not know about this visit.' Her grandmother's voice held a great urgency, and Theda listened with care. We have learned of a significant danger to your life. A journey you take will end our bloodline and send us into oblivion. You are to save us, Theda.'

'She is too young. It is a great responsibility!' Another female voice cut into the calm atmosphere.

'Hush. You have seen the future. Without her, we are just voices; our powers will wither and die. If she survives, our spirits live on,' replied her grandmother.

'Theda, it is said you will carry Ingulf's child; we must hope it has the blood of the white witch. To weaken the dark side, you must kill Ingulf and his father, Beorhtraed – a man intent on killing you; both have dark magick in their veins. Dark magick will destroy all we protect.'

Stunned by what her grandmother said, Theda sat upright.

'But that will make me no better than the dark side. And I am not ready to become a mother!' she declared, fearful of what they asked of her. She trusted her grandmother, but her words frightened Theda, whose breath came fast and furious. She wanted to unhear their request and clamped her hands over her ears.

'I think you should leave now,' she whispered, flapping Ragnis away. A tear rolled down her cheek and dropped onto the blanket.

Ragnis flew to the window ledge.

'Stay, Ragnis. We are not finished yet,' her grandmother commanded.

'Theda, you cannot walk away from this – if you do, you will die.'

Not ready to give up her life, Theda tried to calm herself and focused on the whispering voices. There had to be a way of avoiding such a request. Her body tensed, and a chill ran down her spine. Could she survive alone? What if she did as they asked and was caught? She would die a criminal. But if she did kill four people, according to her grandmother, hundreds, including herself, would live.

The whispering began again, and not wanting to hear anything else, Theda kept her hands over her ears. All she wanted was to lead a simple witch life, gathering healing herbs, creating spells for the good, and hunting the woods for food. She was already a skilled hunter – she was known in the village as their 'redheaded warrior'. It was apparent she had no choice in the matter; she had to listen, and their magick overpowered her desire to turn back time.

Coloured lights swirled behind Theda's eyelids as each woman spoke, telling her of their horrific journeys through life. Cruel and vicious attacks, sly and cunning accusations, each one a lie which had cost the witches their lives.

As she lay quietly listening to the owl, Theda knew she had completed her journey into womanhood; she was now ten and three years old. With that, came the dread of being handfasted to a man and no longer free to run in the woods, a child in awe of nature. Theda curled into a foetal position, finding comfort in sleep again.

Another voice interrupted her thoughts.

'Our choices are a bloodline with a weak, dark side – your child's – or drift on the wind with our magick lost forever. We will be lost to one another forever. Theda, you are the last of our kind; you must live and guide your child as others will do for theirs in the future. Time will decide when to end this battle; until then, we must protect ourselves.'

A curdling of acid rolled inside her stomach, and Theda squeezed her eyes tight in thought.

'Kill? You want me to kill two men?' Theda asked, her voice barely a whisper.

'Them, and your parents. Their greed has condemned you to death, Theda, a drowning on the waters to Denmark – you and the child you will conceive. We need to balance the scales of evil against the good, not just for our bloodline but for those connected to us by the thin branches of our tree. Hundreds of people will be drawn into the dark hole the Longe family have prepared. They will feed them and form an army to kill white witches around the world. Your magick must erase four lives; you are born to this task. Your mother's tainted blood is stronger than I realised.'

Theda's heart dipped and bounced in her chest. What they asked was too much for her to carry out.

'I cannot do it. I cannot,' she whispered in fear.

'Close your eyes again, and let me show you what your parents are doing right now, and then you can decide.' Theda felt her grandmother's hands brush across her cheek, and she willed her body to relax, and soon, she felt the deep sensation of astral travel – something she usually welcomed – but this time, feared for its outcome, now that the ancestors had spoken.

Rising above her body, looking down on a place in the forest, Theda allowed her astral experience to take hold and waited to witness what was happening while she slept.

With the fleeing of the Laird to London to try and win himself a place at the new king's table, the village needed structure. This made it ripe for the Dane Beorhtraed Longe, who had landed in the country to support Cnut the Great, the appointed king of England during the previous winter, to take control. He threatened to take the land and increase taxes if the village could not provide a bride for his youngest son, Ingulf.

Ingulf was wild, bullish and aggressive. Everyone had seen him swagger around the girls in the village, declaring his manhood the largest of his brothers. He fought anyone who looked at him in a way he disliked. Parents feared him around their daughters – all except Theda's.

During her astral dream, Theda saw her mother and father sitting and listening indifferently to people dishonouring her nature.

'Theda is strange. She talks to animals.'

'Theda hunts like a man.'

'Theda is wayward; she never visits the church.'

'Theda needs a Dane to show her a better path.'

'She is strong; she will survive.' This statement from her mother received a round of applause, and people shouted out their agreement.

'Send her to Denmark; she is the bride for Ingulf!'

Once the frenzy of calls eased, it was time for her parents to speak up in her defence.

'My daughter needs taming; she needs a husband,' her mother said, without hesitation, and her father held up his hands to quieten their voices – a master of self-indulgence.

'She needs a stronger man than I to settle her urge to run free and wild,' he shouted. 'You are right; she will survive. She will be Ingulf's bride and save our village.' Her father's arms thrashed about, as if to emphasise he was a man of great power.

Theda waited, hovering over the crowd, anticipating a change of heart, but her parents never fought for her.

'We submit our daughter into the hands of the village and the Longe family. My Danish family of the past will help this village,' her father said, puffing out his chest and holding up a quill.

Both parents signed the agreement and walked away. Theda looked down at the men and women, thanking her parents, patting her father on the back like he was a hero.

He is proud of what he has done to me!

Removing herself from the scene and relaxing deeper

into the cosmic sleep, a voice in the room whispered, 'Now you will meet the man they will tie your hand to for your lifetime.' Theda breathed slowly, allowing her body to rise again and drift across the rooftops. She hovered above a man staggering from barn to bedroom, deceiving young women with his drunken charm. Once in his grasp, he beat them to submission, his large hands around their necks.

She travelled across the water but could not see land; her body temperature dropped, and she struggled for breath. Looking down at the water, she saw herself floating in bloodied water, and Ingulf cheering on a large vessel. No magick could help her; this was the moment of her death.

'No!' she cried out, reaching out into the darkness.

'Settle, child. You are safe, but only if you heed our warning. Once done, take yourself to the village of Warburn and find Plumtree Cottage. It needs repair, but it belongs to our family. Take it as yours, hide away. It will be assumed you perished along with your parents. Use your fire energy, Theda. It will save you.' Theda's grandmother whispered soothing words of comfort as she brought Theda's mind back to a calmer state.

The dream validated the need to protect herself and future generations, to save the floundering souls of her ancestors. She eased her way from her astral travels and lay still on the bed as her mind settled.

'It will be done, Grandmother. Tell them it will be done,' she whispered before natural sleep took hold.

The following morning, while clearing rocks on a barren side of a field, her father took Theda Netherwell aside. His face offered its usual harsh stare. Cold grey eyes pierced her soft green ones. Was he truly her father, her flesh and blood?

'Daughter, you are to be wed on the morrow, and he will take you to his homeland, Denmark,' he said. His voice indicated no reply would be welcome, but Theda, being Theda, chose to ignore his instruction. He could answer questions if he no longer cared about her place in his home.

'Married? Denmark! Who is taking me to Denmark? I am but ten and three years old; can we not wait a few more years before I am shackled to a man? Does he speak English?' She stood with her legs astride and her hands on her hips, a stance she had seen taken by many women bold enough to challenge the men in their village. Granted, it earned many a swipe of the face, but it was a risk Theda was willing to take.

'You will find out later, and I assure you, you will do as he says once you are married.' Her father's tone was sour and threatening. His hand raised.

Her father had never treated her well; today, it was as if she were a stranger to him.

As tempted as she was to inflict an injury on him, Theda held in her energy, though her fingers tingled, a fire she released daily, but only in the confines of a small copse in the forest.

Her father gripped her shoulder.

'I am your father. What I say will happen. I have their

blood in my veins. It is a union of families once more. Go home. Help your mother prepare.' He hesitated then. 'Your husband will not tolerate your insubordinate behaviour, believe me.'

Theda dipped her knee, but she had no intention of returning home. She needed time to compose herself for fear of revealing her secret.

'Smile, Theda,' her father instructed.

The last thing Theda wanted to do was smile as they approached the two men at the far side of the village, ready to hunt for the wedding feast.

'Greetings, Beorhtraed,' Theda's father addressed the eldest of the two men. The man grunted his response.

Her father then turned to the younger of the men, and gestured at Theda.

'Ingulf. Meet Theda, your bride,' he said, gripping Theda's shoulder. 'Ingulf's father taught him well,' he told her. 'He is a fine hunter and speaks English; I have chosen you a fine husband.'

She recoiled at her father's simpering around the redheaded Dane with piercing blue eyes.

'I like them tall, and she is womanly for her age,' Ingulf said, his deep, loud voice husky and his English stilted. He walked around Theda as if inspecting a horse. She cringed when he touched her breasts. The men around him laughed.

Theda's heart felt nothing but the weight of sadness.

These ill-mannered men now tainted their homes, rampaging through the area seeking out trophies to prove their strength. They soured the place Theda had loved from the moment she took her first steps.

'Greetings,' she said, then dropped a slight curtsy, lowering her gaze towards the ground.

'Come, let us celebrate this fine union,' her father said. Theda shuddered at the thought.

'A union I will enjoy on the morrow. Your dottir has a pretty face. We will have a fine wedding night,' Ingulf said arrogantly.

'And if my son cannot, I will fulfil his duty!' Beorhtraed said and bellowed out a loud bray of a laugh.

'I am certain our day will be a fine one, and Ingulf will perform his duty well,' Theda said, and another false smile flashed across her face.

Beorhtraed frowned at her. Theda guessed he did not like bold-speaking women.

Her mother appeared then, and grabbed her arm.

'But first, we must hunt,' she said. 'Excuse us.'

As her mother dragged her away, she snapped out her annoyance.

'Show respect, child. You do not know what your wedding night will be like; now is not the time for you to speak out of turn.'

Her words were wasted because Theda was unafraid of Ingulf or the marriage ties. She already knew what would happen from her vision the previous evening. From the moment she woke, Theda had improved on her plan.

First, she achieved her goal of gathering everyone together at the wedding party to enjoy a hunt, explaining that this was her wish as it was the last opportunity for her. To her surprise, but knowing how he liked to boast, her father agreed and encouraged the event.

'I have ale for you to enjoy before we leave,' she said to her father, and the men gathered around the table nearby while she served them from a pitcher of ale steeped with a remedy to agitate the bowel. Once inside the woods, they would need to seek out privacy and this would allow her to bring each one down with her practised power of fire energy.

She poured a tankard for her mother.

'You too, Mother. Enjoy my day. Let me see you relax before I sail the seas away from you for the last time. It is a day of mixed emotions, is it not?' Theda asked.

Her mother raised her cup to her lips and stared across the rim at Theda, who gave her a beaming smile, prepared to block what she guessed was suspicion.

'I am lucky to have parents who have found me a fine husband. Thank you, Mother. I am scared, but the hunt will help my courage return. You and Father taught me well.'

Theda knew flattery was crucial for her to stick to her plan.

She watched her mother approach her father. Together, they drank and patted one another on the back for a job well done. Theda's first task was complete.

She approached the table where Ingulf sat and pretended to drop her handkerchief. Bending to the ground by his feet, she released the contents of a charm pouch before standing behind him.

'Do my deeds as I speak them,' she whispered. 'We will go hunting without the others.' Ingulf turned and looked at her, and as she stared into his eyes, she watched his pupils change size and back again. He broke the gaze and turned his attention to her father.

'Let's go! Theda can show me the forest. I hear there are plenty of deer to be had,' he said.

'There are new laws. We must not kill the—'

But Ingulf's father's large hand landed heavily on Theda's father's slim shoulder.

'They are not our laws to follow. Ingulf will kill deer and feed his wedding guests.'

Beorhtraed turned to Theda and snatched at her chin, lifting her face with his great paw. She slapped it away, and he laughed.

'Your dottir looks to me more of a great warrior than you, and she must know the paths and hidden places. Girl, show your man where he can hunt and bring down a young doe.' Theda saw the sneering lift of his lip; he was dangerous, but she had courage for company.

Ingulf sniggered and leered at Theda.

Child! You are not fit to be my husband even at ten and eight years.

Chapter Five

'Hunt wisely, Theda,' her father called to them as Theda and Ingulf approached the forest entrance. Ingulf belched loudly and laughed.

'Or be hunted,' he said into her ear. His closeness made her cringe.

Tutting, Theda looked up at the vast frame of a man and directly into his piercing blue eyes.

'Or feared,' she said, then ran ahead laughing, enticing him further down the path. 'Come on, brave warrior.'

As she watched her parents and Ingulf's party walk a path to the left of the woods, she guessed her father would guide them to his favourite hunting area. So far, her second part of the plan was working well.

Bending down, Theda lifted a handful of soil.

'Bless the land we walk upon. My thanks to you, Mother of the Earth, and the gods who keep us safe,' she said before she kissed the soil and scattered it around in front of her.

She reached out and snapped a few wild betony heads, their pink-purple glinting in the sunshine, and pushed them into a leather bottle along with other flower heads and berries she had already prepared before leaving home.

'They will steep for the headaches after our wedding feast and quench a thirst,' she said as Ingulf watched her.

'Get moving. I am bored,' Ingulf grunted ungraciously.

'Patience. I have not been shown the way yet,' Theda said. Lifting her head and whistling loudly she heard the comforting rustle of the leaves in a nearby tree.

'Rsk. Rsk.'

The moment she heard it, Theda smiled at the sound behind her and turned to Ingulf.

'Meet Ragnis, my eyes and ears. He shows me the right pathways to follow for the largest deer. My father is always impatient and goes to the same place. The deer grows wise to him, but I hunt where the bird flies,' she said, turning around and clicking her tongue.

The large head of Ragnis appeared from between leafy branches and blinked at her.

'Greetings, Ragnis. Meet Ingulf, who will soon be my husband. Come, keep us company,' she called out.

Ragnis blinked again, then flew towards them. Theda watched as he circled Ingulf's head.

Ingulf objected and flapped his hands, shooing Ragnis away.

'Go back to your tree; my wife does not need your company, death bird,' he said, growling at the bird nestling onto Theda's shoulder.

'Ah, Ragnis, he thinks you threaten him with death. Our warrior king is afraid of you; we must show him it is me he needs to fear.' She laughed, and flicked her arm playfully towards Ingulf as she ran from his company.

Her mind raced as she worked through the next stage of her plan. She had to work fast with Ingulf and run to find the others. Already, Theda sensed the warmth of her fire energy grow inside; her agitation had started the spark. She took another look at Ingulf, a brute, and knew if she did not go ahead with killing him, she would be dead by nightfall, drowning in dark water. A flash of heat surged through her body, and she did not suppress it as she might have in the past.

'Time to hunt!' she called over her shoulder. Ragnis flew ahead, sitting on a branch to wait as she grew closer to him.

'It is time, Ragnis,' she whispered.

'Rsk. Rsk.' her bird called back, relaying his intention to stay by her side.

Although Ingulf was tall and well-built, he was nimble on his feet. He caught up with Theda and pulled her to heel by her long braid.

'A wench with fire in her hair and a fearless heart. We are well matched, Theda Netherwell.'

Inside, her stomach fluttered, her hands began to burn with energy, and Theda knew it was time to set her plan. She freed herself from his grasp.

'If we stop here for a while, we might see the deer through the trunks of the trees over there,' she said, pointing across a patch of lush green grassland.

'You watch out for one, and I will hunt it down!' Ingulf roared with grand bravado.

Fool. You have already frightened every animal in the woods away.

'Be quiet, or our guests will go hungry,' Theda warned.

'We will sit here and wait for the deer and doe to come to me, the mighty Ingulf,' he declared, slapping his chest. He sat down on a fallen log and patted it for her to sit beside him.

Theda sighed and ignored him. While he wasted time singing his own praises, she gathered feathers and white stones before she insisted they set off on the hunt again.

'We will lose light soon. Do you want to look foolish and tell your father his soon-to-be *dottir* had to kill one for you? Because I am ready to hunt one down. I am not going home empty-handed. It will have *my* tip in its heart,' she said in a voice that teased.

Halfway into the denser part of the forest – a place Theda knew well, and that she had seen in her vision – Ingulf grabbed her arm. He pushed her against a tree and, with a fierce hand, cupped her between the legs. Theda let her heart settle into a steady rhythm to regain her thoughts. Fear was not to be her companion, or she would fail at the task ahead.

'I will be the hunter soon,' he said, pushing his groin against her, and Theda felt the rough bark of the pine tree pierce into her back through the thin cloth. She pushed at him, and despite his muscular arms, she managed to create a distance between them.

AMBER RAVEN

'But you don't want to frighten the doe, my lord,' she said. 'A little kindness first might be in your favour.' She licked her lips, inviting him to kiss her to play for time, and as he moved his head towards her, she dropped more of her charm spell contents from the pouch around his feet.

Ingulf leaned down and kissed her hard on the lips, manoeuvring her to lie down for him. Deftly, Theda manoeuvred herself from his grasp and stepped to one side.

'We are not married yet, Ingulf. You have only a short time to wait,' she said with a gentle smile, 'I do not know the man I am to marry. Tell me about Ingulf Longe. Show me what you find so wonderful inside forests. What is your favourite animal? I want to know more about you.' Her voice was soft, enticing him to tone down his bullish behaviour. What was about to happen was already written, but she wanted it to be a moment she might enjoy. Surely conceiving a child was a pleasant event between two people?

'By the gods, I am marrying a thinker,' Ingulf said with a cheerful laugh. 'You want to know more about me? And I you.'

'You will soon know me, Ingulf. Give me time.' Using a soothing tone, Theda said to keep him focused, 'I know you are a great warrior from Denmark, but what are your other skills?'

'You want to know about me. I follow the stars, walk with the wolf,' he said, and lunged at her. 'And bring down does in the woods.'

Before she could wriggle away, he pushed her to the

ground. Theda did not move; her mind already knew his intentions.

She knew he would howl like a wolf as he forced himself inside of her, so she lay accepting her fate.

She clicked her tongue twice, and Ragnis flew from the nearby tree into the forest. He would wait for her next call.

After Ingulf had satisfied himself, Theda got up and moved away to sit calmly in the crevice of an old oak tree – it was her favourite place to sit and practise her rune casting and manifestations, and it gave her comfort. She was sore and angry, but remained steadfastly in control of her tears, reminding herself of what lay ahead. She did not wish to look back at what had just happened. Ingulf repulsed her, and she was not about to give him the satisfaction of gloating. He sat staring at her, and she watched his face studying hers. She had seen the same stare when her father had waited for her to say one wrong thing and earn her a harsh swipe of his hand. Ingulf was no different. She despised both men.

She took a sip from the leather drinking pouch, not reacting to what had happened.

'Here, drink this,' she tossed him the pouch. 'Ale with herbs – a thirst quencher.'

'Ah, my wench, she thinks of her king,' Ingulf said and took a long draft of the concoction before he laid back on the mossy mound behind him.

'I will always think of you, Ingulf,' Theda replied, surrounding herself with white stones, feathers and a protection charm powder.

'What are you doing?' Ingulf asked as he drank more of her potion.

Theda looked at him, watched his eyelids droop the more he drank, and she smiled sweetly.

'It is a blessing, a wish for a child. Who knows, mayhap your seed has already been planted, and we will have an heir for you, my lord,' she said coyly.

She knew the next step she took would become a turning point in her life.

'Hunt for me so I can feast with my father,' Ingulf demanded sleepily, untying and dropping his axe beside his hip.

Patiently, Theda sat until she heard his gentle snores and knew her sleep remedy had taken hold.

'Oh, you will sleep, but your father will never eat with you again. Nor mine with me,' she whispered.

Theda gently tapped her fingertips, alternating the movement by sliding them down into her palms and upward again. She lifted her alder wand, a branch crafted by her grandmother to aid her success with weather patterns. Gradually, Theda felt the anger and released a surge of energy from her palms to her fingers, and as she repeated the moves, a sudden flash of intense, silver-gold lightning struck across the sky. She looked across at Ingulf, but he slept deeply.

Inhaling, Theda closed her eyes and lifted her arms high, again feeling the energy release from her body.

'Now Ragnis! Save them!' She called out.

A flurry of noise surrounded her as she heard Ragnis

and other corvids screeching out their message. As she worked her hands, deer, hare, rabbits and boar fled past. Birds flapped their way to the other side of the woods in their orderly flocks, their noise loud, but Ingulf still slept. Ragnis flew ahead of them all and called them to safety.

Theda's heart leaped with excitement, over which she had no control, and when another crash of thunder and a streak of lightning joined forces above her head, she released a long breath. Thunder blast after blast raged above them.

A storm was in full force, and it was Theda's doing. Her magick emboldened her.

'The weather is wild and unforgiving,' she said as Ingulf roused himself, picking up the pouch and drinking the remaining potion.

He looked at her with a confused stare and Theda felt a wave of satisfaction.

Walking over to him, she stood astride his body and looked down at him. Her hands tingled, and she felt another energy surge.

Ingulf stared up at her, dumbstruck. The drink had paralysed him. She stood steady and controlled her breathing before she spoke. She no longer had any doubt about what was to be done. Survival of the fittest was key.

She swept her arms outward around her. 'This will be your burial ground – I have learned a truth from my ancestors, and today, your doe-hunting conquests are over.'

As Ingulf fell back into a deeper sleep, Theda sent another surge of her natural energy towards the treetops and took stock of the raging storm. It was time to destroy the man who had intended to kill her. She had witnessed her parents selling her, so she had no doubt the drowning vision she had experienced was her future, too.

She stood back and watched the old oak tree nearby split in two and feed the fire with its dry trunk. She scooped up a handful of exposed acorns nestled by its roots, placed them in her pouch, and then ran towards the other hunting party. They were huddled in a copse, each one of them asleep. The ale had slowed them down, and the deadly nightshade drink inside their water pouches had killed them.

A new sensation of revenge and resentment ran through Theda's body, and then a fleeting moment of shock hit her as she looked at her parents.

Pacing in the realisation of what she had done, she reminded herself that they had taken so much from her by selling her to Ingulf, she was not a daughter to them, she was a commodity – an item to be exchanged, bullied and raped for the sake of greed – and the shock of what she had done left her.

She felt no guilt or shame; she felt nothing but the burning inside her body, forcing its way to the surface of her fingertips. Once again, she spread her palms and watched the gold flames flicker into a blazing ball as she flung it towards the bodies.

'To my enemies, your time has come. The gods will deal with your spirits, but I will return your flesh to the soil. By the fire from my soul, I return you to the Earth Mother!'

Another fire burst around her and engulfed the bodies.

Seeing a section of the beautiful Horsford Woods burning around her, filling her heart with sadness. It had always been a place of safety from her father's anger and her mother's beatings, but it was also the place where she had enjoyed learning about the beauty of nature from her grandmother. She waited until the flames became too hot to stand beside.

She heard screams from across the farrowed field. Men shouted and blew horns to alert others of danger.

Theda closed her eyes and cast her mind for rain as she had in the past.

'Now it ends. May the rains fall on duty done, as is my wish,' she whispered and watched calmly as heavy rain fell, dowsing out the flames surrounding her. Soon, the ground hissed with dampness.

Reassured that Ragnis had played his part in saving the animals and birds, Theda slid into the shadows and ran towards her new home. Her mind spun with emotions, and she vowed to make amends for their deaths. She would do only good in the world; she would love and heal her fellow man, woman and child. Plumtree Cottage would become a safe haven for all Netherwell witches. She would seal her blood within the bricks and protect the walls, which would protect her and generations to come.

'No matter how many times I read Theda's story, I do not think I could do what she did. I suppose times were harsh for medieval women, especially a warrior type like her. But, thanks to her we are cosy in this cottage,' Myrtle said to Nightshade, who sat licking his paws beside her. 'I have so many more to read, but I'm ready for my bed. Come on, you, let's go.'

Chapter Six

The following day, when all her chores were complete and she had visited Eve and enjoyed a brief chat with Harry, Myrtle settled down to write more of her story in the book.

In the back of her mind, she wanted to learn more about her ancestors rather than write what were sometimes painful memories, so she laid down her pen and turned to a random page.

Willow's Story

My name is Willow Netherwell, and I lived by Mother Earth's guidance. Some called out my mother as an evil witch – they hunted her like a beast when she was a mother supporting her child, conceived through an attack by Edmunde Longe, the master of the house where she worked. After her death, the Weybourne sisterhood kept me safe.

In my dreams, I learned of other brave Netherwell women who suffered and fought dark demons before my mother was born. Their stories and my mother's are written down in my grimoire. I hope my daughter and those of the future will do the same.

My story is much like other women of our bloodline, all of us duped and abused by men. As I grew into a comely girl, my guardian warned the boys away from sniffing around my skirts.

The flowers were head-bobbing above the high grass but I could still see Samuel Day. Even as a child he was tall, and I saw him watching me from across the meadow. His eyes drew me to him, and he lived in my mind for five more years.

When I reached ten years and seven, I had another vision of Samuel, but this time within the flames of the Beltane Eve fire as I danced with the women of our coven to celebrate fertility and lovers. That night, I knew Samuel was the man I was meant to lie with, the man chosen to give me a child, and I courted his attention when I saw him at the market.

Once I had conceived my child, though, I rejected his advances, and Samuel's fists laid heavy on my body. Unlike Theda, I was not brave enough to kill him; instead, I ensured he came to rely on strong ale, which stupefied him into sleep. One day, I arranged for him to be transported to join a ship sailing for foreign shores, and he was never heard of again.

My greatest joy now is living here with my daughter Daisy. My mother speaks to me through Ragnis, and I feel her heartbeat within the great oak where the ashes of her physical body were once buried.

Myrtle glanced at the clock; it was late – eleven o'clock already – but she was reluctant to put down the book.

'One more story, Nightshade, and then I will settle down for the night. My family history is like no other I've heard of, and it fascinates me. I want to read about Brigid now.'

Chapter Seven

Brigid Netherwell

Weybourne 1647

When Brigid Netherwell met Edmunde Longe coming out of his bedchamber, his smile charmed her.

His eyes shone and his lips danced with a warm smile, yet something about him disturbed Brigid. As he moved closer to her, she noticed a grey aura shimmering around his body and sensed something familiar about him. Was he like her, born with natural powers, those that heal and those that manifest goodness, or was he a man who performed demonic acts?

Brigid's body shivered as Edmunde's stare intensified.

He knew!

He saw her aura, too, the one her mother once described

as the soft pink shades of blossom. Her kindness. Her mother also warned her never to allow her anger through as it was powerful enough to wilt the blossom and could bring with it death. Her aura shadow was the light of past ancestorial powers clinging to her soul, protecting her from a dark evil.

Was Edmunde aware that he was a powerful man, capable of weakening her into a state of subservience with his mind? Was he a sorcerer or a fellow of witchcraft? Or was he ignorant of all and had allowed the Otherworld dark forces to slide into his being, waiting and ready to pounce?

Either way, he unnerved Brigid more than the witch hunters bent on removing women whose hearts were pure. Brigid's bloodline – white witches intent on good. Her magick grew each year, and her lessons with her mother and grandmother enabled her to practise daily. She was surprised at first when they sent her out to work for Longe. They were a self-sufficient family, and money was of no interest to them, or so she thought. But she soon learned that they shared the money with the poor in the village, and never accepted payment for their remedies or treatments.

'You are the new girl – or are you a woman now you have lived six years and ten?' Edmunde asked, his grin widening into a leer.

Brigid felt a flush of fear surge around her body. She wanted to run, but she was rooted to the spot.

Determined to shake off his stare, Brigid gave a swift bob of a curtsy and remained head down, staring at the floor. She tingled from head to toe as she sensed his stare forging a way into her mind. Her body trembled – whether he was to become a friend or a dangerous foe, there was something foreboding about her employer.

'Sire, I bid you morning on this fine day,' she said, rising from the curtsy.

Again, he stared briefly at her, lowering his eyelids, making her uncomfortable. Was he trying to read her mind?

When, a moment later, he brushed past her, she felt a surge of heat transfer from his body to hers, and her breath lay static inside the centre of her chest as she turned and stared after him.

Brigid pulled out her charm pouch filled with herbs of protection. She held it tight and whispered.

'I protect myself. I call on my ancestors to protect me against my master—'

Edmunde's grinning face reappearing from behind large red and gold drapes startled her.

'You need no such protection. You need the man your mother warned you against,' he said, his arm clamping down on hers and pulling her towards the room he had exited earlier.

When Brigid returned home later to her mother and grandmother, she was apprehensive, wary of telling them about what had happened between her and Edmunde.

Her mother turned to her grandmother. 'I told you she should work elsewhere, and we'd never keep her safe.'

'Edmunde Longe has been away for years,' her grandmother snapped back.

'It cannot be, he...' her mother muttered.

Confused and afraid, Brigid tried to understand what distressed her mother.

'His father was no better, nor his grandfather,' her mother said. 'All have dark magick in their blood.'

'Why did you send me there?' Brigid asked, still confused, her voice cracking with emotion. She rolled up her sleeves and showed them the purple bruises on her arms.

They both stared at her.

'If he filled your belly, you carry more than a child!' Her mother spat out the words.

Brigid stared at the floor, the heat of shame burning her face.

Her mother calmed down enough to explain that she and Brigid's grandmother had been raped. Brigid's father and her grandfather were part of Edmunde's family

'The cycle goes on,' she said, with tears in her eyes. 'Now you, Brigid...'

Weeks later, once it was confirmed that Brigid was pregnant, her mother sought sanctuary for her outside of Weybourne, where she gave birth to a daughter named Willow. When Brigid returned, she requested a meeting with Edmunde and presented him with his daughter and he was kind to her – he seemed almost pleased at the news and they began to meet secretly.

But when household gossip about Edmunde and Brigid walking in the woods together reached Edmunde's rich wife, Evida Longe, she flew into a jealous rage and mounted a hate campaign against Brigid. Edmunde, nervous about losing the vast inheritance he and his wife would receive on the death of his father-in-law, began fuelling the campaign with lies of Brigid's spells and potions seducing him and rendering him helpless.

———

'Guilty!'

The words hit Brigid Netherwell's ears heavier than a knight's angon. The lance had pierced and shattered her heart without touching her.

From across the room, Edmunde Longe's voice cut deeper – twisting like a sharpened knife as he condemned her to death.

Brigid turned to look along the bench of spectators. She spotted Evida sitting in her best clothes, finery more suited to a wedding celebration. She stared at Brigid, giving her a smug and satisfied smirk and raising a finger to point at her.

'Witch!' she roared.

In response, the courtroom resounded with the cries as if in a rally of war, resulting in a complete loss of control. Evida Longe rose to her feet.

'Witch! Witch!' she repeated until Edmunde demanded Brigid be taken away.

The woman had won her revenge against her husband's mistress. The girl who had given birth to his bastard child. A child he denied and renounced as contaminated with witch blood. Brigid's heart now turned to stone as she listened to Edmunde choosing to save himself and deny any truth about his daughter, Willow.

In a pompous speech, he insisted he had been placed under Brigid's spell from the moment they met. Indeed, he was, he said, a victim of her demonic sorcery.

He told the court's elders that Brigid was a dark witch who had promised his soul to the devil if he did not comply with her wishes. He knew this, he said, because he'd had Brigid's cottage searched. The ensuing report had shown findings of racks of herbs, potions and witches' offerings on what looked like a hidden Viking altar.

Edmunde's knights, too, told stories from neighbours about blatant lies bordering on the ridiculous.

Brigid laughed at him for his lies.

This was her downfall.

Edmunde Longe ordered the imprisonment of her mother and grandmother for their part in witchcraft and decreed that the child, Willow, was first to watch her mother die – so that she may live by the lesson learned – then be imprisoned for life, away from temptation, and to set an example to other witches in the area.

Fearing their wives would learn they had also lain with other women, local men joined in. Each man called for Brigid to be publicly hanged as all witches of the past had been. Buoyed up by his lies, Edmunde added to them with fresh accusations against her. By the time both he and his wife had finished spouting false stories, the whole village declared Brigid a witch of the worst kind.

The witch hunt came to a climatic frenzy.

'She is beyond evil – from another realm. Even God fears her. We must suppress the devil – for that is what she is!' roared Edmunde. 'Hanging is not sufficient; she will find a way to stay alive and destroy us all! I suggest we burn her alive so that we can see her soul rise and the devil die. We must let the church show no fear. Execution by fire on God's day is the only way to save our children. Save our souls!'

He talked on, of knights he knew who had made pilgrimage to countries where they burned witches at the stake and his men backed these stories. Eventually, Edmunde persuaded everyone who stood in judgement of Brigid that burning her at the stake was their only option.

Outside of the dark dungeon, Brigid was dragged through the crowds who greeted her with harsh, deafening chants of 'Hag!' and 'Devil's whore!' They fed off one another in frenzied excitement as her grandmother's familiar, a raven named Ragnis, flew ahead, reassuring Brigid that she was not alone.

Ragnis swirled around Brigid, protecting her from the stones and rotten foodstuffs thrown with force at her.

Willow was brought to her, and before Brigid stumbled onto the towering platform supporting the unlit bonfire, she looked down at her baby and wept.

'We will meet again,' she whispered.

A woman from the village stepped forward and placed something around Brigid's neck.

'Blessings, child. When you are ready, bite this to kill the pain. We will protect Willow. Your mother and grandmother are waiting for you.'

A guard pushed the woman away.

'It is time,' he growled as he wrenched Brigid's arms behind her.

Ragnis perched himself on her shoulder.

'Trust us, the sisterhood of your ancestors,' a gentle voice whispered in her ear.

Brigid braced herself. The Netherwell women were with her and she felt a strength flood through her. Though her head was pounding and her energy waning, she was suddenly determined not to fail these women. She lifted her head high and spoke loud and clear.

'To all the women of my blood, and those who are to follow. I cast that you only carry daughters – strong women with our given name – let no man rule thee. This spell is set and bound beyond my death for eternity. Cast me to the Tree of Life and I will nurture you all from beyond, as will each Netherwell woman who follows me into the realm of the spirits. I wish you blessings from the moon, the power of water, the warmth of the sun and the nourishment of our mother, the earth – so mote it be…'

Ragnis gave a shrill, powerful cry before flying to a tree just as the fire was lit and the spectators cheered.

Brigid stared down at the spiralling smoke beneath her feet, and she knew it was only a matter of time before the searing flames would lick high enough to take her to sit amongst the stars. Though she was terrified, she again lifted her head high, doing her best to ignore the searing pain in her legs as the fire took hold of the hem of her skirts. She had bitten into the root around her neck before her hands were tied, and it helped lift her focus from the agony.

Brigid's death was close, but her duty on earth was not complete. Drawing upon the fire's heat energy, she needed to summon the elements to come and claim her spirit.

With the last of her strength, she called out to her ancestors.

With their help, she could expel words into every ear within the village – words that needed to be heard.

'Ancestors, help me!'

A sudden burning raged inside her, and Brigid felt renewed energy. Something was happening outside of her control and not connected to the fire rising higher by the second.

To her left, the man who had brought her down looked at her with triumph and her anger grew traction. How dare he gloat when she had done nothing to harm him. She drew breath as she cried out her plea.

'Earth Mother, hear your dutiful daughter and do right by her. Bring justice to the wronged! Let my judge and jury suffer the darkness they have brought upon themselves. Come to me, sisters, in our battle against the unjust!' she yelled, then let out a bloodcurdling scream to bring attention to the moment.

Not one villager who had stood by to watch her burn to death would go unpunished. People whom she and her mother had helped survive grave illness or injury with their healing skills now denied her the right to live. Their nightmares would stay with them forever.

'Come sisters, come to me!'

Slowly, each ancestral voice whispered from a distance, reassuring her they were by her side, then once united as one, burst into a mighty roar, releasing dark smoke spirals to twist and turn amongst the crowd. Brigid's pain left her body and vented itself out into the crowd. People screamed, rubbing at their skin, bewildered when they saw no cause for their agony.

As the moment's frenzy took hold, dogs howled, and screaming children ran to safety. Only the adults remained unable to move as they experienced the revenge of one of their own. Brigid had no intention of dying a weak woman. They would remember her, and she would ensure Willow would be protected from beyond the grave.

As her body succumbed to the flames, Brigid sensed her abilities as a witch intensify. As she felt the heat around her body subside, she saw a dark power merge with hers, and there was no turning back. The ancestors had released their suppressed dark force, their hidden power – a woman her grandmother had once spoken about, her ancestor, Theda.

Brigid watched the chaos, her hair whipping around her face as she embraced the raw energy of a fresh new wind surging through the woods. Great gusts fanned the flames away from her body and tore down trees. Her eyes fixed on the swirling mass of branches and leaves before her, and the woodland groaned in protest, tree limbs thrashing like wild beasts as if battling for dominance.

Each blast of air carried a flurry of leaves, creating a kaleidoscope of colours as they danced and twirled. The air was now thick with the sound of hissing, like giant angered serpents slithering through the undergrowth, their sinister presence heard but unseen, adding to the mix of creaking wood, a sign of nature's fury.

Brigid sensed the dark energy coursing through her veins again, invigorating her spirit and filling her with a sense of awe and admiration for the untamed power and rage of the natural world. As the blackened clouds swallowed the sun, casting a shadow over the woodland, she saw the fear on the faces of her victims and experienced a surge of exhilaration as though she had merged with the storm itself.

She knew she would soon succumb to the fire, but until then, she would fight to show those who turned their backs on her that they had done her and her family a great wrong.

With the unnatural darkness surrounding the village, the flickering flames of Brigid's deathbed became its sole source of illumination.

The swirling blackness weaved through the trees while hailstones the size of hawthorn berries descended upon the ground, encircling the fire. Her blood witches had formed a basic protection circle around her, signalling their presence. She felt empowered, and her courage amplified to a new height.

She stared upwards and watched the dark sky drop lower; the air was heavy and had a foreboding atmosphere. Horses whinnied and scraped their hooves on the ground beneath her. Her blood throbbed in her ears as her heart threatened to burst from her chest, but with the support of the sisterhood, she knew to trust the future. Their voices filled her ears.

Curse them! Curse them! Curse them!

Through the haze, she saw the crowd still struggling to flee the scene, but they were grounded by a weighty fog – and unseen hands held them still as they raised their eyes to watch the woman they knew burn to death.

The sisterhood was in control. Over hundreds of years, voices and energies merged into one. A chorus of unity rang out as their voices called out, and words slithered into the ears of the stunned witnesses. Through the throng, Brigid saw Edmunde, dumbstruck, seated high on his favourite horse.

She watched as gripping fingers he could not see twisted his face upwards to look at her, forcing him to look at the injustice he had brought to their Netherwell sister.

Sear this within thy soul; see her death. Sear this within thy soul; see her death.

No witness would fail to hear and see what they had brought upon her. Women as far back as Theda were their judge and jury.

Lifting her shoulders and showing herself bold and fearless, Brigid manifested an air of command as she raised her now free and burning arms skyward. With the combined energy of the Netherwell ancestors, Brigid stared across the heads of those who had condemned her to death straight into Edmunde's eyes. White light glowed behind him, her guardians holding him still.

'I curse the womb of your wife and the liver of your son. May he suffer my pain, and they both endure the disease of insanity. My life beyond will haunt them for eternity, and I curse thee, Edmunde Longe, as you lay with me, so you will die with me!' Brigid called out.

A crash from above the clouds sent sparks to the ground, and the crowd gasped as Edmunde's horse reared up and threw him from its back. It pawed at the floor around him. Another thunderbolt saw the horse rear again, then crashed to the floor, crushing its owner to death.

Satisfied she had done all she could, Brigid bit into the sedating root of the necklace and screamed her final words.

'As I wish it so mote it be...'

Chapter Eight

When she stepped inside Marigold's room, Myrtle took a moment to inhale the earthy smell.

She wanted to clear and clean the room alone before emptying and decorating it. Her sister's woodcraft items were stored away, ready to go to a children's home, and her besom was placed outside the front door.

Then, Myrtle opened the wardrobe. An array of dungarees, old shirts, one ceremonial navy dress, and plucked jumpers were stacked on the bed. They smelled of lavender and fresh air. It had been an exhausting time mentally and physically, and Myrtle lifted one of the jumpers and inhaled its fragrance. She rolled memories of them knitting together and playing in the woods around in her mind.

Memories to be recorded, never forgotten. Marigold may have been troubled and possessed, but she had been a part of Myrtle and her story needed to be heard, too.

As Myrtle looked at each item of clothing, wondering which, aside from the ceremonial dress she could give to charity, more memories of her sister's darker side returned. Myrtle knew that allowing them to flow through her was a way of releasing grief and the darker thoughts that threatened to haunt her.

———————

Unlike Myrtle, as a teenager Marigold had no interest in being fashionably dressed. During a conversation with fellow witches at a moot for localised covens, a woman casually commented on Marigold's untidy appearance.

Marigold's sudden outburst of anger caught everyone off guard. She stood tall and gave the woman a hard stare while quietly muttering. After taking a few steps backwards, the woman dropped to the ground and began clutching her chest.

'Marigold, stop!' Myrtle hissed at her sister and rushed over to the woman.

Her mother, Moonstone, turned to Marigold.

'Undo the spell!' she demanded.

Marigold stared at her and said nothing.

The other attendees gathered in a huddle, and Moonstone rushed to them. She grabbed the altar wand and hastily marked a protective circle moat around the women.

'Fill it with salt, and don't move!' she commanded, then ran back to Myrtle.

'Is she dead?' she asked in a frightened whisper.

Myrtle shook her head. 'No, she's awake, but she said her chest hurts.'

'Stay with her; I need to get Marigold back under control.'

Myrtle glanced over at her sister, who stood with a smug smile across her face.

'I told you, undo the spell, Marigold. She meant you no harm,' Moonstone ordered her.

'I am not a tramp. I am Marigold Netherwell. A witch,' Marigold said in staccato sentences.

Moonstone sighed.

'You are right, you are not a tramp. However, you were wrong in hexing a circle member,' she said. 'If you don't remove the spell, she will always suffer.'

'So mote it be,' Marigold said, walking towards the path home.

'Myrtle, go with her, get her to clean out the barn, keep her occupied. And stay home! I will explain when I've dealt with this,' Moonstone said, waving her arm around the meeting place.

'Will Bess be okay, Mum?' Myrtle's voice trembled at the thought their friend might have to suffer long-term pain.

'I can reverse the spell, but I need time. Marigold has shown her new capabilities, and our lives will never be the same if I cannot undo her curses. Go, do as I said!' Moonstone said sharply.

Later that afternoon, Myrtle watched Marigold like a hawk. She was mentally recording her sister's every move to relay back to their mother, who had sent a message to say Bess was now back home and fully recovered.

Seated on a haybale in the barn, Myrtle felt her eyes grow heavy, and the overwhelming urge to sleep became a battle. At one point, she saw Marigold staring at her and grinning.

'Myrtle's tired – wake up, sleepyhead.'

'I am, and I don't know why,' Myrtle said suspiciously.

'I'm doing it, making you sleep,' Marigold taunted, waggling her fingers in the air. 'I can do and undo it whenever I want.'

'And you will stop it this instant!' Their mother's angry voice rang out as she marched into the barn. 'Your powers are not a toy!' she said, then turned to Myrtle.

Myrtle stood up and stretched her body.

'I'm feeling wide awake now. Was that you or her?' she asked her mother.

'Me. Marigold, remember what you send out into the world returns to you threefold. Hexing on a whim is not wise. Grow up alongside your powers and learn control. You are sixteen years old now, not a child!'

Myrtle knew her sister would ignore her mother's warning; she saw it in her face. Marigold had a way of switching off if something didn't suit her. She looked at Moonstone, whose face was flushed with annoyance.

'Myrtle, go and find your friends. Marigold and I need to have a private chat,' her mother said.

Myrtle did not hesitate to run down the lane to the shoreline, where she knew Eve would be.

'You made it!' Eve called out, encouraging Myrtle to join the group she was sitting with. Always urging her to join them, her best friend never allowed her to slink away from events. Taking a deep breath, Myrtle wandered over, trying to avoid the stares of those around her.

Myrtle was something of an outsider with the village teens, and she suspected her lifestyle was the cause.

'Okay, Red?' one of the boys near Eve said, and Myrtle enjoyed the attention he gave her. Giving her a nickname made her feel part of the group.

She gave him a shy smile, flattered by the six-foot, floppy-haired blond boy with a wannabe rock-star attitude.

'Budge up, Barry, let Red sit down,' the boy demanded of his friend, who Myrtle could see was holding hands with Eve.

'I like that: Red. Suits you, Myrt,' Eve said, following her beaming smile with a soft wink.

Though she felt awkward, Myrtle decided humour was the way to go.

'Thanks, but I am not sure why he is calling me Red,' she said flippantly, returning the wink so the boy could not see.

'Is she for real?' he asked and burst out laughing. Composing herself, Myrtle put on a straight face and turned his way.

The boy blushed. It showed her he had a sensitive side.

'I'm for real – um, Red,' she said, touching her cheeks before laughing. 'Oh, you mean 'cos of my hair – I understand now – we share the same name 'cos of your red cheeks,' she said and sat beside him.

'Touché!' Eve said, giving a light clap, 'Dan, she got you good there.'

Dan grinned and nodded. 'She did, and I get the hint, Myrt.'

Older than her by a year, Daniel Scott challenged Myrtle's inner emotions. She had never felt the flutter of interest in her stomach whenever a boy spoke to her. When they did, it was often to find an answer to a question in class. Now, she sat beside one of Sheringham's most popular sixth-form students.

'Are you celebrating something?' she asked, looking at the lager bottle in his hand.

'Yup, no more exams!' Dan shouted, raising his bottle in the air. Then he nodded towards a pack. 'Help yourself.'

Myrtle, having attended a beach gathering once before and not wanting the alcohol on offer, produced a small bottle from her pocket. 'Thanks, I don't drink, only water,' she said, 'with elderflower.'

Dan took a swig of his drink. 'Hops for me, none of your poncy flower power stuff,' he said, and some of the group around him laughed, Eve included.

Myrtle frowned at her. 'What's yours, Eve?' she asked.

'Lemonade shandy,' Eve replied as Barry reached over and poured lager into her near-empty glass.

Surprised that Eve was drinking underage, Myrtle chose to say nothing. Seeing her mother overindulge had put her off, and not being in control of her senses around Marigold was unwise.

'Ah, cheers then,' she said, sitting and sipping her drink, listening to the chatter about life aspirations, pop groups and the brands of cigarettes on offer in the corner shop. After a while, Myrtle realised, aside from the records she listened to at Eve's house, and the Celtic sounds of the coven, she did not have anything to offer to the conversation; she did not smoke nor want to, and she hadn't given her future a thought.

She had passed her exams with good grades, but her mother made it clear there was no money for college or university, and her place was at home, helping grow the family business – a market garden, skin creams and craft creations. Myrtle offered no argument; she accepted her path in life.

After that evening, Myrtle attended all meet-ups in the village. Eve and Barry were close, and Dan would seek her out to wander along the shore without the group. He was unlike some of the lads, whose banter around the girls bordered on personal and embarrassing. Dan chatted about travel and places he had visited with his parents, Spain being their favourite.

'Dad loves it 'cos the beer's cheap, Mum loves the sunshine and Sangria,' he said. 'They've been talking about getting a place out there – for holidays, it'll be far out. Spain's kinda groovy.'

'It sounds exciting. We don't go on holidays – Marigold can't even cope with school or going into Sheringham,' Myrtle said.

Dan placed his arm across her shoulder as they walked. She had never experienced a boy or man expressing affection, and her body stiffened with uncertainty.

'Maybe one day you will have a holiday in Spain,' Dan said as they walked.

Not sure what to say, Myrtle turned her head towards the sea. A streak of silver shimmied across the water, and the extreme heat of the July air stroked her skin. People walked hand-in-hand along the beach, and children scampered across the green fields beside them. Everything at that moment was perfect. Contented, Myrtle sighed.

'Don't sigh, Myrt,' Dan said, misunderstanding. 'We can get train tickets if you get a job and save. Travel by night ferry through France and train to Benidorm. It'll be a blast.' He squeezed her shoulder.

'It sounds wonderful,' Myrtle said softly, knowing she would never be allowed to go.

Suddenly, Dan spun her around and looked at her.

'Me and my girl in Spain, yeah, that's worth saving for,' he said and leaned forward, kissing her.

The world stood still for Myrtle; she had no doubt Dan had kissed a girl before, that his lips and tongue had discovered other people's mouths, but she did not care. This was her first kiss, and he had called her his girl. Love wound through her body like a butterfly seeking out a flower. Her heartbeat ticked faster than usual, and life became bearable once more.

A few weeks later, she confided in her mother.

'Mum, can we talk?'

Her mother looked at her, and Myrtle wondered if she would bother listening to her daughter's news. Nowadays, mead was Moonstone's staple diet, especially when Marigold battled against her.

'I've found a new friend to talk to, and we go for walks. His name is Dan,' she said and flopped onto the sofa. 'He's kind and funny.'

'That's nice. Just be careful he doesn't take advantage of you. Do you hear me?' her mother said, looking at Myrtle with a serious face. 'And keep him away from Marigold. She will get jealous of him, not you. She'll curse him the minute she thinks he will take you from us.'

Myrtle laughed. 'Take me from you? Mum, I met him a few months ago. He is seventeen and not ready to take me from you – well, maybe to Spain in a year, but honestly, he's just a great friend.'

Myrtle did not want to say that Daniel Scott brought a glimpse of what life might be like beyond the cottage walls, and she was biding her time to see where their relationship was headed.

Her mother huffed and shook her head. 'Carry a defence

pouch with you and keep it close to him,' she said, her voice guarded and serious. Annoyed her mother did not question her comment about Spain or show any interest as to why that particular country, Myrtle walked out of the room. Her mother cared more about Marigold's growing fascination with dark magick than what was happening in Myrtle's life.

When Marigold found out Myrtle had a boyfriend, their mother warned her to be pleasant to him if they ever met.

But Myrtle made excuses to Dan about visiting the cottage and meeting her twin. She knew she couldn't avoid it for long, though, especially now that Dan had invited her to meet his family. Her excitement increased, and she dropped her guard around Marigold, who had noticed her new energy.

'I can feel a change in you,' she said, her voice loaded with suspicion. 'Has *he* kissed you?'

Myrtle ignored the question and applied her eyeshadow.

'If you must know, I'm going to a music concert with Eve; Mum said I can stay out a bit later than normal. I'm excited; that's what you can probably feel. It's an emotion you aren't familiar with, I realise that.'

She was fed up with always having to explain herself to Marigold, but regretted her sarcasm as soon as it came out; antagonising Marigold was not wise. 'I'd say you could come, but it will be noisy, and besides, you don't like my kind of music.'

'You can keep your music; it's trash, just like whatever it is you are wearing,' Marigold replied, waggling her fingers in front of Myrtle's carefully chosen tank top and bell-bottom trousers.

As she pushed her feet into her new platform shoes, Myrtle tried to settle her energy levels and calm her nerves. She had managed one awkward hurdle with Marigold, at least.

'See you later, then,' she said, rushing out of the door before Marigold could say anything else to bring her down.

At Dan's house, his family could not have been more welcoming. Their home was modern and filled with new technology, and their loud banter and laughter around the table were a breath of fresh air.

The meal was Spanish-themed, and Dan's father talked about a new venture of his in Spain.

'Life in the sun appeals more and more,' he said. 'This heatwave we're having is a freak one, and it has made me long for Spain again. The sooner we find somewhere, the better,' he said passionately, exchanging a glance with Dan's mother, who nodded.

'If we get a place there, you could bring Myrtle out with you, Dan,' she told him, offering Myrtle a cheerful smile.

Dan grinned and Myrtle gave his mother a shy nod. She was happy. They had offered her the opportunity to spread her wings, travel abroad, and enjoy the company of a family not tied to fear.

'We're saving for a trip, so yeah, one day. Maybe next year,' Dan said and put his arm around Myrtle, who basked in his love.

'I'd love a new adventure with you next year, Dan. Your dad made it sound so exciting,' she told Dan later that evening as they were snuggled beneath the stars, hidden in a corner of Sheringham Park. It was a place they often stopped to kiss before parting ways.

'Yeah, well,' Dan said, 'Dad's got it all planned out.'

But Dan began letting her down and not turning up for outings. When they did meet, and she moaned about standing around for hours in the extraordinary heatwave they were experiencing, he insisted he couldn't help it, that he had important commitments to his family.

Myrtle threw herself into beachcombing and making sea-glass jewellery, which sold well and boosted the savings she had stored in a tin beneath her bed. August came and went with only snatched moments together with Dan, and when she invited him to spend time at Plumtree Cottage, he made excuses not to visit. After they went a few weeks without seeing one another, Myrtle began to worry about their relationship. Was she about to face her first heartbreak?

At the end of August, Dan sent a message via Eve, who gave it to her during a coven meeting.

'He said to meet him in your usual place tomorrow at

seven,' Eve said. 'I think he's frustrated that you don't have a telephone at home.'

Shrugging, Myrtle made a fed-up face. 'Mum won't even have a battery-operated clock; we still wind ours up. A telephone and a television are the last things she'd have. She's so uncool!' she said.

Eve giggled. 'She's not; she's just thrifty. Don't forget, she doesn't have a man's wage to pay for luxuries, at least that's what Mum says.'

'True, but it's still annoying,' replied Myrtle. 'Anyway, thanks for the message. I'll be there. I've not seen him for ages. How are things with you and Barry?'

After hearing Eve relay her dates with Barry and their fun together, Myrtle felt a pang of envy. She and Dan appeared to have drifted apart, and his attention to her was nothing compared to Barry's towards Eve.

The following day, Marigold was being obstinate, and their mother scolded her for not cleaning her bedroom. Myrtle spent over an hour picking up items thrown from Marigold's bedroom window and taking them back upstairs. Eventually, she stood back and looked at her mother, quietly cleaning the altar area and talking to herself.

'I'm out this evening, meeting Dan,' she said, 'and I am not clearing up after Marigold anymore. You can keep telling me to, but I won't. I keep my room clean; she can do her own. I'm not her skivvy.'

Taking a deep breath, she waited for her mother to turn around and give her usual list of reasons why Myrtle should support her twin, but nothing happened. Her mother kneeled straight-backed, and her head held high.

'Marigold will never conform to the rules of the house – or the world,' she said over her shoulder.

'Then I will take a leaf from her book and enjoy my life more. My chores are done, my room is clean, and I am about to take my turn clearing beneath the Tree of Life,' Myrtle retorted and turned to leave the room.

'We all carry burdens,' her mother said, 'Marigold is yours.'

In a flash, Myrtle felt an anger rush through her body.

'She's yours, not mine. I feel her twenty-four hours a day – her presence inside me, the other half of me – the cruel half, the unkind version of me is not a burden, it is a curse!'

Both of them jumped when the hall door was flung open with a loud bang, and Marigold stormed into the room.

'You are the curse on this family, the unwanted one, the snivelling people pleaser!' she bellowed at Myrtle.

Suddenly, the atmosphere changed, and the air became stifling. Myrtle looked at their mother, who now stood and stared at Marigold and then at Myrtle.

'This battle between you two needs to stop. It is tiring. I don't understand you. And as for you, Myrtle, I think it is time you stopped seeing that boy; he is a bad influence. He distracts you. When was the last time you practised spell work?'

Marigold's laugh resonated around the room. 'Spell work? Myrtle wants to leave us and run away from

Weybourne. She doesn't want to be a witch, I know. I can feel her guilt.'

Her rage slithered away, and Myrtle focused on suppressing her words. Anything that left her mouth now would drive a permanent wedge between her and her family. Marigold and her mother were all she had in the world. They were far from perfect, but they were hers. Walking over to her mother, she kissed the top of her head and saw the empty bottle and glass. She made a mental note to talk to Eve's mother, the one person who might be able to make their mother see sense.

'I'll see you later. I will continue seeing Dan; he is not a bad influence; I am just not good at creating spells. Marigold does that enough for both of us.'

Ignoring her sister, she walked from the room. Her family would have to cope without her for one evening, and there might be a time when they will have to cope without her forever. Life in Spain appealed to her – if Dan was the one for her.

During their walk, Dan was quieter than usual, but the warmth of his hand holding hers felt comfortable and reassuring.

'You're quiet tonight,' she said as they sat on a bench watching a woman throw a stick for her dog.

'Lot on my mind – nothing to worry about – jobs and that sort of stuff,' Dan replied, 'Mum and Dad are putting the pressure on about next year, after college.'

It was one of the rare times when Myrtle did not envy

him. Her life was mapped out at Plumtree Cottage, but then she thought of the alternative, a life with Dan.

'Maybe I had better start thinking about a better-paid job, too. Save for our holiday in Spain,' she said, nudging him and leaning on his shoulder.

'Mmm, yeah. Right, gotta go. Are you okay walking home? It's a bit dark tonight.'

'Don't worry about me; I can find my way home with my eyes closed. Ragnis is waiting in the tree, so I'm safe enough,' Myrtle replied.

'Anyone tries to attack you, he'll peck their eyes out, I'll bet,' Dan said with a laugh.

'Something like that,' Myrtle said and joined in with the laugh.

From the edge of the park, she watched him walk away. He had barely kissed her, and his mood was miserable. Something troubled him, and he left Myrtle with a niggling worry that he was biding his time to finish with her. Maybe she had better do it first, save him the awkward moment. She had enjoyed their time together and knew she had deep feelings for him, but before he broke her heart, she would give him the out he appeared to need.

Chapter Nine

'I've invited Dan to meet you both this evening. I know you think he is a bad influence, but I want to show you he is not.'

Myrtle looked at her mother, trying hard to exude confidence. Marigold stared up at her from her kneeling position in the vegetable patch.

'Well, I won't be meeting him; we don't have men around here,' she said, her voice sniping and unfriendly.

Myrtle's mother stood upright and eased her back.

'We will meet him. A bit more warning would have been appreciated, though. And we will not alter a thing. He accepts us as we are, or he will not be welcome again.'

An excited Myrtle rushed to her mother and hugged her.

'Thank you. I know you'll see why I like him so much!' she said.

Marigold gave a disapproving grunt and continued weeding around a patch of carrots.

Her attitude disturbed Myrtle.

'And I'd like you to be friendlier, Mari,' she said and walked away. 'I'll bake a few things, Mum. You won't have to do anything; just smile.'

Myrtle walked away before Marigold made another snide remark. She could not believe that after she'd opened up to Dan about her worries about them drifting apart, he had agreed to meet her family. All thoughts of finishing with him flew out of the window when he accepted her invitation, promising him it would only be an hour.

After baking more than could be eaten in a day, Myrtle piled sweet herb biscuits and cheese straws on a plate, sliced some jam sponge, and prepared a cocoa mix ready to heat when Dan arrived. She had tidied the lounge area and refreshed the hanging herbs above the altar. She sprinkled lavender oil onto a cloth and wiped the wooden surfaces in the room, deep breathing as she worked. She lit lamps rather than the harsh electric lights, and soon, the room felt calm and inviting.

Selecting a candle coated in rose petals, she set it into the candle holder and sprinkled rose quartz crystal chippings around it. She then kneeled down. Lighting the candle, she closed her eyes and embraced the room's peace.

Something distracted her from her quiet moment, and the room grew cold. Myrtle jumped to her feet to check the log fire, but the cheery flames flickered in the grate. Puzzled by the change in the atmosphere, Myrtle looked around. In the corner of the room, she saw a dark shadow.

'Marigold, if that is you, come out now!' she demanded

and walked towards the image. As she grew closer, her body tensed, and her heartbeat gave three firm bumps in her chest. Myrtle stopped walking.

'Who's there?' she called out, but the chilly atmosphere and dark shadow still lingered.

Snatching up her mother's grimoire, she searched for the banishment spells and chants; finding the one she wanted, Myrtle took a deep breath and read the words.

> *By moonlight's grace and sun's bright ray,*
> *With earth's pure power and winds that sway,*
> *I call upon the ancient might,*
> *To banish darkness, bring forth light.*
> *By fire's flame and water's flow,*
> *I cleanse this space, let evil go,*
> *By star's bright gleam and crystal's glow,*
> *No demon here shall ever show.*
> *Spirits of old, heed my call,*
> *Break the chains, let shadows fall,*
> *With sacred herbs and blessed rite,*
> *I cast thee out, into the night.*
> *By strength of heart and mind so clear,*
> *No wicked force shall linger here,*
> *From this home, be gone, take flight,*
> *I seal this spell, by magick's right.*

An elongated shadow moved along the wall and appeared to slither away beneath the door. Slowly, the warmth returned to the room.

Satisfied she had done all she could to secure the room, she began wondering who or what had entered uninvited. As her mind worked through her thoughts, Marigold and her mother opened the door and stepped inside.

'Mmm, smells delicious in here,' Marigold said, 'really *friendly and warm*,' she said, and Myrtle heard the twist of sarcasm.

'Was it you? The shadow casting fear and unkindness into the room?' Myrtle demanded.

She heard her mother inhale and give Marigold a swift glance. Marigold muttered something.

'Speak up!' Myrtle shouted, exasperated. Her mother raised a hand to stem their voices.

'Stop. Stop it now. This room needs cleansing before your friend arrives. There is too much negative energy. Marigold, go and wash! Myrtle, get out your grimoire, read your friendship chant from the door, and I will smudge in here. Quickly!'

Myrtle lifted her book of shadows from the shelf, rushed to the door, and read from the peace and friendship section of the book.

> *Earth below and sky above,*
> *Fill my heart with warmth and love.*
> *Waters clear and fires bright,*
> *Bring me happiness tonight.*
> *By the light of the sacred moon,*
> *Air that whispers, winds that sing.*
> *Bring me bliss in everything.*

By the power of three,
As I will, so mote it be.

When she had finished, she hit the bells in the tree, and Ragnis appeared.

'Ragnis, watch for the shadows. Marigold has cast a spell on the house. Mum has more faith in my spell work; we might need a warning.'

Blinking his eyes, Ragnis shuddered, flapped his wings and flew to the highest point beside the cottage's chimney. A sensation of reassurance warmed Myrtle, and she went back inside.

'There'll be a frost in the morning, and if she keeps it up, Marigold will feel its sharpness,' she said harshly. Her twin had gone too far.

Her mother gave her a sympathetic look.

'She'll behave. I've cast a calming spell. This poor home of ours will fall. It is burdened with so much energy hovering over it tonight. Go and have a freshen up and wait for Dan. I will make her invite him inside, as she has the strongest power, and it will counteract the dark one we've cleansed.'

For the first time in a long time, Myrtle felt supported by her mother.

'Thanks, Mum, I am grateful. You'll like him; I know you will!' she said and rushed to her room.

She watched from her bedroom window as Dan propped his bike against the inside of the fencing.

He looked so handsome in his flared jeans and patchwork jacket. His wavy hair sat neatly on his shoulders, and she noted new platform shoes, not as high as David Bowie's nor as outrageous, but still on trend. Her heart flipped with excitement and a smidgen of anxiety.

An evening with Dan and Marigold in the same room might be difficult. She rushed downstairs, and her mother held up her hand to stop her rushing to the door.

'As I said, your sister will invite him across the threshold. Marigold, open the door.'

Myrtle stood just behind her sister's shoulder.

'Merry Meet! You must be Dan. I am Marigold, Myrtle's twin. You are welcome to enter our home.'

Myrtle smiled as she stepped out from behind her sister, and Dan stepped across the threshold.

'We're very much alike but not identical,' she said, seeing the confusion in his face.

'I thought you had grown a foot overnight,' Dan said, laughing. It's nice to meet you, Marigold.' He held out his hand, but Marigold walked away.

'She's not socially fit for purpose,' Myrtle said jokingly.

Dan looked down at his shoes. 'Do I take them off?'

Myrtle shook her head. 'We only have rugs, not posh carpets like your mum and dad,' she said, glancing down at his shoes. 'They're nice. Your haircut is nice too,' she said shyly as he kissed her lightly.

Suddenly, she was shy about having him in the home.

The mention of posh carpets reminded her of what was beyond the dated kitchen. Although it was quaint and cosy for them, for Dan, it might look like something out of a Hans Christian Anderson storybook.

'Mum's in the kitchen – but the baking is my effort,' she said shyly.

'Great, lead the way,' Dan said with a confidence Myrtle envied. She pushed open the door and watched his face as he took in the hanging herbs, the oil lamps and the well-scrubbed wooden oak furniture.

Moonstone gave them both a beaming smile, and Myrtle noted the glass on the draining board. Either way, a glass half full or empty, her mother had shown her intention for the evening. With her too relaxed, Marigold would take advantage.

'Mum, this is Dan,' she said, hoping her mother had enjoyed only one drink.

'Mrs Netherwell, it's nice to meet you,' Dan said, stepping forward and holding out his hand.

'Moonstone. Call me Moonstone – and it's Miss Netherwell,' her mother said.

Myrtle's stomach sank to her boots. She had never mentioned that her mother was unmarried. A brief shockwave flitted across Dan's face, and a flicker of shame gripped Myrtle. Then she reprimanded herself. There was no shame to be had; her mother was an unfortunate victim, as many of their ancestors were.

'Moonstone. You have a lovely home, very, um, unique,' Dan said and smiled.

'We lead a simple life,' her mother said and lifted her glass. 'Let's go into the other room; it is cosier than standing in the kitchen,' she said.

'I'll get Dan a slice of cake first,' Myrtle said, giving Dan a look so he could stay with her.

'Bring it through,' her mother said. She walked into the next room, her long, colourful skirt swishing across the floor and her head held high. For a brief second, Myrtle noted how faded her mother's red hair now looked and how much weight she had lost. From behind, she could have been an older version of Marigold.

'Do you want cocoa with that?' Myrtle said, cutting a large wedge of sponge. 'It's strawberry jam, our own – in the middle.'

Dan stood by the table, and Myrtle could feel his eyes watching her every move.

'Cake and cocoa, the way to a man's heart,' he joked.

'I'm on the right path, then,' Myrtle quipped back and pushed a plate his way.

She picked up her mother's and Marigold's and entered their sitting room. The lavender rose fragrance and gentle woodsmoke from the fire hugged her soul. Dan's family might laugh a lot, but their house did not have the beating heart of history, of family lives lived before; it was modern and stark. Suddenly, she no longer felt awkward about Dan seeing how they lived.

'As you can see, it's a room steeped in history. The old fireplace and grate are hundreds of years old; the original building base is medieval, and only our family have ever lived in it – our ancestors. Mum might look older, but she's not that old,' Myrtle said with a laugh.

Marigold shifted in her seat, and Myrtle noticed a sly grin across her twin's face. 'The Netherwell witches added to it.'

When Dan did not react to what she had said, Marigold frowned, and Myrtle tensed. 'Mum had a new bathroom installed where the animals would have slept.'

'Farting sheep and cowpats while you sleep is not ideal,' Marigold said, and Myrtle looked at her horrified.

Dan coughed out a laugh. 'Pretty rank,' he said, taking a bite of his cake, 'but this is not. My mum needs the recipe; hers come out like cowpats – no pun intended.'

The room vibrated with laughter, and Marigold joined in.

'So, your parents are buying a holiday home in Spain, I hear,' Moonstone said, and Dan nodded as he took a last bite and chewed.

'Dan's parents have invited me to stay there,' Myrtle said quickly, 'I'm saving my sea-glass jewellery money to go.'

Her mother looked at her, and Myrtle sighed inwardly; it was Moonstone's negative look.

'It'll be a year or more before I have enough saved,' she added.

'My dad's really keen, and Mum's excited, too. It's great fun out there,' Dan said.

'Well, I hope it all goes well for them. So, what are your

plans, Dan?' Moonstone asked, steering the conversation away from Spain.

'Not sure. Dad's giving me ideas at the moment. I've been wondering about what I'd like to do, the future and that. I've stopped my paper round and I'm helping him in his workshop; he mends bikes now ... since losing his factory job.'

'Well, I hope you find something that suits you.' Moonstone cleared her throat. 'Right, then. It's been nice meeting you, Dan. Marigold and I are going to bed down the animals. Myrtle, can you do the chickens ... once you've said goodbye.'

With her mother's unsubtle implication that it was time for Dan to leave, Myrtle pushed down her disappointment as she ushered him out of the door. As they walked down the garden path, she slipped her hand into his.

'Why does your sister call your mum Moonstone?' he asked.

'Mum's wanted us to call her that for years, but I can't bring myself to do it; she's Mum, and I can't call her anything else.' Myrtle hesitated. 'I hope they didn't put you off,' she said softly.

'Put me off, they're amazing – witches and shit, wow. There's nothing your sister doesn't know about gardening, and your mum must have been a real sixties chick. She's still got the flower power vibe going on.'

'Mum's a bit out there, but she has taught us how to survive without a man, you know, a dad, to take care of things.' She desperately wanted to change the subject. 'When will I see you again?' she asked.

'Um, well, I'm busy at the moment, helping Mum and Dad with the garden, but I'll get in touch soon, promise. Night Myrt.' Dan bent and kissed her cheek.

Myrtle watched as he rode away. There had been no passionate goodnight between them, and she missed his affection.

'You can't have it all,' she whispered to herself. 'Marigold invited Dan in, and Mum stayed sober.'

She went and closed the chicken coop.

'Night, Ragnis,' she called out, before going back inside, where she felt the warmth and affection from past generations welcoming her.

Her mother was lying full-length on the sofa, while Marigold sat opposite in the armchair.

'He's an odd one,' Moonstone said, as Myrtle walked past her.

'Odd?'

'Dressed up like a fancy Nancy,' Marigold said and laughed.

'I'm not sure he's for you, Myrtle,' her mother warned. 'Time will tell, but don't get too involved with him, and don't give your heart away.'

Chapter Ten

'Barry has asked my dad if we can get engaged!' Eve squealed as she and Myrtle prepared the coven altar for the weekly meeting.

Myrtle stopped what she was doing and looked at her friend. Eve's face was alight with happiness.

'Engaged?' Myrtle hid her shock. 'That's fabulous news! When's the wedding?' she asked with a light giggle.

'We've said not till I'm twenty-three, at least – time enough to save for a place of our own,' Eve replied happily.

Myrtle hugged her friend. 'Exciting,' she said. 'Congratulations.'

'It will be you and Dan next. A double wedding, here under the oak tree.' Eve touched the trunk of the Tree of Life.

Myrtle copied her, laying her hand flat on the trunk, wondering if Eve had ever felt the vibration of the Netherwell energy beating through the tree.

'I'll tell Dan when I see him next,' she said, with a false laugh. Dan had been busy working with his father, and she barely saw him. Depending on the weather, they met once a week on a Sunday afternoon at either his house or along the seafront. His affection had cooled and if Myrtle was honest with herself, she knew he had lost his fun spark. To while away the time, she'd been focusing on creating sea-glass jewellery and skin creams from rose petals. Every now and then her heart would flutter when she thought of Dan, remembering how he'd opened up a new world for her, one outside of Plumtree Cottage and Marigold.

Realising that Marigold's powers were growing stronger, Myrtle had also been spending her time away from Dan practising her magick, and a visit from their grandmother one night reassured her she was right to do so.

As she lay sleeping, Ragnis's tap on the window disturbed her, and she rose to let him in. It was unusual for him not to be with her mother, but lately, he also watched over her.

'Is there something wrong, Ragnis?' she whispered as she pulled on her dressing gown and felt around with her feet for her slippers.

'Hush, Myrtle. It is your grandmother, Agnes; go back to bed. I need to speak with you. Relax, and Ragnis will guide my voice and thoughts your way.'

Myrtle stood bewildered; she looked at Ragnis. The bird had spoken to her.

She stared as he flapped his wings and hopped to sit on the bedstead post. Myrtle kicked off her slippers and scrambled beneath the covers, waiting to see what would happen next. She closed her eyes and took a few calming breaths as her heart pounded against her ribcage.

'Blessings, Myrtle. Listen and refrain from speaking; I cannot stay long. The ancestors are worried. Your twin is going too far with her destructive ways and is encouraging danger to cross the boundary between life and death. Our elder, Theda, is the most powerful amongst us, and she has sensed a dark demon feeding on your sister. And your mother's energies are failing, she can no longer always hold off the dark spells Marigold casts. In time, you will be the chosen one, the new high priestess, and Theda has chosen you to receive a thread of fire energy to boost your magick; use it wisely to suppress Marigold. We fear the outcome will be devastating for you both, but we are with you, Myrtle. Do not be afraid.'

The voice died away, and Myrtle heard Ragnis leave the room. She curled beneath the covers and let the drowsiness transform into a deep sleep.

When she woke the following day, Myrtle felt surprisingly refreshed, clear-headed, and eager to embrace the day. She tried to remember her dream but could only recall the smell of her grandmother's favourite perfume, Lily of the Valley, and the mention of Marigold – connected with dark magick.

Needing time to work out what had happened the night before, and resolving the urge to sit beneath the Tree of Life, Myrtle slipped unseen into the woods and sat with her back against its trunk, absorbing its calm energy before returning home and completing her chores.

'Your sister is grumpy this morning, I warn you,' her mother said as Myrtle mentioned collecting rosehips.

'What's new?' Myrtle replied and left her mother writing at her desk.

As she walked through the garden, she spotted Marigold. As she came closer to her, she heard her sister muttering to herself, and simultaneously Myrtle felt a sudden drowsiness..

'Stop it, Marigold. I can feel you practising on me again,' she warned.

Myrtle had been experiencing this drowsiness for a few weeks, the onset often preceding a minor disaster for someone who had annoyed Marigold somehow. Too many people were suffering because of her sister's disregard for their witchcraft abilities.

'Just because you can't use magick, weak witch... Ouch!' Marigold cried out, holding her hand.

Myrtle stood tall over her sister. 'Bee sting?' she asked, playing innocent. She had made it happen.

'Take her indoors, Myrtle, and draw out the sting,' said Moonstone, who had come outside, 'And no arguing, Marigold.'

Once inside, Myrtle checked Marigold's hand.

'The sting is still intact. Keep still.'

After scraping the skin to remove the venom sac, Myrtle cleaned Marigold's hand with apple cider vinegar and soothed the area with honey.

'There, all done,' she said.

Marigold withdrew her hand from Myrtle's and stared at her, making Myrtle uncomfortable.

'You told the bee to sting me,' Marigold whispered angrily.

Myrtle, not willing to allow her sister to get the upper hand, tilted her head to one side in question.

'And how could I do that? What bee is going to do as I say?' she asked, playing innocent.

'I could get a whole swarm of bees to attack you,' Marigold hissed.

It was true, Marigold could and would do that and Myrtle wasn't sure she could hold a swarm at bay. But Marigold could not have the upper hand. She needed calming.

'No, Marigold, you do not need to do that. It is unkind, and I have done nothing wrong,' Myrtle said softly. 'We are sisters and fighting between ourselves is not a good idea. I've looked after you today. Think about that, not what next spiteful thing you can do to me. Be kind, Mari, be kind.'

'Has the soreness gone?' she asked Marigold, as her sister paced the kitchen floor.

'What did you do? I know you did something to stop me,' Marigold said, her angry tone rising.

'Listen, a bee stung you because you were close to the flower it was harvesting. Mum asked me to help you because she reckons I'm a natural healer, and an empath. You are lucky I am, or you'd have a hand filled with bee venom, so get over whatever you think I've done, and let's help Mum. She looks exhausted.'

Myrtle placed the small bottles back into their medicinal box and went to the back door. 'Coming?'

She heard Marigold grumbling behind her in the garden, and felt a rush of satisfaction. She had managed her first suppression. With a renewed determination to become the best she could at her craft, Myrtle promised herself to continue studying ancient spells and adapting them to keep Marigold's dark art at bay.

───────────

It was October. And while her mother and Marigold attended a coven meeting one evening, Myrtle sat at home and lifted down *The Netherwell Book of Voices*.

She had read two or three stories about her ancestors in the past but had yet to take in the facts. Now that she had communicated with them, she became curious. She knew the women were not married when they gave birth, but they had men in their lives.

Scouring the pages, she looked for a true love story but

eventually decided hers and Dan's was the one she wanted to nurture.

She had not seen Dan for over two weeks, and her mother's speculation about whether he had met someone else worried her, even though Eve reassured her she did not know, hadn't heard of anyone else on the scene. Although tempted to invite him to join the Samhain end-of-summer and harvest ceremony at the end of the month, Myrtle was unsure how he would cope. It was a powerful event, with bonfires warding off unwanted ancestors set to harm the living. With her ancestral history, there was always a chance the Longe family increased their powers by finding other, linked bloodlines from their Druid and Celtic family trees. Her ancestors walked in peace; theirs would not. The ceremony their coven held leaned more towards the traditional Celtic rather than the modern, and inviting the dead to the feast always meant plenty of food and drink on offer. Dan would enjoy that side of the festival, but although she was extremely fond of him, she was not sure she could trust him to keep the ceremony secret. The coven was not ashamed of its roots, but some people never understood their way of thinking or trusted women who called themselves witches.

On the last day of the month, her mother stopped her on her way to tend to the animals.

'Are you inviting Dan to the Sah-wen ceremony tonight?' she asked. 'If so, you must make sure he knows the privacy rules. If you are serious about one another, he has to know your roots, but equally, you must trust him completely, Myrtle.'

Myrtle shook her head.

'No. I've not asked him. I'm meeting him for the fifth of November fireworks. It's easier that way – it protects the other coven members. It is still in the early days – maybe next year, when he will understand our beliefs more.'

Her mother stroked Myrtle's cheek. 'Thank you for being such a thoughtful daughter,' she said, and the rare compliment and gesture of affection moved Myrtle.

She decided it was time to bring magick into her relationship with Dan. Before she left for the Samhain celebration offering respect to the dead, Myrtle felt that love for the living needed her attention first. She wrote words on pink paper.

> *Show my love to one man: Daniel Scott,*
> *Bind him to me with a heart filled with love,*
> *Let his eyes see only me.*
> *As I will it, let I be.*

She rolled it into a scroll, placed it with rose petals and small chippings of rose quartz in a small hessian pouch, and put it in her pocket.

At the ceremony, held a short distance from the Tree of Life, the area was softly lit by the waxing gibbous moon, biding its time to become the moon her coven referred to as the Frost Moon.

All around her, women were clothed in autumnal

colours, many opting for flowing dresses or capes. The fire licked high, and the music was loud. When dancing and singing in the spirits around the fire began, Myrtle joined in, embracing the freedom it gave.

> *Stars shine, bring light to gentle spirits of mine.*
> *Guide them through the veil.*
> *On Sah'wen night, bring gentle spirits to reunite,*
> *Let them feast at our table filled with love.*

Later, she sat with her mother and friends, listening to more songs and enjoying the feast offered.

Part of her wished she could have shared it with Dan, but the other part enjoyed the coven's secrecy, which never mocked anyone within the sisterhood.

Five days later, she met Dan.

'Have you missed me?' he asked, and Myrtle nodded.

'I have. A lot. Life's boring without you around.' She leaned in to encourage him to kiss her. 'I've brought a blanket so we can lie back and see the fireworks; let's go over there where no one can see us.' She pointed to an area away from the main walkway of the shoreline, where the shrubbery gave them privacy.

The cold November chill did not dampen their eagerness to lie together on the blanket and cuddle and, carried away by his affection and the passion he'd kept from her for so long, Myrtle allowed herself to go further with Dan, basking in his warm, soft lips on hers, and his sensual embraces. When his hands touched her body in places no one ever had, she felt her control crumbling, and became overwhelmed by desire.

When they had finished making love, Myrtle curled into Dan's body as he stroked her head affectionately and kissed away her happy tears with such tenderness that she thought her heart would explode.

She was full of happiness as they spoke about a future together after their trip to Spain.

'I think next September I should have enough money to travel, how about you?' Dan asked.

'Definitely, I am going to apply for my passport in January. Next year, I hope to see many changes in my life!' she said.

'Have you thought any more about moving out of Plumtree Cottage?' Dan asked. They had talked about it, though really Myrtle could not imagine ever leaving her mother and sister.

'I'm not against it. Sometimes I think a flat in Sheringham might be nice,' Myrtle said, as she imagined nights around the fire reading poetry and working on craft projects together. 'But I've never lived alone.'

'One day we could live together,' Dan said, urging her into a second bout of lovemaking. Myrtle felt happiness flow through her body, and allowed her thoughts to turn to a brighter future.

By December, Myrtle couldn't pretend that since they'd started sleeping together Dan was more attentive and sweet. In fact, he was cockier, not as sweet, when they met. She had read the magazines that told her once a boy gets what he wants he loses interest. But surely Dan wasn't one of those boys?

Halfway through the month, she and Dan met at his parents' home while his family were in Spain. When they stepped inside the house, Myrtle hesitated.

Something had changed. The house felt cold and uninviting, and the downstairs rooms looked different. It was a brick building with basic furnishings, no longer a home.

'Have your parents started packing already?' Myrtle asked, wandering around the lounge and touching spots where there used to be family photos, but now only dust marks remained.

'Yeah. Pictures and bits,' Dan said. 'They've taken some stuff out to Spain.'

An open suitcase with what she recognised as Dan's clothes in it lay on the dining room floor.

'Going somewhere?' she joked, with a light laugh, tapping the case with her foot.

'I haven't got round to unpacking from the last trip to Spain,' Dan said flippantly and shrugged his shoulders, 'not that it has anything to do with you.'

Shocked by his tart reply, Myrtle felt unsettled.

'Sorry, it was just a question,' she said.

'You and your bloody questions,' Dan replied, leaving her staring at the case.

She was silent, wondering what the matter was.

'Drink?' he asked, waving a beer bottle at her. Myrtle shook her head.

'Please yourself, party pooper,' he muttered.

Over the next half hour, Dan seemed disinterested as she chatted about her week, hardly offering any conversation. It seemed bottles of lager were the only thing holding his attention, and she noticed his cheeks were redder than usual. He must have been drinking for a while.

'Mum wondered if you wanted to join us for our Yuletide festival on the twenty-fourth,' she said, 'it's a family tradition night.'

Dan sighed.

'Let's not waste time talking about boring traditions. Come here and kiss me,' he said, grabbing cushions and laying them across the floor. He patted them as an invite to join him, and Myrtle obliged.

Leaning against him, Dan brushed his hand against her breast and sent shivers throughout her body. Signs of the Dan she loved were back, and a spell of heavy petting confirmed her feelings for him. But then, suddenly, he pushed away from her.

'Don't you ever get tired of living like your mum, still living by her old-fashioned ways, spending all day running around after your sister, living in a hovel?'

He flipped her silver necklace off her breastbone and frowned. 'And why do you always wear the devil's necklace?'

Taken aback by his sudden attack, Myrtle sat up and glared at him. As she did, her body heated inside, not with passion but with an anger she had never experienced. Using calming techniques that her mother encouraged Marigold to use, she inhaled and exhaled three times, then clasped her hands together. The rage subsided, but the hurt remained.

'Old-fashioned? It's part of who I am, and that hovel is our home,' she said and lifted her necklace. 'And this is a silver pentagram worn by coven members and has nothing to do with the devil – don't be so rude!'

Dan gave a sneering laugh. 'Witch voodoo more like. Woo-hoo, voodoo.'

'Dan Scott, take that back!' Myrtle said, shocked by his words. 'That was horrible of you, and you know it's not true.' She was confused. Dan never usually took the mickey out of her family's beliefs. There was something off about him.

'Why, is it a sin against your religion or summat?' he asked mockingly.

'Don't be so mean. Our parents have different views on life, and I never laugh about yours, so stop making my mum seem strange,' she said, her voice rising.

'She *is* strange. Everyone I know thinks the same. She's a hippie. A drunken wild child,' Dan continued, cruelly.

'That's enough,' Myrtle said quietly. He'd had too much to drink – which she'd noticed made him quite mean sometimes – and they had a future to plan. 'Let's not argue, Dan.' She snuggled up to him. 'And don't be mean.'

'Mean?' he said, a bit theatrically. 'Come here, then, and I'll make it up to you.' He pulled her into his arms.

The longer they kissed, the more passionate and agitated he became; the gentle whispers of encouragement he usually gave her were replaced with an urgency she had not experienced from him before. Within minutes, he had manoeuvred Myrtle beneath him, pulling at her underwear. He smothered her mouth with his, and she had to push him away to breathe.

'Slow down, Dan,' she pleaded as he pushed his pelvis against hers. 'Be gentle!'

But he ignored her, intent on satisfying himself quickly, leaving her confused and frustrated. As soon as he'd finished she pushed him off her with such force it startled them both. She leaped to her feet and snatched up her knickers, pulling them on, trying hard to ignore the uncomfortable, damp sensation between her legs.

'What is wrong with you?' she demanded.

Without speaking, Dan got up and walked into the kitchen to get another beer. He flipped the metal lid from a bottle and drank as if slating a desert thirst, before flipping the lid of another bottle and sitting on one of the only chairs in the room.

'You were rough with me. You ruined—' Myrtle couldn't finish her words for fear of crying. She realised she was shaking with the shock of what had just happened.

'I've got things on my mind,' Dan said finally, moodily.

Myrtle shuddered at his moody response. She deserved better, an apology at the very least, but something told her she would not get one. Dan had a coldness about him.

'That's no excuse to be so rough with me,' she said. 'And you didn't even wear a condom!'

'Give it a rest. Nag, nag, nag...' Dan said, indifferently.

'What's the matter with you? Do you want to break up, is that it?'

Something told her the evening was not going to end well. If ever she doubted her ability to cast spells, it was at that moment. Her love spell had failed.

Dan swigged at his beer and then spoke.

'Dad's renting out this house, and he and Mum are going to be living full-time in Spain,' he said. 'I'm going out to join them.' He stared at her. 'We're not coming back...'

Myrtle stared at him in disbelief.

'What? When?' she asked.

'I'm flying out tomorrow. It's been planned for ages,' he said.

'Tomorrow! What about us?' Myrtle's throat constricted with emotion.

Dan looked uncomfortable. 'There is no us,' he said. 'They don't want me seeing you again, and I have no choice if I want a roof over my head. They don't understand your spiritual crap. You don't fit, you are...'

He trailed off and looked out of the window and the casual devastation released Myrtle's suppressed anger.

'You arse,' she said, grabbing her coat. She was determined to resist employing magick to somehow fix this situation. The best thing was to just get out of the house.

She had to save face, walk away and not look back.

It was obvious to her now that she had been used and, after tonight, she could add, abused.

Dan had never had any intention of taking her to Spain. Myrtle Netherwell had amused him when it suited him and had probably fed her a fake dream to satisfy his needs. A rush of shame rampaged through Myrtle, and her anger fizzled into a pit of realisation. Her desperate longing for love had led her to give herself to Dan too soon, mistakenly believing his affection was a genuine expression of love. It was nothing more than lust.

Steadying herself in the lounge doorway, Myrtle looked at Dan, swigging back another bottle of beer and felt nothing but disgust at the situation.

'I hope you and your family have a good life in Spain, Dan. Thanks for showing me the truth about you. Guess what? I'm better off without you. Merry Day, Daniel Scott, and Happy Yuletide,' she said, emphasising her last word with heavy sarcasm, and she ran out of the front door.

She hesitated at the end of the drive for a few seconds to see if he came after her to prove her wrong, but when she saw him close the curtains and shut her out of his life, Myrtle ran towards the park and let the anger and heartbreak burst out in the form of a primal scream.

It was then that she heard Marigold's laugh inside her head – a deep, spiteful cackle of a winning opponent. Her sister had overpowered the love spell.

In the week leading up to their Yule festival, Myrtle was bad-tempered, angry at herself for being so naïve with Dan and grateful she had not made the journey to live with him.

Eventually, what happened to her became too much of a burden, and she told Moonstone the truth.

Once her mother understood how serious she had been about Dan and the promises he had made, she allowed her time to grieve the break-up. Still, Marigold, who when confronted had denied over-riding the love spell, constantly tormented Myrtle over having lost a boyfriend.

Tired of the unrest in their home, Moonstone stopped the teasing and distracted Marigold with a woodcraft project, whittling wands for the witches of the coven. She instructed Myrtle to work out her issues and focus on self-healing.

To everyone's relief, life at Plumtree Cottage slowly regained a balance that suited them all. For the family and sisterhood, Yule was a time of reflection and a celebration of the dark days giving way to the light. The sun sat motionless, almost as if resting before it gave the best of itself once again. The Winter Equinox's restful period gave Myrtle time to reflect and consider her future. At the Yule festival, she absorbed the atmosphere of love and gratitude surrounding them and embraced the warmth of the fire.

Chapter Eleven

1980

By the end of February, Myrtle realised, to her horror, that she was pregnant.

She took long walks through the woods, sitting amongst nature, attempting to remain calm, but her body shook with emotion, cold and fear. The courage she needed to come to terms with being pregnant often failed her, and a profound misery cloaked the voice of positivity.

One chilly afternoon, she sat on a high point overlooking the village and tried to imagine herself walking with a child along the beach pathway or running along the shoreline, seeking out pretty shells. She envisaged herself teaching a daughter the importance of woodland greenery, blending herbs, and listening to the birds singing in the seasons, and imagined sitting through the night holding a baby under the moonlight to soothe it to sleep – sharing with it everything her mother had taught her.

She watched a hare leap across the fields below and the smoke from chimneys play chase amongst the clouds. Life moved on regardless of what was going on inside of her body. Her reputation as weird and strange was not as fierce as it once was amongst the village teenagers, but if it became obvious she was pregnant, tongues would start wagging. One thing she knew for sure was that she would not implicate Dan – she did not want him in her child's life. As far as Myrtle was concerned, the child had been conceived through abuse. The baby deserved love, but not from him. She doubted he would care, anyway, he had not made contact with her since leaving the country.

Even when she had come to terms with her situation, there was Marigold to worry about. Her sister had never hidden her dislike for children, and Myrtle worried she would hate hers even more.

Myrtle took to wearing a necklace of crystals and herbs under her clothing. Around her waist, she tied a protection pouch filled with bergamot, juniper berries, marigold flowers, cinnamon, cloves and echinacea, all carefully chosen to block out negative energy, increase her mind power, and protect the baby.

She chose to forage alone and went to regular coven meetings, surrounding herself with as much protective witchcraft as possible. Myrtle knew her energy was not strong enough to fend off Marigold's powers, but she put anything she felt might help her child in place.

The day had come when she couldn't keep her condition to herself anymore. She had to tell her mother and her sister the news. Today was the day she needed protection the most. Inhaling and exhaling slowly, she first expressed words to ensure the house was surrounded by positive energy, and then she went to find her best friend.

———

'I'm shocked, Myrt, and so angry for you; what a horrible thing for Dan to do!' Eve put her arm around Myrtle. 'I don't blame you for cutting him out of your baby's life. It's for the best. Listen, your mum is a good person. Just tell her. She'll support you; you know she will,' Eve said.

'I know, but I'm worried about her; she has so much to deal with, especially when Marigold is in a temper. Not only that, but I also heard her throwing up in the bathroom this morning. She looks awful. It would be just our luck if she's pregnant too!' Myrtle said with a dramatic flair.

Eve clamped her hand over her mouth, 'No! Do you think?' she said.

Myrtle shrugged, 'We'll have to hope not. Marigold hates babies. One will be too much for her, two will push her over the edge. I'll have to tell Mum, though, 'cos I am keeping mine.'

'Be sensible, take time to think this through, Myrt. A baby. Is it what you want to be, a single mother?' Eve asked.

Myrtle nodded.

'Not because it's Dan's, but because it is mine. Besides,

Netherwell women have had babies from a young age for years,' she said.

'Then you'd best tell your mum as soon as you get home, 'cos if she's pregnant too, that's a lot to deal with – especially with Marigold, and, well, you know her quirky ways.' Eve chewed on her lips. 'I'll come with you if you want.'

Myrtle shook her head.

'Thanks, but I'll manage. I'll have to speak with her today, or I'll chicken out and hide away,' she said.

Eve looked at her in horror. 'If it doesn't go well, and before you run away, speak with my mum or someone from the coven; they will help. Hey, but your mum is so cool; she'll have you knitting bootees before you know it!' she said and hugged Myrtle. 'Go, be brave. You deserve the world, Myrtle Netherwell. Don't you forget it!'

As she approached the cottage door, the witch's bells jingled when she walked past, and Myrtle stopped to compose herself before letting herself inside. She looked around the room and felt a sudden sense of calm. Her nervous queasiness eased.

In the quiet of the room, she encouraged herself to be strong. 'You can do this. You can share your news,' she said.

Listening out for her mother, Myrtle noticed their altar was in disarray.

'Mum?' she called out, looking around the room at the

unusual mess. Dishes were in the sink, washing in a heap on the floor; no bread was in the oven, and the fire beneath the cauldron was barely alight. Chores that their mother usually automatically did were untouched.

'Mum, you home?'

Realising her mother was not indoors, Myrtle refreshed the altar and washed the dishes. She placed the clothes in a bucket to soak and swept the floor. Mixing a bread batch, she set it aside to prove and then relit the fire. Heading outside to the barn, she found Marigold milking the goats alone.

'Mari, have you seen Mum?' she asked.

With a nod, Marigold directed Myrtle to the woods.

'Mushroom picking,' she muttered.

Just as Myrtle arrived at the end of the pathway, she saw her mother walk towards the chicken coop. She was pale, and her hair was unbrushed and tangled.

'Mum, are you okay?' Myrtle called out and gave her a wave.

Moonstone leaned against the fence and shook her head.

'Help me inside, Myrtle. I feel faint. I'm so cold.'

'Did you touch something? Lick your fingers. What is it?' Myrtle said, struggling to hold her mother upright.

Her mother shook her head.

'Marigold, Mum's not well; help me take her inside,' Myrtle called to her sister.

'She's probably drunk again,' Marigold muttered.

'Let's just get her indoors,' Myrtle commanded.

Once back inside, she encouraged Moonstone to have a

bath, and Marigold returned to the animals. Myrtle was grateful for the time alone with her mother.

Just as she was about to work the dough she had made earlier, her mother called out for help.

'Myrtle, I can't get out!'

Rushing to the bathroom, the sight of her mother's thin frame shocked her. Her mother was definitely not pregnant, in fact she'd obviously been wearing layers of clothes to hide her near-fleshless bones.

'I can't get out,' her mother said. 'I'm so tired, and my legs gave way,' she said, lifting a feeble arm for Myrtle to take and support her as she tried to get out.

'How long have you been like this?' Myrtle said, knowing she had been so caught up with Dan that she had not noticed much in her home.

'Get me upstairs to bed; we can talk there,' Moonstone said.

An hour later, a stunned Myrtle sat with the news that her mother sensed she had cancer growing inside, and the ancestors had confirmed what she thought, that her time on earth was nearly over.

When Marigold settled down to a task early in the evening, Myrtle warned her that Moonstone was unwell and not to be disturbed.

'She's dying,' Marigold said bluntly, and Myrtle was too startled to deny it.

'How long have you known?' Myrtle asked, waiting for some emotional reaction, either verbal or physical, from her sister.

'I heard her talking to you when I returned for my gloves. I'll be left here alone, won't I? When you chase after a man again,' Marigold said.

'No, Marigold, I'm staying here,' she said.

Marigold shrugged, 'There's not enough space for all of our energies; he said you will have to leave.'

'He? Are you talking about our dead dad again? Get in the present, Marigold. Mum is dying. I have no time for you and your dark fantasies. Dad is a dangerous entity, understand? I need your focus and energy to help with Mum!'

Giving a simple but unnerving laugh, Marigold held out her hand for Myrtle to hand her a plate of food.

'Everything will be different soon; he wants you on his side,' she said.

Not giving Marigold the satisfaction of extending the conversation, Myrtle went to check on their mother.

'Knock, knock,' she said as she tapped on the bedroom door.

Myrtle heard the faint 'come in' and entered her mother's room. The comforting smell of lavender greeted her as she moved towards the bed.

'Can I get you anything?' she asked her, who was semi-upright against the pillow.

'You can sit for a minute and tell me how Marigold is doing? Does she know?'

Settling on the edge of Moonstone's bed, Myrtle nodded. 'She does, she overheard us.'

Her mother sighed.

'I need you to promise me you will look after your sister. I know she is hard work, but Marigold must never go into care, and those who do not understand her will try and take her away...' Her mother's voice petered out as she fought for breath. 'Promise me...'

Myrtle touched her mother's face, which was now damp with tears.

'I'll do my best. I won't let her go into care,' Myrtle said. 'Get some rest. We'll take you to the meeting tomorrow. Your friends will help us.'

After leaving the room, Myrtle made her way to her own. She stood by the window, gazing at the world, lost in thoughts of what life would be like in the coming year.

She was not yet an adult herself, and by September, she would be both a mother and a carer to her sister. She leaned against the cool windowpane and whispered the words into the room.

'Goddesses and gods, ancient and wise, Grant me strength; let it rise. In shadows deep and fires bright, empower my might. Fear and doubt, I now release, In confidence, I find my peace.

'So mote it be, this sacred rite, Confidence and strength, ignite. As I will, so shall it be, In magic and truth, blessed be.'

Chapter Twelve

Myrtle gathered a blanket, her basket filled with crystals and suitable items to create a humble altar.

Marigold insisted on carrying Moonstone on her back, and Myrtle was amazed at the gesture and her strength.

As they approached the heart of the woodland, nature's breath hung in the air, showing a glistening tapestry of frost-brushed cobwebs and branches that sparkled under the pale sunlight.

A soft hush enveloped the scene, interrupted only by the occasional caw of a crow. The ground, a carpet of untouched hardened snow, crunched beneath each step, echoing in the stillness that embraced the woods. The air itself seemed to hold its breath as if in awe of the beauty painted by winter's icy brush.

On arrival at the Tree of Life, Myrtle laid down a waterproof sheet and blankets beside the trunk, and

Marigold helped their mother onto it and sat beside her. Myrtle had never seen her sister behave in such a compassionate manner. Something did not sit right with her, but she pushed the nagging thoughts to the back of her mind and concentrated on easing her mother's discomfort.

The women who arrived for the ceremony displayed a wide range of expressions. Each displayed shock, sadness and concern as they listened to Moonstone explain her situation.

After accepting the invitation to sweep the clearing anticlockwise with her besom to remove negative energy, Myrtle picked up her mother's athame, placed the tip of the knife to the ground, and drew a large circle as she moved clockwise. She then joined the women as they formed an inner circle with crystals around Moonstone, now lying on a thick mattress made from dry moss and bracken and covered in sheepskin blankets.

Four large rocks represented North, South, East and West on the outer edge of the circle, and four different coloured candles represented air, fire, water, and earth flicked against them.

The women lit a fire laden with branches to fend off the chill from the thick frost. A white mist wove around them, dampening their faces, but it wasn't long before the comforting warmth of the flames and the delightful aroma of the pine burning mingled with the wintry air.

Once satisfied that everything was in place, Myrtle and Marigold were invited into the inner circle with the newly nominated priestess, who stood beside their mother, and listened to the blessing of their family.

'Hear us greet you, Mother Gaia. Take Moonstone's hand and give her comfort and strength as she battles death with weak arms. Grant her final days with peace. Bless her daughters Marigold and Myrtle with strength and courage as they face an uncertain future.' The priestess called out her words, and the tinkling of bells and the song of a robin seeped into Myrtle's soul.

She closed her eyes, taking in the new aroma of sandalwood burning on the altar, and listened to the crackle of the fire. This was the place she was meant to be – a place where her heart beat to the rhythm of united love.

The murmurings of the priestess and the other women singing softly, one strumming at a lyre and another tapping the leather of her Shamanic drum, made her want to stay in the heady state of comfort forever.

The chill of the cold air nipped at her nose, but the rest of her body was wrapped in a warmth that didn't come from the fire.

Mesmerised, Myrtle felt her body lifted from the weights holding her down and rose above the ground. She gave into the embrace of her surroundings. A warm hand touched her forehead, and another had her hands, lifting her skyward. Her body danced in the mist, and she brushed against the branches of the highest trees.

Not daring to open her eyes for fear of breaking the beautiful sensation of the magic enabling her to soar above her troubles, Myrtle let herself drift. Her mind saw the world beneath her; she watched her mother's chest rise and fall with what little breath she had left, and although she was pale and weak, there was a radiance about her, a beauty Myrtle had never noticed. She could also see herself and Marigold holding Moonstone's hands and the dreamlike way the witches moved around them, scattering tiny chippings of crystals blended with dried petals at their feet.

'Mother of the winter snow, of the sun which warms us, and the rains to quench the thirst of the soil. The bringer of day and night, give us the strength to carry our sister Moonstone Netherwell and help her pain,' the priestess chanted loud and clear.

Her words tingled inside Myrtle's ears and again gave her peace of mind that she was not alone.

A sweet voice sang a song about trusting the future and spoke volumes to Myrtle. Had she got a future here with the women of Weybourne, the sisterhood of witches? Could she offer something to the coven?

Her powers might not be as strong as Marigold's, but the child growing inside of her told her she had the power to conceive and to know love.

Another woman sang of a mother nurturing a child, of the child comforting the mother – the circle of life and the ebb and flow of nature. Myrtle took a deep breath as her soul floated, absorbing seeds of knowledge and storing them away before the ceremony ended.

As her body descended, Myrtle became aware of something disturbing the calm and tension in the air. She looked down again and saw a dark shadow surrounding Marigold, an image tarnishing the gentle side of her twin from earlier. Was her sister releasing dark powers during their moment of astral travel? If so, why?

Pushing the troubled sensation to one side, Myrtle knew she had to allow her soul to re-enter her body untarnished, still within its cleansed state. A natural tremor told her she had returned whole and she opened her eyes. Slowly she rose to her feet and gave the group a soft smile of thanks. They returned her smile with wide ones of their own. Glancing over at Marigold, she was relieved to see the dark shadow no longer surrounded her.

She moved her focus back to her mother and kissed her warm brow.

'He's here; it's Ingulf,' Marigold said to Myrtle and kneeled beside Moonstone. Myrtle sensed excited agitation in her sister.

Moonstone remained in her own deep, peaceful sleep, and Myrtle couldn't help but feel grateful for the strength of the protective boundary surrounding them, keeping the Longe family's demonic determination at bay.

Then Marigold broke the peace. She began cursing Myrtle – accusing her of blocking the Longe's rite of passage – their opportunity to seek revenge. With Moonstone no longer able to soothe Marigold's anger, Myrtle felt helpless. She now had to care for both her mother and sister – with an unseen dark force hovering over them all.

Aware that all eyes were watching her twin with disapproval, Myrtle appealed to the priestess.

'Marigold is angry about our mother's health, she is struggling to control her feelings, and I am afraid she is prey for a dark presence – according to Mum, my father dabbled in the occult – is it possible he is amongst us now?' she asked. 'Please, can you protect her?'

The priestess nodded.

'We will do our best,' she said and beckoned her fellow witches to her side.

The six women stood huddled together and then slowly moved in on Marigold, holding out their hands and offering comforting words. They embraced her and encouraged her to sit with her mother and ignore the voice in her head.

To Myrtle's surprise, Marigold remained still and silent, her eyes fixed on the women as they joined hands, united in reinforcing the protective circle. They cast the same soothing sleep spell on her as they had on Moonstone, and the ritual began again with mother and daughter lying side by side.

In awe of what she had witnessed and the ease of the women, as they joined forces to calm her sister, Myrtle was grateful once again for the power of the coven and knew it was her duty to try and dedicate her life to the Weybourne Witches.

A week later, their mother passed away in Myrtle's arms.

Marigold had yet to mention Ingulf since her sleep spell. However, Myrtle feared it was a battle that would be fought another day. Her sister moved around muttering to herself and Myrtle was convinced she heard her hiss hexes at her as their paths crossed. She knew it was only time before one would take hold.

Myrtle scrubbed and cleaned their mother's bedroom, crying at every small thing she came across which triggered a happy memory. Her mother had kept very little in the way of mementoes, but those she had were connected to her daughters when they were born. Silver teething rings, two small sets of booties, a woollen bonnet and two dreamcatchers made from bird feathers. Myrtle placed them in boxes and stored them in a wardrobe. Once Marigold had showed signs of settling, she would get them out and share them with her.

Marigold, meanwhile, worked every day inside the barn, and Eve's mother and a woman from the coven supported them both in their grief. By now, Myrtle had entered her tenth week of pregnancy; the nausea worsened, and by the end of each day, she was exhausted.

After the cremation of her mother, Myrtle did as others had before her and scattered her ashes beneath the sprawling canopy of the Tree of Life.

Going through her mourning process, Marigold refused to change her clothes and looked like a clown in the oversized dungarees and red jumper. With nothing on her feet and no overcoat, Myrtle worried her sister would freeze, but as always, no amount of pleading with her changed Marigold's mind.

When they arrived at the Tree of Life, Myrtle watched her twin leap and jump around like a toddler at a birthday party, and observing Marigold's wildness increasing, she contemplated how long the banishing spells would last.

Eve's mother kindly arranged for a drumming ritual to be performed, and each drum vibration resonated through Myrtle's body. Her grief for her mother consumed her, and she couldn't shake off the weight of the responsibility she had willingly agreed to shoulder. Life was going to be tricky with a baby and Marigold.

She longed for one good day.

'It is not too late to find a good home for Marigold; there is no shame in it,' Eve's mother said as if she'd read Myrtle's mind. The woman placed an arm around Myrtle's shoulder.

Grateful for her kindness, Myrtle knew she meant well, but her words upset her. She gave a slight nod. 'I promised Mum I'd take care of her; it was the last thing she asked me to do.'

Eve's mother turned to face her. 'She was dying, dear; she was clinging onto hope. Moonstone told me herself what hard work Marigold was; it was unfair of her to burden you with her for life.'

'I know you mean well, but Marigold is my twin. We are one person inside two bodies. If she goes into a home, I might just as well go with her; we are bound to one another.' Myrtle gave her a soft smile. 'But thank you for caring.'

Eve's mother shook her head.

'You are a better person than me, and I think the authorities will have something to say, as you are both under eighteen, and Marigold has needs. Your mother was perhaps in denial about that fact, but it has been obvious to the rest of us,' she said, patting Myrtle's hand. 'Think about having a chat with a doctor. It won't do any harm.'

The last thing Myrtle wanted to do was discuss her situation with a doctor, and she wondered how soon some authority would be knocking at her door. Myrtle was determined to keep her baby and Marigold at her side. She had to devise a plan to prove that life at Plumtree Cottage was stable for all of them.

Myrtle headed into the woodland two weeks later to sit by the Tree of Life.

Striding out against a wind that had a bite to it and pushed against her body as she walked, Myrtle felt older than her actual age. A dread inside her gnawed at her daily.

Once at the tree, she kneeled on the blanket beneath the large branches and leaned facing the trunk. Sprinkling the area around her with protective sea salt and crushed crystals, she then took a moment to bless the tree. Folding her arms around the trunk as far as they could go, she leaned her forehead against the bark and inhaled the musty smell of the woods.

'I wish you long life, oh mighty oak,' she said. Then she

took a deep breath and began to pour out all her fears and concerns to the tree.

'Wise tree, I need your strength today. My sibling is draining the life from me, and caring for her is like climbing a mountain without breath in my lungs.'

The wind rippled through the leaves, and Myrtle paused, taking in the peace the Tree of Life and its surroundings gave her. Ragnis called out from the top of the tree.

'The darkness of the Longe family is growing stronger through Marigold,' she whispered. 'Help me protect my baby. Give me a sign, strength, anything, to restore peace in our home.'

Remaining calm as the ground vibrated beneath her, Myrtle released a breath and straightened her back when she heard a loud sigh from the greenery at her side. It flitted around her like a leaf free from bindings, and a voice interrupted the sound.

'Myrtle Netherwell, you can do great things and must not let fear and doubt hold you back. Trust in yourself. Serve the sisterhood, and they will show you the way. I, Hazel, am at your side.'

Myrtle felt a sense of peace and a renewed determination to face the challenges ahead.

Chapter Thirteen

Marigold

They think me a fool. I sensed a change in my sister soon after our mother died. No matter how I try to push my way into her mind, I cannot break the wall she had built between us. Myrtle has a different energy, and it is growing stronger. The Longe men are worried and are increasing their powers to destroy her through me.

I noticed happy days and sad days with her, and then the ache inside her body travelled through to me. It was a dark ache. Maybe it is her sadness over losing Dan.

I asked the Tree of Life to take it away and danced in the rain to wash away my sister's pain, which lived inside of us both. Eventually, I found happiness again in my other world, which some say is a crazy one, but I must remain connected with Myrtle despite this pain. It is our destiny.

Our father's spirit told me he could not take me into

their world, away from the sisterhood who did them wrong, if they did not have both of us under control. I want to be with our father; he fascinates me and encourages me to learn about dark magick. I work in the garden, and Myrtle thinks I am content, but I am not, I am consumed, excited, by dark magick.

I want to cast fear on people and make them see me as I am – a powerful witch, not a mumbling girl growing vegetables. When I feel invisible, I am not alive inside. If I feel anger when it is released, so is the tension inside my head. Father understands me. I know he is dead, but he has a strong spirit, and we grow closer every day.

My sister no longer cares about me, and this divide will worsen.

Today, Myrtle told me she is pregnant. This is my punishment for breaking the love spell.

She knows I cannot cope with babies; they smell sour and they scream. When they are around me, the inside of my ears tingle, and my hands twitch. I want to hide them away so they don't hurt my ears.

I did that once, and my mother was furious. I took a pram from the park. The screaming baby stopped crying when it saw the trees and the birds in the woods. I couldn't understand why everyone was angry with me; the baby and I were both happier.

Mum said she would not take me to the park again, so I have never returned; I built my own swing. I told them I would never go anywhere outside of the home again, and I didn't. I put my hands over my ears when people try and make me.

Then, I set my anger free.

A demon stokes the raging fire inside and takes me on journeys into the night sky, where I draw fresh power from the darkness. I am too weak to fight him, so I accept his energy and hear his voice – it is not our father, but he is part of us; the Netherwell and Longes are mixed-blood, which he – Ingulf the angered one, the one slain by Theda – says cannot be denied.

Myrtle and I are different; she was not born with fire in her belly like me. We are twins bound by blood, but our parentage and ancestry shred the tying strand. It is a lifetime battle of revenge from both families, and Myrtle and I fight on opposing sides. It's who we are. It is our destiny.

The Longe bloodline grows more potent inside me, and I accept that it is who I am, the child of the man who lives in the Otherworld. Myrtle's child, if it is a son, he will be ours; he will inherit the power of revenge. If it is a girl, she must not be allowed to live.

I can feel the Tree of Life tremble beneath my hands; it fears what lies ahead. Tradition follows Brigid's curse, and only girls are born to our bloodline, but this is the first time for a set of twins.

Is the curse broken? Will a male emerge for us to draft into the battle and break the connection with Myrtle?

I am excited about the future!

Chapter Fourteen

Some days, Myrtle thought about building her small cottage craft seasonal business into something more. She needed financial stability now more than ever, and increasing sales of Naturally Netherwell products was the only job she could envisage herself doing while caring for her sister.

Myrtle's sleep became unsettled with anxiety – and heartburn. She wanted her child to grow up feeling safe and loved, but Marigold's hostility towards her grew stronger the more her abdomen swelled. It was a struggle to remain calm when Marigold ranted about her bringing a child into their home, making threats against the baby when it was born. Myrtle was frightened by her sister and what she was capable of. And although the coven members surrounded her, she felt alone with her problems.

Rising early one morning, she pulled on her clothes and stepped outside, barely noticing the inclement weather. She ventured into the woods without Marigold noticing. She walked with weighted shoulders to the sanctity of the Tree of Life.

Touching the tree with both hands against its cold, gnarled trunk, Myrtle focused on reaching beyond earthly realms as she spoke.

'Blessings of the day. I hope someone can hear me. I ask for your wisdom and guidance in my daily life. Please help me follow one path and not stray. I need a sign or something to give me a purpose.'

Myrtle sensed an unnerving presence nearby, but keeping her hands firmly on the trunk, she absorbed the tree's natural vibrations. Slowly, the rustling leaves increased their sound. Ragnis circled a few feet above the canopy of trees, and a chill wind danced around the base.

Clouds formed above the tree, and darkness fell. The atmosphere became pensive, and Myrtle sensed more activity around her – a voice filtered through.

'Do not be afraid, Myrtle. It is the way. Your daughter will be birthed into the world by you and is to be nurtured by another. It is feared Marigold will destroy her with her jealousy and dark powers. Protect your child. Make the sacrifice and save her. Keep Marigold close. No matter where she lives, she will find a way to bring your daughter down. The Longe family must not close in on her. When time decides, our name will become hers, and you will reunite. Giving her up saves her from the demon Marigold nurtures. Trust in the faith of your ancestors, Myrtle. Trust we will guide you. I, Hazel, will protect you, so mote it be.'

Tears streaked Myrtle's face and she wiped them away,

then she stretched and inhaled the musty air disturbed by the breeze. Her hand sat naturally on her pregnant belly. Her daughter. She now knew it was a girl. Her child was not to be raised by her – she was to sacrifice her right as a mother to save her child. Marigold was not to be trusted around her daughter.

'How can I bear this? Why me?' she cried out.

Voices swirled around her like the leaves from the tree.

'Trust.'

'Save her!'

When the voices faded, fatigue overwhelmed Myrtle, and she sank to the floor. To give up her child was too much to ask of her.

'How can I give her up?' she wailed, though deep inside, she felt the inevitability. It was already foretold; her future was already mapped out, and the ancestors knew the outcome but could not control it – could not control Marigold.

Lying on the ground, Myrtle felt something happening, something fast and furious, and she struggled to focus. Soon, she could not move…

'It is a good job Eve found you,' said the doctor. 'I understand you skipped breakfast before your walk, and it brought on a faint?'

Sticking to the story she had told Eve, Myrtle nodded.

He talked on about the perils of skipping meals, but

Myrtle barely registered what he was saying. She felt she was losing control of her pregnancy. When Eve had by sheer luck been walking in the woods and found Myrtle collapsed, she had involved her mother, who'd been firm that Myrtle needed to put herself in the care of medics now.

'You should tell your doctor about Marigold, too,' Eve's mother had said. A specialist residential home for her might make life easier for you.' She had hesitated then, squeezing Myrtle's hand before she added, 'Have you given any thought to giving the baby up for adoption? You are so young, Myrtle, and without your mother to help you... Give both some thought, dear.'

Myrtle knew she meant well, but hers was not meant to be an easy life.

'I am not giving up on my sister or baby,' she said later to the doctor.

'I understand—' he began.

'With respect, I don't think anyone understands, not when it comes to my sister. She needs me,' Myrtle replied.

'So does your baby,' he said, gently but firmly. And from what you say, it will be vulnerable around her.'

Myrtle's attitude softened.

'My choices are limited. I cannot, will not, hand over Marigold to care. No one but me knows how to handle her when she becomes agitated. If I have to choose, it is my baby I would find a caring home for, not Mari. Neither of us would cope if we were separated.' She knew that explaining about dark forces of nature and spirits who haunt her sister would have them both assessed for mental competence so she tried to remain calm.

Doctor Henson smiled at her. 'Your courage and loyalty are admirable. I wonder, if I found a kind and caring home with a couple who would adore your baby as their own, would you consider adoption? Especially if you had contact with the child throughout its life – say, as an aunt?'

Myrtle gave a sad nod, wondering if her heart would break.

The GP paced a little, and looked nervous about something.

'What is it?' she asked.

'This is a little unusual,' he said, 'but would you agree to meet my wife?'

'Your wife? Why?'

'I think she … that is to say, 'we', can help you. Sadly, Sheila is – we are unable to have a child, and in the four years of trying, we have discussed adoption at great length. We could offer your little one a good home.'

Myrtle could see he was uncomfortable with his suggestion. She leaned back in her chair and looked up at the ceiling. She hated the thought, but handing her baby over would protect it from Marigold's darkness. She breathed out, then in, then out again.

'Would it mean my baby will live locally?' she asked the doctor.

He nodded, 'Holt – so, not far away.'

It was ten minutes away. Her child would grow up nearby, and she could still be part of its life.

He smiled. 'I would say this, but my wife is a lovely lady,' he said. 'Kind and responsible. The baby would be very loved – by both of us.' He hesitated. 'Would you like to meet her? My wife.'

'I...' Myrtle's mind raced. Meeting the woman would not harm; it was not a binding contract. And it would be better to place the baby with the doctor and his wife rather than have it go to an orphanage before settling with strangers.

She nodded carefully. 'Yes, I'll meet Mrs Henson, but I am not promising anything,' she said, and stroked her belly.

Chapter Fifteen

Myrtle's meeting with Doctor and Mrs Henson went well. She considered what they offered, and after three days of consideration, and encouragement by Eve's mother, she agreed to sign the adoption papers. She knew it was the right thing to do, but she did feel moments of regret.

'When she is old enough, I want her to know I had no choice,' she whispered as she pushed the signed papers across the table to Richard Henson.

'You are predicting a girl, Myrtle?' his wife, Sheila, asked with a smile.

'I am. Netherwell women tend to have girls,' Myrtle replied. 'I don't want to give birth in the hospital, and I would like the midwife who delivered me and Marigold to be with me. She's an old family friend.'

'I know Annette well, she trained locally. I'm happy for

her to help deliver your baby, and with a home birth, dare I suggest here, in our home? said Doctor Henson. It will be more comfortable for Marigold, all things considering.'

Grateful for his consideration in her needs, Myrtle agreed.

When she requested a meeting with Annette at Plumtree Cottage and explained the situation, Annette held out her hands and took Myrtle's.

'You're a brave girl. The sisterhood will help you and Marigold, just as Moonstone helped us. Come and join our meeting this afternoon and enjoy a picnic at the altar. Get your coat. Marigold looks busy enough; I'm sure she can cope alone for an hour,' Annette said, looking at Marigold digging over a patch of land.

Myrtle joined the company of the women. She knew most of them from her mother's healing and funeral ceremonies. During the meeting, individuals shared poignant stories of their past relatives, recounting their ancestors' harrowing experiences of being relentlessly pursued, like foxes by hounds. Their fates were equally brutal and fatal.

Myrtle learned about various parts of Norfolk she had never heard of, although she knew most of the stories about witches who had lived in constant terror during earlier centuries. The ruthless hunt and executions led by the

Witchfinder General, Matthew Hopkins, and his supporters shocked her when she heard some of the women now were the great-granddaughters of those who'd been executed.

The criteria for labelling someone as a witch were alarmingly broad. The hunters employed cunning methods to win favour with the Witchfinder General. The more stories Myrtle listened to, the more she realised she and Marigold would have been accused because they were twins, and Marigold more so for her outrageous behaviour.

'Just think, our great-great-great grandmothers and beyond did the same thing we are doing today,' one woman in her eighties said as she pulled chickweed from the ground. 'I remember doing this with my mother and grandmother when I was your age, Myrtle. Chickweed always brings back memories of my childhood.'

Myrtle smiled, 'The first flower I remember picking and tasting was gorse. The almond nut flavour always brings back good memories.'

Another woman of around sixty years old said, in a soft Norfolk accent, 'My first full memory was of the Bricket Wood Coven. Well, more of the stories told to me about the New Forest. It was my mother's part of the world; she met my father there, but after a year, they moved to Norfolk and continued to follow the ways of the Gardnerian Wiccan. I was born here and love that my parents taught me their magick.'

'My relatives told me about Fye Bridge in the county,' said another. 'Ducking stool stories gave me horrible nightmares.'

The atmosphere around them altered. A quiet hush went around the grounds, and Myrtle shivered.

'The stories are dreadful, and I am thankful daily for our freedom,' she said.

'We've learned over the years that united women can survive anything by supporting one another. You will have all the help we can offer. Moonstone was kind, and you are very much like her, Myrtle. Whatever happens next, you will cope,' Annette said.

During her time with the women, Myrtle knew she would be guided well into doing what was suitable for her and the baby.

When she returned home, she prepared a new altar for a fresh start in life. She selected a blue candle decorated with small birds she had painted in silver. She was drawn to the candle's representation of calm, communication and dreams. She anointed the candle with lavender oil, rolled it in dried marjoram for protection, and lit the wick. She held a crystal in her hands, each one representing calm and love.

'Bring peace and joy into Marigold's life. May our future dreams be calm and settled. As it might be.'

Selecting a large bay leaf and a black marker pen, Myrtle set them down outside on the back step and then wrote a message on the leaf,

Help me forgive Dan.
Strengthen my powers so I might fight the dark demons.

She laid it into the well of a large shell and set fire to it, willing the spiralling smoke upwards.

'Take my words and help me on my journey of forgiveness, and to find happiness again.'

Chapter Sixteen

August 1980

Myrtle tidied the cottage as quickly as she could, eager to get outside for fresh air. A niggling ache in her lower back had troubled her during the night.

Once she had finished with the basic cleaning, she sat at the table to create smudge sticks, humming quietly as she worked. When she had finished inside, she pulled on a lightweight jacket and joined Marigold, who was clearing out the goat shed.

'Morning's blessings, Marigold. You were up and about early this morning,' she said, dragging a small hay bale from a pile in the corner of the barn.

'Weather too good to waste,' Marigold replied and continued scrubbing the concrete floor.

'Here's the hay. I'm off to get the last of the blackberries. Ouch!'

Marigold stopped sweeping and leaned against her broom handle, staring at Myrtle, who was rubbing her back.

'Hurt yourself?' she asked.

Myrtle took a moment to compose herself.

'Yes, I slept funny, then pulled my back, lifting the hay. I'll walk it off in the woods. See you later.'

When Myrtle arrived at the Tree of Life, she sat down. The peace of her surroundings soothed her, and she rocked gently back and forth to ease the backache, guessing the baby was settling into a different position. Six weeks remained until her due date.

Ragnis hovered and then decided on a fallen trunk.

'I can feel this one kick most days, but she's quiet today. I have done the right thing for her, haven't I, Raggy?'

Ragnis ruffled his feathers and blinked at her.

An onset of dizziness overcame her, and Myrtle took a deep breath. Suddenly, an intense pain seared across her back, moving swiftly across her abdomen. She took a deep breath.

These pains are not practice pains! she thought, panicked, and struggled to her feet, staggering sideways. Pain after pain attacked her body, and she could not move.

'*She's mine; her Viking blood is strong,*' a menacing voice whispered in her ear, and Myrtle shuddered.

'Go away!' she called out in between breaths.

Sliding down to the ground, she soon realised she was in labour, and there was nothing she could do about it except deal with giving birth alone. She pulled out her foraging knife, dried it on her skirt and laid it on a cloth covering her wicker basket.

'*She's mine,*' the deep gravel voice said again, and Myrtle's skin tingled with fear.

'I banish you from this place!' Myrtle shouted but knew her powers were weak.

A spit of rain fell on her forehead. Above, thick black clouds choked the sky, smothering the late summer.

'My child is not yours for the taking,' she screamed, above the increasing whine of the wind.

'*She is our blood, mine, too.*' The voice was threatening and Myrtle felt prickles of terror.

'No, her father is not a Longe!' she said, with as much force as she could.

But with the presence of this dark force along with hers, Myrtle had the sudden, horrific realisation that Dan's family was somehow connected to their past.

Abruptly, her body gave a powerful, natural warning she could no longer ignore.

Getting onto her hands and knees, Myrtle pulled at her underwear and gave her first push. Rain lashed down around her, and she screamed when a searing pain tore through her. Something was wrong.

The frenzy of birds screeching and fluttering above her became a frantic noise, but Myrtle tried to focus and crawl to ease the ache, but something snagged at her foot. A large ivy-covered tendril draped down tentacle-like from a nearby tree and snaked around her ankle. She tried to tug it free, but another urge to push took over her efforts. A scream left her lips and left her fighting for breath; this was a struggle between the dark world and new life. Again, the ivy tugged as she tried to move.

'She's mine.'

Cold air circulated around Myrtle as the words were muttered.

'No. No. Never!' she screamed.

In an instant, the sky on her left turned black. She moved and focused on the unmistakable blue skyline on her right. She needed to overwhelm the dark storm. Frantic with fear, she asked for help.

> 'Blue to blue, I power you,
> Move to meet, and darkness beat,
> As I wish it, so mote it be.'

Lying back exhausted, Myrtle thought she had heard her name called in the distance. The crunch of twigs, indicating someone was approaching, agitated her, and she repeated her words louder and louder.

'Myrtle!'

It was Doctor Henson's voice.

'Myrtle!'

As she turned to face him, a whirlwind spun through the trees, and hands grabbed at her body, and Myrtle screamed.

'Myrtle, try and be calm.' Doctor Henson's steady voice helped her draw breath.

'Something wrong. Baby. Dead.'

'It's all right.' Richard Henson's soothing voice filtered through the noise of thunder now clattering above them and through blurred vision she saw his wife was with him.

'We are here to help you both. You are not alone. Granted, the conditions are not ideal, but we can do this together. You are far too along to walk home, and we can't carry you,' he said, and placed his hand on her abdomen to monitor the next contraction.

Sheila spoke. 'We came to see if you were ready to come and stay at ours until baby arrives, but here we are, amongst the leaves. Marigold said you would be here beneath a big tree – you must be a creature of habit.' Sheila gave a light, nervous laugh. 'Hold my hand dear, squeeze it when the pain is unbearable.'

Myrtle squeezed the warm hand and puffed out her pain. 'Marigold…'

'She's fine. Quite happy in the garden. Here we go. Now push,' the doctor instructed.

Pushing as hard as she could during the worst of her contractions, Myrtle did as instructed.

Suddenly, a loud wail echoed through the trees, and a chilling breeze swept through the woods, carrying with it the scent of damp earth. A feeling of impending doom swept through Myrtle.

Ink-black clouds reappeared and soon swiped out the blue, and the air crackled with an unnatural electricity. She heard a guttural growl but noticed neither of the Henson's reacted.

'I banish you from this space! I banish you from this place! Sisters, hear me, save us!' she screamed out.

'Hush now, don't worry about the storm. You are in safe hands. Let's get your baby out and home in the dry.'

Myrtle heard the concern in Doctor Henson's voice.

'We are in danger, do you understand?!' she cried out again.

'It's a storm. Nothing more. Breathe and push, there's a good girl,' Sheila said gently.

Myrtle sensed a rage brewing inside her during a deep breathing moment, but it was not something she had induced. Had it come from Marigold being stimulated by Myrtle's intense pain?

'I banish you from my mind and body! I banish you from my body and block you from my mind, as I will it so it shall be!' she cried out. 'Ragnis, tell them!'

'Richard, she's deranged. Banishing her child, what on earth is she saying?'

Sheila's agitation and concern brought Myrtle back to her situation. She had to push her baby out and get it away from the woods. The sooner she was in the safety of the Henson home, the better. She heard Ragnis call from a distance, a rallying call to the sisterhood.

'Child be born!' she yelled.

'That's right, come on, Myrtle, push!' Richard Henson urged.

Myrtle pushed again, and frantic whispers filled the air. The ancestors were drawing on their strength to aid her.

Hailstones fell. Then, the sun reappeared, followed by more hailstones.

'That's all we need: freak weather!' Richard Henson shouted above her head.

Myrtle gritted her teeth and gave another push, then inhaled.

'She is not yours!' she cried as the cackling laughter surrounded her.

'Richard!' Sheila's voice rang out in shock.

'It's the pain. She doesn't mean it, darling. This baby will be our child. Just comfort Myrtle, don't fret.'

'Sisters! I need you!' Myrtle shouted and touched the Tree of Life. She felt it vibrate and saw the shadowy figure step backwards, its strength fading. Somehow, her ancestors were attempting to suppress its power.

And then, with an abrupt silence, the storm ceased. The rain halted, the wind stilled, and the clouds dispersed. The Netherwell women had won an invisible battle by blocking the Longe family from using the Tree of Life as a portal.

With one last push, Myrtle delivered her child.

'It's a girl as you predicted,' Doctor Henson said, his voice loaded with emotion, and Myrtle knew he was ready to be a good father. 'She's a rosy-cheeked little thing. Sheila will stay with you. I'll go to the train station and call for an ambulance.'

'No!' Myrtle said firmly. 'No hospital. Just take her to

your home, check her there. Telephone Eve to come for me. She will tell Annette. Check on me later. I cannot take the risk; Marigold will not tolerate a baby in the house. Besides, the darkness has already tried to take the babe's spirit!'

Agitated, she shuddered with exhaustion.

'Hysterics won't help you, Myrtle. Talk of baby's spirit and mythical nonsense is not useful,' Sheila said.

'*Sheila,*' Doctor Henson's voice held a warning.

Suddenly, her little daughter gave a mew of a cry, and Sheila smiled.

'Attention-seeking already. Hold her, Myrtle. I thought about Lucy as a name, but what about her middle name?' Sheila bent down to Myrtle.

Myrtle shook her head; she was in no emotional state to hold her baby.

'Hold her, or your heart will break. She is still going to be in your life. We promised,' Sheila reassured her.

Myrtle reluctantly accepted the child and saw her mother's face staring back at her.

'I was going to call her Gaia Mystia,' Myrtle said, her voice cracking with emotion.

'That's an unusual name. Is it a family one?' Sheila asked.

'Yes. Two women from my mum's side. I've always liked the names. Gaia means goddess of the earth, and Mystia was a Netherwell who lived in the woods. In my head, she will always be Gaia.'

Richard lifted Myrtle's wrist and rechecked her pulse.

'They're fine names, aren't they, Sheila. I'll call Eve from the station; it'll be quicker than waiting until I get home,' he said.

When Myrtle finally arrived at her house, she assured a waiting Eve she was in no physical pain.

'I'm just tired, but I'll relax by taking a soothing bath. Where's Mari?'

Eve pointed to a figure at the end of the garden.

'Where she always is, talking to her flowers.' Eve laughed. 'Now, let's get you to bed.'

Once Eve was satisfied Myrtle was safe and resting in bed, she left.

Feeling completely drained, Myrtle slept until her sister began banging on the bedroom door, demanding food.

'I had the baby, Mari. Leave me to rest. Get a sandwich until Eve's mum comes later,' she said.

'So, I must eat bread and cheese because you had a baby,' Marigold shouted.

Myrtle listened to the sound of Marigold stomping her way downstairs and allowed self-pity to swallow her, pulling the covers over her head. She had no mother, no boyfriend and no child. What she did have was a psychotic, demanding sister. Nothing had changed except herself – now she was a woman who had given her child away.

Ragnis appeared at the open window. He peered inside, shuffled along the windowsill, and then sat at the end of her bed.

A fragrance she recognised filled the room.

'Mum?'

'Rest Myrtle. You have been brave, and I am sorry I am

not at your side to help you through it all. Keep Marigold calm, and we will do our best to hold back the dark side. Your Gaia is protected. We will watch over her.'

Myrtle caved into a deep sleep with heavy eyes until Richard called out from downstairs.

'Hello, Myrtle? It's Doctor Henson,' he called out.

'Come up,' Myrtle replied and listened to him tread the stairs, then tap on her bedroom door.

'Come in,' she said and sat up in bed with a ready smile – a fake smile to ensure his visit was swift.

'I saw Marigold as I came in; she hurled her usual welcoming go away, no men welcome,' he said with a laugh. 'I take it she heard about the baby?'

Myrtle shrugged her shoulders.

'She's angry I did not make lunch for her after I told her I had the baby, but she has not said anything else about it yet,' she said.

The doctor patted a bag by his feet.

'Sheila made you a large flask of chicken and vegetable broth to aid your recovery. There's enough for both of you. Now, get a good ten days' rest, remember.'

Myrtle burst out laughing.

'Ten days? I will be in deep trouble if Marigold hears me talking about staying in bed or resting for ten days, but I promise I will not overdo things. Thank Sheila for her kindness today,' she said.

Richard Henson nodded. 'Do reach out to us if you need help; never be afraid of doing that, Myrtle.'

She smiled. He was a good man – the kind of man she

would wish to be her father, so she had no qualms about him bringing up her child.

'How's the baby?' Marigold asked, dipping her spoon into her soup.

Myrtle looked at her hunched over a tray at her bedside, a wild child devouring every mouthful as if it were her last.

'Eat slowly, Mari,' she encouraged. 'Your niece is healthy and has good parents in Doctor and Sheila Henson.'

Marigold stopped eating and looked at her.

'You okay with that, strangers bringing her up?' she asked.

Taking a spoonful of her food, Myrtle took a moment to think about her reply.

'I am sad. Sad to the core. She is beautiful, and I would have loved to have her in my life, but I have you, Mari.'

'Does she look like you, or Dan?'

Marigold's apparently healthy interest and her questions threw Myrtle slightly, but she was touched.

'She's like Mum. You can meet her one day if you want.'

Marigold shook her head.

'I don't like children. Not even yours.'

Myrtle gave her a soft smile.

'Technically, she is no longer mine, and it would not be fair on either of you. Gaia would sense your tension.'

'That's her name?'

'Gaia Mystia, but the Hensons are calling her Lucy.'

'Nice.' Marigold laid down her tray on the bed and stood up.

She rummaged in her pocket and produced a grubby napkin wrapped around something.

'You can give her that; I was bored,' she said and handed the small package to Myrtle, who stood stunned. Never in her life had Marigold given a gift unprompted. She took a moment to appreciate what had happened. Marigold had accepted her niece into the world, just not into her life.

Unwrapping the napkin, Myrtle stared at the wooden half-moon attached to a brown leather strand. The small moon was carved with stars, and the wood was smooth and polished. Myrtle stroked it. 'It's beautiful, Mari. Truly beautiful. Thank you. I will see she gets it and is encouraged to wear it when she is older.'

'She might not like it, and don't think she can come here because of a piece of wood,' Marigold said. Before Myrtle could comment, her twin walked away.

Myrtle returned the necklace to its protective wrapping. She intended to cleanse and bless it before she handed it over to the Hensons. A guilty flush ran through her for not trusting her twin had not cursed the necklace, but she was not prepared to take the risk.

Chapter Seventeen

1981

Eve requested more beauty products for her mother's shop, prompting Myrtle to create new facial-care recipes.

With her mind occupied, it helped whenever sadness and the little regret over Gaia's adoption kicked in or when Marigold had tested her nerves for more than a day.

When she delivered the newest items to Eve, her friend handed her a leaflet.

'I think you should apply for a place,' she said, tapping the local college flier. 'They are offering new-business classes. Mum and I think it will be ideal for you to learn how to expand Naturally Netherwell. It would help to have something to occupy your mind outside Plumtree Cottage. Plus, you get official certificates.'

'I'm okay. I don't need anything new in my life,' Myrtle said, knowing the words were not entirely true. She was miserable. She no longer wanted to laugh, even at the small things. Nothing made her happy anymore.

'Come on, who are you kidding? What have you got to lose? A few hours a day, three times a week. It's a bike ride away,' Eve said, 'You can learn how to expand as you've always dreamed of, and Marigold will be okay for a few hours; I'll check on her.'

'Hmm. Business classes?' Myrtle mused, skimming through the brochure.

'It's perfect for you, Myrt. Try it for a term; leave if you don't like it,' Eve said.

Myrtle pushed the brochure back to her friend.

'I don't think so – it will be over my head – business studies – not sure that's my thing,' she said.

Eve pushed it back to her.

'Whatever you learn in that time will be money well spent. You can put it into practice to expand your Naturally Netherwell skincare range into a proper company. Or it will give you the skills to get a job with someone else,' Eve said.

Myrtle pulled a face. 'I will never work for someone else. How can I? I can't leave Marigold alone for too long.'

Eve gave an exasperated sigh. 'Then train to become an employer. Just stop moping about; what's done is done. You've given up on life, and it's sad.'

'I'll think about it. Thanks, Eve, thanks for trying, and for being there for me.'

Myrtle folded the flier and placed it in her jacket pocket.

'How is Gaia? Have you seen her lately?' Eve asked as she glanced through the fresh batch of facial products Myrtle handed her.

'She's growing fast and is sitting up unaided now. Sheila keeps her spotless and is a good mother, but she never shows her any affection, not like Richard.'

'Maybe she feels awkward showing it in front of you; it can't be easy having the birth mother visit,' Eve said.

Myrtle shrugged. 'Perhaps. It's not easy seeing my daughter with her, either, but she's a happy child and safe; that's all that matters.'

Life at home ticked along with daily chores, keeping Marigold on an even keel and away from the general public, and coping with the mess she created when crafting inside the home. Myrtle's savings increased from selling her skincare products, and she set aside money to build Marigold a workshop. Her wood whittling had taken on a new life, and the pieces were growing.

One late afternoon in January, Marigold walked indoors, her face red, and Myrtle could see she was highly agitated.

'He's back, Myrt. I heard him, he's back!' Marigold shouted.

Something clutched at Myrtle's heart as she spoke and froze on the spot.

'I take it by you yelling out he's back that you mean Ingulf?'

Marigold shook her head. 'It was Edmunde this time. I tried to ignore him, but he said he wanted *me* to join him when he takes Gaia. But I don't want to go without you,' Marigold pouted.

Nerves tingled, and Myrtle's body tensed.

If more Longe men communicated with Marigold, it would not bode well for Gaia or Myrtle.

'Has Edmunde communicated with you before?' Myrtle asked, not sure she wanted to hear the answer.

'Ingulf's father, Edmunde, Samuel Day, so many of them have merged with the dark one, Ingulf,' Marigold replied. 'I've told you, they want us both – and now they want Gaia, too. The only way you can protect her is by giving in. The Hensons and their friends are safe – unless I tell everyone their daughter is a natural-born witch,' Marigold taunted, adding a spiteful smile.

Myrtle's throat felt constricted. A panic attack threatened her ability to think; she bent forward, trying to concentrate.

Fight Myrtle – ignore Marigold; do not let her into your head. Collect your thoughts. Breathe. Breathe. She is weakening you.

I draw on my strength as a woman in battle. Keep the demons from me and my child. Breathe. Breathe.

'Worried about something?'

Her sister's smug question infuriated Myrtle, and she took two more deep breaths.

'Marigold, listen to me. You must never, I mean *never*, speak to anyone outside of our home about me giving birth to Gaia. Gaia is not to know I am her biological mother. Promise me,' she said.

'Pinky promise,' Marigold said childishly, waggling her little finger at Myrtle. 'But the Longe family will take her anyway. She cannot live – she has your blood.'

Myrtle rushed into the sitting room, picked up her black salt dish, and took a handful, pushing it into Marigold's dungaree pockets.

'Find anything to protect yourself, Mari, do some spell work. Just as I thought our lives were getting easier. Damn the Longe family. Damn them!'

'Some say damn the Netherwells. Do you really think I care about protecting myself? I am my father's daughter; he lives through me. Black salt won't work, sister dear.' Marigold gave a sharp laugh which ripped through Myrtle's body like a vice. Her sister had increased her threats thanks to their father and his ancestors' hold over her. Myrtle had to find a way – find renewed strength to protect Gaia without the Hensons knowing.

That night, when Marigold snored enough to prove she was asleep, Myrtle crept into her bedroom carrying a poppet doll and carefully tucked it at the end of Marigold's bed.

Retain your demons. Store their venom and hold onto their drive to kill.

She lit a black candle outside Marigold's door to ward off any lingering demons and went to bed in the hope that she had stifled the Longe voices while her sister slept. She intended to carry out the ritual until she was satisfied that her effort had helped suppress the Longe family in some small way.

———————

By the end of March, spring poked its head through the ground in the form of colourful bulbs, and slowly, the countryside looked alive again. The protection-laden home and night-time spells appeared to have held off the Longe threats. Marigold appeared calmer, and Myrtle looked forward to a peaceful spring.

She took a collection of tiny ragdolls to Gaia. They were all spell-protected with the crystals Selenite and Amethyst, wrapped in cloths steeped and dried with the herbs Angelica and St John's wort, and turned into protection poppets hidden inside the doll.

On a visit one afternoon, Sheila took Myrtle to Gaia's bedroom and showed her the dolls sitting on a shelf along one wall.

'They are sweet but too good for Lucy to play with just now, so Richard built a shelf for them. You have many talents, Myrtle, and your needlework is exquisite,' she said, and her kind words touched Myrtle.

'Thank you. I meant to say they are for show. I should have said that when I brought the first one. It is good of you to accept them for her. It helps me, as I feel I am doing something for her when I sew. If it's okay with you, I would like to make her a quilt one day,' she replied.

Sheila smiled. 'That would be lovely. Now, let's go downstairs, and you can tell me about the college course. Do you have everything you need?'

Myrtle left the visit reassured that her daughter had enough protection from outside influences while Myrtle was not around.

Life was less stressful, and Marigold threw herself into her spring and Ostara projects.

Having accepted her college place, Myrtle was preparing for her course, which was due to start at the beginning of April.

When she'd mentioned it to Marigold, her sister took it surprisingly well but flatly refused to have Eve's mother keep her company. They agreed on a routine, and Myrtle counted down the days.

On her first day at college, Myrtle was on edge. She touched the carnelian crystal in her dress pocket for reassurance and to absorb its gift of self-belief and motivation.

The large, modern building did not give off welcoming warmth, and as she turned to return home, she managed to walk into the path of a very tall male, winding him in the stomach.

'Watch out down there,' he quipped, looking down at her with large brown cow-like eyes. He had the longest and thickest lashes she had seen on a man. His teeth were white and straight, and his smile was wide. The welcoming warmth she had looked for was in him.

'I am so sorry. I was just, um. Oh, I am sorry.' She stuttered out her words, and the man still smiled down at her. She looked at the floor, not out of shyness but in the need to ease her aching neck. He was well over six feet tall.

'You are forgiven, oh Copper Queen. I'm Harry, business studies,' he replied and held out his hand in greeting.

Myrtle hesitated, then took his hand; it was warm, and she felt a friendly connection. Nothing sinister fed back from him.

'Hello, Harry Business Studies, I'm Myrtle Netherwell,' she said with a laugh as she shook his hand.

Harry laughed too, and it echoed around the characterless building. He brought the space alive for Myrtle, and the urge to run home left her.

'Clever. Very clever,' Harry said. 'So, what course are you studying? Hairdressing?' He cast his eyes over her head.

Conscious of her freshly washed red hair sitting glossy, halfway down her back, she forgave him for thinking it may be a course she would follow. As far as Myrtle was concerned, her hair was her best asset.

'Actually, I'm also studying business studies,' she replied, 'no one would want a haircut from me, that's for sure!'

Looking up at Harry gave her a pleasant shiver. He was a good-looking man, and his smile and soft voice suggested he was a kind and caring person.

Then she remembered Gaia, Dan and her past. Flirting with someone was not the way to start her new life.

'Do you know where our lecture room is?' she asked, looking towards the stairs ahead.

'First floor, room two,' Harry replied. 'Let's go in together; it's less nerve-wracking.'

Myrtle smiled. She had little doubt he was the nervous type, but he was sensitive enough to see that she was too, and had extended the hand of friendship.

'Lead the way, Harry Business Studies,' she said and followed him up the stairs.

'Ready?' Harry asked as they peered inside and saw several heads seated in anticipation of their first lesson.

'As I'll ever be. Okay, let's do this,' Myrtle said. As Harry held open the door for her, she was fully aware of all the heads in the room, turning around to see two complete opposites walk into the room and sit side by side.

Harry leaned into her and whispered, 'Do you think they noticed how alike we are?'

Holding back a belly laugh, Myrtle turned and grinned at him.

'Hard not to,' she replied.

Harry became the reason Myrtle looked forward to her college days. Life at home was calm, but Myrtle realised that unless she had chats and giggles with Eve, she had no banter-style conversations with anyone else. She did not need a string of friendships, but she did want to build on the one with Harry.

One morning, when she and Harry sat in the college canteen, they chatted about the classes they had enjoyed during the past term.

'Until I came here, I had no idea about running a legitimate business. The rules and regulations that go with it scare me,' she said.

Harry gave a nod of agreement.

'Tell me about it. Mind you, I envy your skills at remembering stuff and writing notes you can actually decipher; mine are crap.'

Myrtle laughed. 'You have other skills. Look at how you manage the economic side of things and the tax info. That makes my eyes bleed.'

'It will be needed when I set up my garden centre,' Harry said and pulled out a tatty notebook from his backpack. 'It's all in here, my life plans for Tye's Delights.'

Myrtle stared at him, 'Tye's Delights? Is that set in stone?' she asked carefully.

Harry shrugged, 'No. Why?'

'It sounds, well, I don't know, a bit porn-shoppish, or something like a cake shop. I can't relate it to a garden centre...' Myrtle blushed. 'Sorry. My small venture is Naturally Netherwell. It's not great, but it suggests something about the product is natural. I get orders via my stockists every week.'

'Lucky you. Grow your empire! Okay, what better name can you come up with for mine?' Harry asked.

Myrtle sat thinking.

'Go simple. Why not Harry's Garden Centre? Customers immediately know the owner's name and what the business is. Gradually, it will become their go-to place, and they will just call it Harry's.'

'You're a genius,' said Harry,

Myrtle smiled. 'It's a shame my sister isn't more of a social person. You and her would get on great. There's nothing my sister can't grow. You'll have to come and see her gardens. They are seasonal, and she grows the herbs and flowers for my products.'

'I'd love to meet her,' Harry said.

'Mmm, well, you might see her but won't meet her. She's, um, shy.' Myrtle said, crossing her fingers against the white lie she had told. There was nothing shy about Marigold.

'Here it is,' Myrtle said. 'Our humble abode.'

'You were born here? It's beautiful. My god, is that a fox over there?' Harry said, pointing at the edge of the woods. 'Oh, it's gone...' He stood back for a better view of Myrtle's home.

Myrtle took in his face as he gazed at the small Suffolk

brick-and-flint home bathed in ivy with its thatched roof and slanted chimney pot, which added to its quaintness. It sat in the centre of the garden, now showing signs of yellow spring blooms breaking through fresh, vibrant greenery, and it all added to the chocolate-box image of a quaint British olde worlde property. She got a shimmer of pleasure seeing Harry admire her home.

'Every ancestor dating back to the medieval period has lived here. It's been adapted over the years. Mum made improvements at the suggestion of the local council, but we lived without too many modern alterations. Still do,' she said with pride as she opened the front door.

'Wow, that's impressive,' replied Harry.

'If you look carefully behind the chimney, you will see Ragnis, our resident raven,' Myrtle said, watching as Harry walked to get a better view.

'Why is there a man wandering around my vegetable garden!'

Marigold's voice exploded across the grounds from the edge of the woods where she had been foraging. She stood with her hands on her hips and her legs wide apart. Her hair blew wildly from beneath her knitted cap, and her cheeks were flushed red with anger.

'Calm down. Be nice,' Myrtle said softly as she walked towards her. 'This is Harry Tye. He's a friend from college. He's come to meet you, and I promised him a piece of land to grow his fruit and vegetables.'

'They won't be as good as mine,' Marigold said, and when Harry laughed, she gave him a glaring look.

'We're also going to work out where I can have a proper building for Naturally Netherwell because I've learned it is a bit more complicated legally than I thought, so my lessons have already paid off.'

Marigold gave a harumph and a foot stomp in reply.

'Everything is complicated when the outside world interferes,' she muttered, moving towards Harry. 'Mind your feet on the camomile bed.'

Harry smiled at her, and Myrtle froze as her sister stopped and stared at him. She recognised the signs, what would come next, but before she could urge Harry to come inside, she saw Marigold's fists round at her side, and her jawline tightening.

'Why are you smiling at me?' Marigold questioned him.

Harry faltered, and his smile left his face. He looked frantically at Myrtle and then back at the still-glaring Marigold.

'I smiled to say a friendly hello,' he said, his voice filled with nervous tension.

Myrtle quickly interjected.

'Marigold. I told you, he's a friend. Harry smiled because you are my sister,' she said hastily.

Marigold turned away from them both and looked around the garden before turning back.

'He can grow over there,' she said, pointing at an area Myrtle and Harry had discussed earlier and walked away.

'Blimey, I thought she was gonna punch me then,' Harry said with relief. 'She's taller than me! She certainly protects you.'

He smiled at Myrtle.

'She's my twin – I know, chalk and cheese, right? Just like you and me.' Myrtle smiled. 'Marigold has, um, problems and doesn't like strangers. She must think you're okay because she's let you live.'

Harry laughed. 'Lucky me. I thought you said she was shy!'

'Shoot me, I lied,' Myrtle said, grinning. 'If I'd told you the truth you would never have come here.'

'Are you free for a drink tonight?' Harry asked suddenly, taking Myrtle by surprise.

'Oh, no. I'm sorry, I don't, I haven't – um,' her words failed her as she stammered an apology.

'Got a fella? Not surprised, no worries,' Harry said, and Myrtle could see his discomfort in her rejection. She waved a hand.

'No, it's not that, I had… I'm not married, and I haven't got a boyfriend, and actually, I'd love to join you, but another day,' she said quickly before he walked away and she lost her opportunity to say yes. 'I warn you, though, we lead a very different life to many of the girls you might know, and local gossip creates strange stories. Marigold is a handful; our mother died, and I am in charge of my sister's care,' Myrtle finished, breathlessly, having rushed out her words.

Harry burst out laughing. 'There's a rumour you are a witch if that's what you mean,' he said. 'When I first saw you, I thought you were dressed in the latest fashion like the goth rockers. Anyway, being a witch is no different than any other religion. I mean, Goth has followers a bit like you, like I said.'

'Goth? I'm unsure what that is, but I enjoy dark clothing and natural things,' Myrtle said, then decided she wanted to be honest with Harry. He had heard gossip but needed to hear her side of things.

'I'll be honest with you, Harry, 'cos I think I can trust you – and rumours are dangerous things. My family are natural-born witches. I'm not Goth, but I am a practising witch. I tried not to be once, but it worked out pretty bad, so I returned to what I know and understand.'

Harry grinned back at her as he leaned against the fence, 'Right. Really? Tell me more – this is fascinating stuff,' he said.

'Yes, really. Our ancestors were Pagan witches, but merged with Wiccan over the years. Marigold and I were brought up under the guidance of other women and our mum. Each generation of our family was the high priestess until Mum died. Because I've decided to follow in her footsteps, I'm also studying to be a high priestess.'

'What's one of those?' Harry asked.

'Basically, it's the head witch of a group. I'm learning to become a teacher of our beliefs, not preaching but guiding, helping them find their spiritual pathway – understanding our rituals and keeping grounded in a modern world. Honouring Mother Nature.'

'Aren't pagans and witches evil? Freaky stuff, like spells and all that,' Harry said, with real fascination in his voice.

'I think you would know by now if I was evil,' she said

with a laugh. 'I was not the one who got half the project answers wrong last week, and thought I was most forgiving.'

Harry pulled a dramatic hurt face and she belly-laughed.

'Fair enough,' he said.

'Anything you want to ask?' Myrtle said, waiting for Harry to make a swift exit. Instead, she was surprised when he perched himself on an old, upturned barrel and looked at her.

'So, are men called wizards? Was your dad one?' He asked.

Myrtle shook her head.

'There's been no dad in my life,' she replied, 'and men are also called witches. Although we do not have men in our coven, we are very much a sisterhood.'

'Coven?'

'Family of witches.'

'Like a gang or one of them cult things – you know, all sex dances for the devil?' Harry asked and gave a grin.

Myrtle looked at him in horror. She knew people associated paganism with the occult and outrageous couplings, but to hear someone say it out loud annoyed her.

'It's nothing like that; people make up their minds about what they don't understand or have no wish to learn. My sister and I tend to be more solitary in some of our ways. We are normal people doing normal things, coming together to celebrate our belief in the universe.'

She paused for breath, knowing she'd sounded offended.

'Marigold and I follow the seasons and celebrate them. We believe all things natural,' she said. 'Our celebrations are lively and happy events, or they can be quiet and calm, depending on the individual, but we do not dance for or with the devil. Most keep quiet about their belief because they worry about what others think, but some will talk about it openly. I only tell those I trust, and even then only on a need-to-know basis.'

Harry lifted an eyebrow. 'What celebrations do you have?'

'Lammas Day in August is for the harvest period, and everyone celebrates the birth of a new autumn. Samhain – pronounced "Sah win" – is the same day as Halloween and welcomes the coming winter.'

'Hmm, I'm not a fan of winter. Holds up my work,' Harry said, 'but carry on, this really is fascinating.'

'Yule is what we celebrate around the time you celebrate Christmas. Christmas and Yule are a bit alike. Our Pagan ancestors were kissing under the mistletoe long before anyone else. We celebrate the spring equinox around the same time that Christians celebrate Easter. I could go on, but hey, as I said, no devil worship here.' Myrtle laughed.

Harry nodded. 'Yeah, I get it now, a bit anyway. Sorry, I was a bit of a dick. My mother would clip my ear for being rude.'

Myrtle smiled.

'So, still want to take me out for a drink sometime?'

Harry jumped to his feet.

'I'll risk it. Oh, just one thing, is it safe to come here and pick you up in the dark?' Harry said with a wink, and Myrtle laughed loudly in response.

'It is unless Marigold is in one of her moods, but I'll put a burning flame over the gate if that happens. When it does, you had better run home, she's fast on her broomstick,' she teased back.

Chapter Eighteen

'Shall we get some candy floss? My treat,' Harry's voice called out over the noise of the penny slot machines as they made their way outside.

It had been a week since Harry had visited their home, and Myrtle agreed to spend the afternoon with him at the lively Sheringham arcade.

'What's it like?' Myrtle asked, sniffing and inhaling the sweet and savoury smells permeating the air around them. The whole place was alien to her, and her heart pounded with excitement as she listened to the music and the dinging, pinging sounds of the arcade machines around them.

'Don't tell me you've never had candy floss?' Harry asked, frowning at her in amazement.

Shaking her head and feeling slightly foolish, Myrtle gave him a sheepish look.

'Mum never allowed us. It was an expense she could

never afford.' She hooked her arm through his. 'Come on then, show me how magic it is.'

After queuing and watching people walk away with large bags of pink wispy floss, Harry ceremoniously handed her her own large, conical-shaped pack.

Myrtle couldn't wait to try it and quickly unwound the top. She copied a girl standing nearby, and pulled out a large piece with her finger and thumb, folding it gently into her mouth. Before she swallowed, she felt the tingle of the sugar as it melted on her tongue and the sweetness as it burned the back of her throat.

'Mmm, this is delicious,' she said as she pulled another clump and ate it as they walked along the seafront.

'I can't believe this is your first candy floss. We'll get a cola next. Please tell me you've had a cola,' Harry said, staring at Myrtle as she allowed the last piece of her treat to dissolve on her tongue, ignoring the sickly feeling in her stomach.

'Obviously, I've heard of it, but I've never had one,' she replied, and for the first time, she felt embarrassed. 'I'll buy the cola. Where do we get one?'

After they'd bought the colas, they sat on a giant rock beside the water's edge, and Harry handed her one of the two bottles. The drink was lukewarm and fizzled around her mouth, foaming as she took in its flavour. It was very sweet and did nothing for the nagging headache she'd acquired after the candy floss.

'Delicious,' she said and suddenly Harry awkwardly leaned in for a kiss, catching her unawares. She pulled back.

She had deliberately kept it light-hearted between them, but it was obvious Harry wanted more.

'Ooh, sticky lips!' she said and laughed lightly.

Flushed with embarrassment, Harry leaned back and took a sip of his drink.

'Friends, Harry. Let's keep it at friends,' she said softly.

'Yeah, sorry,' Harry said, 'that was clumsy of me.'

Myrtle smiled, thinking it best not to say anything. As much as she liked Harry, she did not need another boyfriend.

'Don't apologise. I had a boyfriend, and my lifestyle and men aren't a good match, put it that way.'

'Because of being a witch?' Harry asked.

'Because of being a carer for a demanding sister,' Myrtle said, her voice flat, wishing she could bring herself to tell him the truth. They got on so well, but she was not prepared to scare him off by telling him she had been pregnant and given birth to a daughter whom she'd put up for adoption.

'Will you tell your sister?' Harry asked.

Myrtle stopped sipping her drink. 'About what?'

'About the candy floss, cola, the arcade – all the things I've experienced since I was old enough to walk, and can't get my head around that you haven't enjoyed any of till now. Will she be jealous?' Harry said.

'Marigold? No, because she will never find out. I've learned a way of blocking her when I have fun,' Myrtle said, 'and this has been the best fun I've had for a long time. Thank you, Harry, you are a true friend.'

'Yeah, sorry about the kiss thing. Forgive me?' Harry asked.

'Never,' Myrtle teased and linked her arm to his.

Back home, Marigold's shouting and screaming from the cottage filled the air, and Myrtle ran down the path, her stomach aching from the sugar treats she had consumed.

'Go away, you evil hag! I will not wear clothes when I don't want to; it's my home, not yours. You keep me prisoner here!' Marigold's voice chanted out loud and strong.

Myrtle raced upstairs just in time to see Marigold pushing Eve's mother away from her as she tried to persuade her to at least wear a dressing gown.

'Ingulf wants me to dance for him!' Marigold shouted, 'Get out!'

Myrtle's heart sank. Marigold's demons were back.

'Mari, put the dressing gown on and listen to me. Can you manage that?' Myrtle said softly. 'We'll go downstairs and make cocoa…' She smiled at Eve's mother and gestured with her eyes to the top of the stairs.

'What happened?' Myrtle asked when they were out of Marigold's earshot.

'I thought I would drop by and check on her, and well, I found her running naked around the garden. It won't do, Myrtle.'

'She hates it when I go out in the evening,' Myrtle said,

'but cocoa will settle her down. I'm sorry you had to experience a tantrum. Thank you for keeping her company.'

Eve's mother shook her head. 'I daren't say what I'd like to, as I respect all you have been through, Myrtle. But truly, don't give up your life for your sister. Enjoy time out with friends, get a life away from her.'

With a shake of her head, Myrtle sighed. 'You know my answer to that; my promise to Mum was not something I just said because she was dying—'

The sounds of Marigold coming out of her room upstairs stopped her.

'Hush, no more talk of me going anywhere; she's coming down.'

Marigold walked into the kitchen wearing a hideous array of clothing, and Myrtle glanced at Eve's mum. 'I'd go home now if I were you. She's wearing what she calls her creative clothes. If I can't get her to sleep, it will be a long night working on one of her projects,' she said with a smile.

'No life for a girl of your age!' Eve's mother said, pulling on her coat. 'It'll end in tears.'

After they had gone to bed and she was in a comfortable sleep, a noise from the kitchen disturbed Myrtle. Confused for a few seconds, she lay still and listened to the clatter and banging. She guessed her sister had gone back downstairs to create something, and Myrtle had no doubt it would be a messy project. Listening to the sounds of pots and pans rattling on the stove, it was an experimental cookery one. She sighed and climbed out of bed. Glancing at her clock, she noted it was two o'clock in the morning.

Opening the kitchen door and seeing what resembled the end stages of a food fight, Myrtle wished she could release the chains of care and enjoy a carefree candy-floss moment.

'Mari, let's have an early breakfast,' she said, and she made a start clearing up her sibling's mess. There was no point in attempting to encourage Marigold back to bed.

After their meal and clearing the kitchen mess, they sat on the back porch watching the sunrise.

'My favourite time of day,' Myrtle said as she watched the sky turn from white and grey to a vibrant pink and orange display of sparkling threads above the rooftops. It was going to be another warm day.

'I like the night,' Marigold replied.

Myrtle looked at her sister, a wild child with no concept of time.

'You always say that, but you can't tend to your garden at night. You love your garden, and animals.'

'Sometimes I'm with our dad at night; we travel together,' Marigold replied.

A shiver ran through Myrtle's body. Her father still controlled Marigold, despite Myrtle's attempts to banish him every night.

'I don't see that as a reason to love the night,' she said. 'Someone controlling your mind is not good.'

'You like the sun; I like the dark. Deal with it,' Marigold

replied, and Myrtle knew it was the end of the conversation. To pursue it would mean agitating her sister.

When she'd finished her chores, Myrtle walked to the Tree of Life to enjoy a moment of calm.

'Greetings, Tree, Mother sun is bright, and I bathe in her glory. I ask that she recharge my crystals and bless the water I bring. I've noticed my sister has more confused days than good ones, and I need to keep her safe from her demons and call on the help of my ancestors. I bless your roots and wish you a long life, so mote it be.'

Myrtle sat beneath the tree before she headed home with a renewed sense of well-being. She sensed a disappointment when she saw the back of Harry cycling down the lane. Too far for her to call him back.

'I saw Harry has been to fix the door on my new workshop,' Myrtle said to Marigold when she checked on her sister inside the barn. 'Did he stay long?'

'Too long,' Marigold muttered, brushing a goat free from dried mud.

Myrtle frowned.

'I hope you were kind,' she said.

'I told him it was time for him to go; I didn't want his company anymore. He said okay and left,' Marigold muttered; her body language told Myrtle she was hiding something.

'Did you force him to leave with a spell?' she asked, not sure if she wanted to hear the answer.

'Let's just say he won't look at you in the same way ever again,' Myrtle retorted and gave a self-satisfied smile.

'What have you done?' Myrtle asked, keeping her voice calm and steady.

'I told him you are not available as a girlfriend because your old boyfriend is coming back to help you with the baby you have together. Then I told him he would meet another girl and marry her – that was the spell. I distanced him from you – he's not taking you from me,' Marigold said smugly.

'You did what?!' Myrtle exclaimed, her heart beating so fast she thought she would faint.

'Oh, don't worry, his lips are sealed on your secret. He won't ever be able to tell anyone. Someone has to protect you. Besides, when we join Dad and the others, Harry won't have to mourn you – it saves him from heartbreak.' Marigold returned her attention to the goat.

Myrtle's body ran cold. Marigold had betrayed her. She had to find Harry to see how far Marigold had gone with her spells.

Inside the cottage, the ticking clock on the wall sounded louder than ever, and Myrtle felt the atmosphere was better suited to a funeral. It dawned on her that this was her future. Every day until death parted them, this would be how she and Marigold lived: rare conversations, friends, they would all be dismissed by her twin as and when it suited her.

Tick. Tick.

Myrtle closed her eyes and inhaled, then let out a drawn-out breath.

Shut up.

Tick. Tick.

Stop it!

Tick…

She swung an angry glance at the clock, which clattered to the floor with a crash.

Myrtle stared at it for a while. Had her anger enhanced her power? Did her passive nature suppress her magick and render it weaker than Marigold's? Marigold was always angry about something. Why was she only realising it now? Anger was a form of protection, too.

'Maybe I should be angry more often,' Myrtle said to the room. Pulling on her jacket, she went to find Harry.

'Keep your anger, Myrtle. Keep it flowing; Harry might need help,' she muttered to herself as she wheeled her bicycle down the path and peddled to nearby Kelling Heath, where she thought Harry may have headed.

Chapter Nineteen

Dismounting her bike, Myrtle looked at the weather-beaten buildings in front of her. Harry's dream was still in its early stages, but he had purchased land and received planning permission to build his garden centre.

Across the central courtyard, Myrtle saw him staining wooden window frames. She watched him while she composed her words, and once she had settled the tremble inside of her, she approached him.

'Hi, not interrupting, am I?' she asked cheerfully.

Harry turned and looked at her. He gave a smile.

'Myrtle, great to see you. I'll be glad when all the frames are coated; it's not the most exciting job on the planet, but it will save me a fortune.'

Myrtle hesitated. Harry's voice was friendly, and there was nothing to suggest that Marigold had upset him.

'Marigold said you'd been to the cottage and fixed the door. Sorry, I missed you and thanks for helping. I understand she kicked you off the premises when you had finished. I'm sorry about her manners. Here, a bottle of fresh apple and pear juice as a peace offering,' she said, holding out the brown bottle.

Harry placed his paintbrush on the lid of his tin and took the bottle from her. As Myrtle looked into his eyes, she smiled. 'So, did she have a chat or tittle-tattle about me?' she asked, watching him closely.

Opening the bottle and drinking a mouthful, Harry gave a slight shake of his head, then lowered his drink.

'She didn't tell me how good this is, and no, she simply stared into my face like a woman possessed and muttered something about girlfriends, and I can't remember much else except she walked me to the gate and told me not to come back. You know, in her usual polite manner.' Harry laughed, and Myrtle felt relief rush through her body. Marigold's ranting had failed to take hold, it had not damaged the friendship, nor had it unnerved him.

'You know you are always welcome at Plumtree Cottage. Now, do you have another paintbrush?' Myrtle asked.

She monitored Harry's behaviour towards her for a month and helped him build his dream business. She gave him plants from her greenhouses and a generous number of Naturally Netherwell products to get him started.

'The new sign goes up tomorrow,' Harry said with pride one morning as they took a break from finishing the last of the cleaning.

'You must be so proud, I'm proud of you. And your first

employee seems nice,' Myrtle said, nodding towards a young woman wiping down a second-hand cash register and filling the sections with the correct money.

'Mel? Yeah, she ticked all the boxes – great plant knowledge and friendly. I had chosen someone older, a man, but the last time I was at yours, I changed my mind and decided on her. It had been a good interview – I like her and think she'll fit right in around here,' Harry said, looking over at Mel. Myrtle felt a pang of jealousy when Mel looked back at him and winked.

This was the girl Marigold had manifested for Harry. So, at least part of her spell tactic had worked. Harry was not to be the man for Myrtle, and it did not take long for her to decide what to do.

'Well, you are busy, and Mel certainly looks as if she's found her feet,' she said, looking over at the brown-haired girl, nigh on Harry's height, who was now spraying water over a selection of indoor plants. 'Good luck, Harry,' she said. 'See you again soon.'

And Myrtle walked away, fighting the tears pricking her eyes.

To cast a spell to reverse what her sister had done was not necessary. As much as she liked Harry, and yes, in time, maybe had forged a romance with him, she had to be realistic. It was kinder for them both to let things be. College was over, and she had won the Female Business Student award. It was time for both her and Harry to look to a new future and practise what they had learned.

Chapter Twenty

With Ragnis still keeping pace above her, Myrtle cycled through her beloved Weybourne.

Nightshade lay curled up in the front basket – her constant companions made her happy, and she felt loved.

Ambling past the flint and stone houses and through the village which nestled within the embrace of centuries-old stories and had a timeless grace, echoes of generations past, Myrtle sniffed the air. It carried the comforting aroma of wood smoke, and the cool sea air caressed her face. She took as many narrow, leafy lanes as she could to avoid the few thoughtless drivers who used the main roads as racetracks, before entering Sheringham town.

She looked up at the blue sky.

'How lucky we are, Nightshade. No matter what happens in life, nature turns its wheel and shares everything with us, to remind us of how blessed we are to live on such a beautiful planet.'

Climbing down from her aged bicycle, she chained it to a metal post a few feet from the craft shop, not that she needed to worry, one hiss from Nightshade would send any thief running.

Myrtle cherished her bicycle and was thankful she had never outgrown it. She loved the sense of freedom it provided her.

With her hands on her hips, she stretched her neck and back, shook her skirt to release it from its folds, and then lifted her bag from the basket attached to the bike. She looked over at Eve's rooftop and smiled when she saw Ragnis sitting on the apex.

Summoning courage, she entered a popular boutique to buy some new clothes – something she had not done for several years.

The late July weather was in her favour – not too hot. However, thanks to her nerves, when she stepped inside the shop, she felt clammy.

She had accepted an invitation to talk at a business event in the college about her journey with Naturally Netherwell.

She pondered the idea of modernising her look and creating a more business-like Myrtle who could confidently give a lecture about women overseeing projects in a male environment, a subject she was passionate about.

In the back of her mind, Myrtle feared that she would flounder and stammer when she stepped onto the podium. Something had to change, and if it meant her style, she needed to talk with the shop assistant about a suitable look for the event. The young woman who listened threw herself into helping Myrtle.

When Myrtle's eyes met her reflection in the mirror, with her hair artfully pulled back in a fluffed-out loose ponytail, she couldn't help but admire the image of a poised and self-assured businesswoman, and the sight of herself in heeled shoes was almost unbelievable.

Agreeing the outfit suited her, Myrtle bought everything, including the make-up the girl had used to give her a fresh look, and hoped Eve and her mother would have the same opinion as the girl in the shop.

She walked down the street carefully in the heels and stepped inside the craft shop. Suddenly, she felt out of place, not wearing her usual comfortable floating skirts and tops. As the doorbell tinkled, a voice called from the back, 'Be right with you.'

Then Myrtle heard a male voice – Harry.

She wanted to turn and run; she did not want Harry to see her making a fool of herself, but her feet wouldn't move. Besides, she told herself that running in heeled shoes was not something she could accomplish.

She grinned when Eve ventured out from behind the curtain that divided the shop from her home. Eve stood still, her eyes widening in surprise.

'Myrtle?' she said. 'You look amazing.'

'Thank you.' Myrtle smiled.

'Woah,' came Harry's voice from behind Eve, 'you look incredible.'

Myrtle's stomach flipped with excitement – at both of their reactions and at seeing Harry again.

He's a friend, she reminded herself, nothing more.

'I wasn't sure about this...' she looked down at her clothes, 'but I'm giving the women's business group a talk on my own business, how I built it up, and I wanted to avoid looking like the local gardener.'

Harry laughed.

'Nothing wrong with what the local gardener wears,' he said, indicating his own grubby clothing. 'Anyway, best be going back to it. I can't leave Mel on her own; we're getting busier.' He smiled at her. 'See you around, Myrt. Good luck with the talk. And thanks for the shelves, Eve.'

'No problem,' said Eve, as Harry left the shop. She waited a second before she turned to Myrtle.

'What on earth went wrong with you two?' she said. 'He's mad about you. Even more now, I bet. You look fabulous. So trendy and powerful!'

Raising her eyebrows, Myrtle sighed. 'Stop trying to matchmake. Anyway, Harry's got the hots for Mel. Me and him, we're just friends.'

'If you say so,' said Eve, just as her mother appeared, giving Myrtle a soft smile.

'You look wonderful, dear, but be careful about making changes in order to gain other people's approval. I know your speech will impress. No errors, only inspiration.'

She held out a brown file. 'In fact, it's inspired me to make a few alterations around here. Your mother would have been so proud of you.'

The compliment touched Myrtle. Eve's mother, a woman who had run her own business for many years, had been inspired by something Myrtle had written.

It gave her the boost, the courage, she needed.

'Thank you, and I promise always to be me,' she said, embracing both Eve and her mother.

Standing at the podium three weeks later, Myrtle took a deep breath, feeling the weight of anticipation from the sea of heads before her. Clutching her briefcase and dressed in her new outfit, she was armed with everything necessary, including courage.

She steeled herself for what lay ahead, but just as she placed her briefcase on the nearby table and took a sip of water, a creak from the lecture room door diverted everyone's attention to the back, where a woman muttered her apologies for being late. As the woman found a seat, Myrtle saw out of the corner of her eye a shadowy figure against the wall.

When the room turned its gaze back to her, unimpressed by the latecomer, the mysterious shadow remained, an ominous presence that Myrtle sensed was connected to the Longes – maybe her father. It moved behind everyone in the room, hovering above their heads. She felt slightly nauseous, and annoyed that this was ruining a significant moment in her life.

Stay in control. You have the power and strength to protect this room, so be it.

Breathe.

Stay in control. You have the power and strength to protect this room, so be it.

A realisation struck her; perhaps she had inadvertently let her guard down during her speech preparation, enabling the dark side to manifest itself again – or had Marigold summoned them and told them Myrtle would be distracted? Had a Longe spirit sensed her newfound courage and sought to claim her spirit before it could grow any stronger?

Through the microphone, she said, 'If you will excuse me,' and retreated to a quiet corner off-stage. She could hear the women whispering around the theatre. Then she heard a man's harsh voice. His voice.

'You will not win this battle. They are mine. You are mine.'

With her eyes closed, Myrtle fumbled for the intention pouch in her pocket, focused on the mental fortress she had built, and added words to help her through the speech.

Please give me the power to be myself, to show my courage and inspire. Grant me a room of peace and like-minded women. Remove the dark shadows wishing me harm. I take back my power. As I will it, so mote it be.

A sudden flicker of light across the stage stirred a murmur from the audience. An electric bulb popped from a side lamp, and a woman squealed as it made her jump. Nervous laughter filtered around the room.

Myrtle took calming breaths as she peered around the wall, looking to the back of the room and then swiftly over the heads of the giggling women. The lurking figure had vanished. Satisfied she had managed to stave off a threat from a Longe male, Myrtle gazed at the eager faces and resumed her place at the podium.

'Sorry about the lights. Someone is back there dealing with it now,' she said. 'So, let's start again.'

Polite applause allowed Myrtle to compose herself.

'Greetings. I am Myrtle Netherwell, the founder of Naturally Netherwell, crafting organic skincare products from homegrown herbs, fruit and vegetables. Our small market garden in Weybourne has just received permission to build a production centre on our land. This means I will employ two women and have a growth plan to enable me to employ more. Without the insights gained from the business studies course at this college, managing something larger than a shelf outside Plumtree Cottage would have been inconceivable...'

As she finished the opening of her speech, Myrtle stood listening to the thunderous applause reverberating around the room like a symphony of support.

Glancing towards the back corner, checking for dark demons, her eyes widened with surprise as she spotted Harry casually leaning against the wall. It was a silent gesture, yet the thumbs-up he flashed spoke volumes. He grinned, reassuring her, before leaving the room, a silent beacon of encouragement.

'I come from a long line of resilient women who were persecuted for their beliefs, finding solace in the depths of Weybourne's woodlands. My ancestors were pioneers, working the land with a profound respect for Mother Nature, ensuring that future generations would inherit the same enthusiasm. When I was growing up, this was my reality.

'But, at seventeen, I found myself caring for my twin, when our mother passed away. Limited choices lay before me, but I had inherited a great abundance of knowledge thanks to the solidarity of women supporting women.'

Myrtle inhaled and slowly exhaled. 'I've witnessed the unique skills women possess, skills men might not even dream of acquiring. I admire women who channel these abilities to uplift themselves with determination, sometimes at a personal and financial cost.

'As the proud recipient of this award'—Myrtle lifted the weighty glass star and waited while applause rippled around the room—'I stand here to champion the women in my circle and to inspire new female students to embrace their strengths. The world needs women who believe and achieve, and men who acknowledge this equality. If we can reach goals and fulfil dreams by respecting and supporting one another, then this college has done more than teach us how to fill in a tax form; it has given us hope. A power we can take out into the world. The power of unity and equality.'

A ripple of loud applause deafened her once again, and Myrtle, basking in the moment, raised her hand to silence her audience.

'But wait, I have something to share with you. Please bear with me again, just for a moment.'

Hurriedly, Myrtle made her way to the side of the stage. There, she exchanged a neatly folded set of her everyday clothing, a long dress embroidered with wildlife and fern leaves, for the formalities of her suit. The transformation was swift. She released her ponytail, shook her hair free, cleansed her face and eyes and removed the business suit. She pulled out one of her more comfortable dresses and pushed her feet into her comfortable pumps. She stepped back onto the stage with renewed enthusiasm, and the room fell silent as she approached the microphone.

'Greetings. My name is Myrtle Netherwell, and this is my usual attire. A suit is not who I am. It is what I am expected to wear in the corporate world. I will never change my inner being, but as you can see, there is a marked difference in my appearance – this is me, the everyday me. Always remember who you are, but if you must conform to what society expects of you, do so without changing your inner spirit, only your clothing, and always support your sisterhood. Good luck, and thank you for listening tonight.'

Again, the applause thundered out. After she had collected her things, she stepped out into the lecture theatre and saw Harry standing in the middle of the aisle with his hands in his pockets. Her heart flipped, but she dared not let him get too close again.

'Well, your name has made a noise this evening. The reception room is full of women wanting to shake your hand,' he said.

'Thanks for coming, Harry. I didn't feel alone when I saw you,' she said. 'Are you coming to the reception?'

Harry nodded. 'If it is an invitation, but if you'd rather I wasn't around. I just wanted to check on you, Myrtle. I knew how scared you were, but I always had faith in your ability. You were brilliant. I watched from the other side of the stage. And changing your clothes, that speech, brilliant move.'

'It was something Eve's mother said to me, which gave me the idea. It doesn't matter what clothes we wear, we must always remember to be true to ourselves and share that with the world.'

Harry nodded. 'Eve's mum's a cracker. I get a lot of advice from her – some of it I listen to,' he said with a smile.

'She told you to come tonight?' Myrtle asked.

Harry shrugged one shoulder and bent to pick up her large bag. 'Now that would be discrediting me for caring for you off my own back,' he said, heading out of the room.

Chapter Twenty-One

1993

Over the years, Myrtle's visits to Harry's garden centre became more regular, she loved to wander amongst the vast array of plants and sprinkle crystal chips and words of encouragement for strong growth amongst them.

She also spotted a new growth – Harry and Mel's working relationship had moved into a boyfriend and girlfriend stage, and it pained her to see them so happy.

'Miss Netherwell, how are we this fine May day,' Harry said as he wheeled a trolley of roses through the courtyard.

'Merry meet, fine sir. I'm well, thank you. Good to see you thriving and looking so happy with yourself,' Myrtle replied.

Harry set down his wheelbarrow.

'Did you have a good birthday celebration? Feel old at thirty?' he asked.

'I did, thanks, although I missed you. I think it is the first one we've not spent together since we met in college – and that was years ago – so yes, I feel old,' Myrtle said and noted Harry's face flush.

'I'm not going to lie to you, the thought of being near Marigold still disturbs me. She curses me – and yeah, I know it's only words, but the last time she did, my back gave out on me and I had blackouts – it felt like the real deal, a proper curse. Mel was amazing and ran this place with the help of my mum, and hers.'

Myrtle nodded. 'I don't think Marigold is capable of mustering up a bad back to keep you away from our door,' she said, more haughtily than she meant. The truth had irked her, and her jealousy irritated her.

'I know, and it sounds crazy when I say it out loud. I just hear a voice in my head warning me to stay away from Plumtree Cottage.' Harry looked uncomfortable and pulled a handkerchief from his pocket to wipe his brow.

'You have probably become anxious about seeing me, and telling me you are in love with Mel, that's what's causing these masking thoughts,' Myrtle said with a feeble giggle, trying desperately to end the conversation.

Marigold had made Harry a target for the Longe family, to get Myrtle to focus upon him and not battle against them. She needed to walk away from any romantic thoughts she had about him whenever they were close, once and for all.

'Mel? Harry's blush was unambiguous. Well, she is pretty special to me… In fact, I'm going to propose to her.'

A hitch in her throat prevented Myrtle from responding immediately, instead, even though she felt stabs to her heart, a reminder of what she had lost, she had to deal with it if she wanted to remain Harry's friend.

'That's wonderful, Harry. Mel will make you a good wife. She's in love with you, I can see that whenever I visit.'

Harry grinned. 'I think she's more in love with my money,' he said.

Cycling home through the back lanes Myrtle finally let her tears flow.

'I love you, Harry Tye. I always will,' she whispered. 'Be happy on the days I will never be. Love with passion, and be blessed with a loving family. As I wish it, so it will be!'

She was ready to confront Marigold.

Back at the cottage, Myrtle fumed as she marched down to Marigold's workshop.

'How could you!' she shouted, pushing back the door so it slammed against the wall.

Marigold looked up from the project she was working on, showing very little reaction – almost as if she had been waiting for this moment.

'Ah, someone has seen her boyfriend,' she taunted and laughed.

Myrtle struggled to contain the anger brewing, it layered itself on top of her disappointment and sadness.

'Harry is going to marry Mel. You messed with his head. Undo your spells on him. The poor man is in pain.'

She put her hand inside her pocket and felt her wand, felt empowered by its heat. She looked at the wooden toys on a shelf Marigold had whittled.

'Don't even think about it,' Marigold growled. 'Or I will make life miserable for you.'

Myrtle threw back her head and laughed, and the heat from the wand dissipated.

'Oh, Marigold. You cannot make my life any worse. You really can't,' she said and walked away.

Four months later, Myrtle stood outside the church with other well-wishers. Harry looked smart in his navy suit, and Mel looked a picture of frothy lace and fake diamonds. Myrtle's heartache was well hidden as she wished them both happiness for the future. She did not stay to celebrate the union, but she did whisper a blessing and even persuaded Marigold to lift her curse. To her surprise, her sister did as she asked.

In the weeks following, Marigold produced more varieties of late summer and autumnal plants, and Myrtle's visits to the garden centre increased, as did Harry's visits to collect them. Marigold kept her distance and soon Myrtle's anxiety settled.

By late November, orders for Naturally Netherwell increased and Myrtle's focus was on nothing but business.

'Yule logs – the real thing. Fresh and dressed with

greenery,' she said to Harry as he opened up his van and she set down a large crate filled with the logs.

'Wow, they'll go down well for Christmas. Did you make them, or did Marigold?' he asked peering into the crate.

'Marigold. There's a box of wooden toys, too. If they don't sell, give them away to customers,' Myrtle replied.

Harry loaded the car.

'You doing okay, Myrt?' he asked.

'I'm happy enough, Harry. You – how's married life?'

'Fine. Mel's stressing over having the family round for Christmas dinner, and spending money as if the world is ending, but it's okay,' Harry said, and his tone told Myrtle things were not 'fine'.

'It's difficult adjusting to a new life,' she said. 'But it will get easier—'

'What's he doing here? Get out!' Marigold's voice broke through her as it thundered down the garden.

Harry sighed. 'I'm off. She scares the heebie jeebies out of me sometimes.'

'Be nice, Marigold,' Myrtle snapped. 'Harry is taking your logs and toys to sell for you. Don't be so damn rude!'

Marigold gave one of her cackling laughs, which always unnerved Myrtle.

'Yes, go, Harry.' Myrtle turned to him. 'She's in an odd mood. And say hi to Mel. Everything will be fine.'

To her surprise, Harry leaned down and kissed her cheek.

'I'd love to have a sister like you. Marigold doesn't know how lucky she is,' he said.

As his van pulled away, Myrtle touched her cheek.

'I don't want you as my brother, but if it means I still get to see you, that's how it will be,' she whispered to herself.

Not daring to go near Marigold for fear of firing up both tempers and creating a hostile atmosphere, Myrtle took herself inside.

She touched the walls, and blessed the ancestors, before cleansing and creating a Yuletide altar.

It had been thirteen years since she'd given birth to Gaia, and Myrtle mused about her daughter, a girl who now had the same soft shade of golden hair as Moonstone's, and the same build as herself at that age.

Over the years, she had watched Gaia – Lucy – grow up in the tender care of the doctor and his wife. Careful not to spoil their stability with her, but keen to be a part of her daughter's life in whatever way she could be. As far as Lucy was concerned, Myrtle was an honorary aunt, a good friend of the Hensons. But was it just a matter of time before she realised the truth, saw the resemblance between them?

Myrtle was grateful that Gaia's hair wasn't as deep red as her own or it would have definitely given the village gossips something to talk about.

Sheila and Richard had thrown a garden party for Gaia's birthday, and Myrtle watched her daughter laugh and chatter with her teenage friends, relaxed and happy and wearing the latest fashionable clothes. Sheila and Richard moved amongst the guests, and Gaia was the first to spot Myrtle as she approached from the front path.

'Auntie Myrtle!' she exclaimed and ran to her.

'Lucy, just look at you, so grown up!' Myrtle replied and accepted her daughter's hug, absorbing her loving energy.

'Mum didn't tell me you were coming. What a lovely surprise,' Gaia said.

'I wouldn't miss it for the world. Your thirteenth birthday is a special day,' Myrtle said.

Richard joined them.

'We nearly had to cancel the celebration, though, so take it steady young lady,' he said, ruffling Gaia's head.

'Dad, stop! I felt a bit dizzy, that's all,' Gaia said and turned to Myrtle. 'It was weird, though. I thought I saw stars and shadows, even though it was daylight.'

Myrtle kept her face steady. 'Oh... Are you all right?'

'Yes, I'm fine now,' grinned Gaia, waving at one of her friends. 'I'll catch you later!'

As Gaia ran to a group of girls, Myrtle turned to Richard.

'Did the dizziness last long?' she asked.

Richard smiled and walked her over to Sheila.

'Teenage years, she'll have a few more each month, I suspect. I think we are safe to assume it is nothing more than a young girl reaching puberty,' he said.

Myrtle nodded but wanted to say he would also have to

watch Lucy more carefully now that she had entered her year of magick inheritance.

Looking around the pristine garden and checking for lurking shadows, Myrtle decided to leave early. The longer she was around Gaia, the more attention she attracted to the Henson household – the Longe family would be aware and waiting.

'Lucy, I have to head home now as Marigold was in a funny mood today.' She hugged her and then took a small cloth bag out of her pocket. 'Here's a little something I made for you. It's to protect you … you know me and my natural thinking.' Myrtle smiled. She had moon-blessed the amethyst crystals and cast a protection spell over each stone she'd threaded through the leather.

Gaia gasped when she saw the gift and placed it on her right arm. She hugged Myrtle tight again and kissed her cheeks. 'It is beautiful, thank you! I love it. I'll keep it on forever,' she said, running off to show it to her friends.

Myrtle turned around to see Richard and Sheila watching their daughter's response.

'Thank you both for today. Now we wait for whatever the future might bring,' she said and laughed, though it was hard to make light of a secret with consequences.

Chapter Twenty-Two

1995

Myrtle was delighted when Gaia expressed interest in the skincare creation side of Naturally Netherwell particularly as it drew her daughter closer to Marigold, whose plant knowledge fascinated Gaia. Myrtle enjoyed watching her aunt and niece bond over a batch of nettles.

'If you are looking for a Saturday job, I'm happy to take on someone so enthusiastic about our craft,' Myrtle said.

'I'll ask Mum and Dad, but I'd love that, thank you!' Gaia said, excited.

The rest of the day was spent chatting about identification and preparation. For Myrtle, it was the perfect day.

During the evening, Marigold expressed her pleasure at Gaia's interest in nature.

'She is quiet. I like quiet. Even the fox sat by the fence and watched us; she only comes to you – I think she knows Gaia is your child,' she said to Myrtle, who sat absorbing the calm of the cottage.

'My fox? I noticed Ragnis also likes to sit nearby when Gaia visits,' Myrtle said, smiling at the thought of her childhood companions watching over her daughter as they'd watched over her and Marigold. Anyone else would have said the vixen was not the same animal, but Myrtle knew that the fox housed her ancestor Willow's spirit.

'I feel Gaia's energy when she is beside me,' Marigold replied.

With a tilt of her head, Myrtle questioned Marigold.

'Do you accept her as family, Mari?' she asked.

'She is your daughter, not the doctor's. Will you tell her?'

Marigold picked at the buttons on her shabby cardigan as she spoke, and Myrtle sensed an anxiety hovering over her sister.

'She will learn about me when time decides.'

'But will you tell her?' Marigold insisted.

Shaking her head, Myrtle reached out and touched her sister's arm.

'It is not my place. If she asks when she learns of her original birth certificate, I will tell her the truth, but until then, you and I will not say a word. You have done well for so many years, Mari. I am grateful, truly I am.'

'She's a Netherwell by blood. She cannot escape the truth.'

Marigold's voice was now laden with threat, and Myrtle shuddered.

'When the ancestors decide it is safe, then it will happen. Keep your mind focused on the garden, not Gaia,' she said, ushering Marigold outside.

Sitting before the altar, Myrtle lit a candle and closed her eyes. She brought the image of the fox and Ragnis to the forefront of her mind.

'Stand with my family for all eternity with my thanks. With my mind, I revoke evil. May my powers grow and the magick within my daughter's soul protect her – as I will it, so mote it be.'

———

The frost continued to bite during the week, but Marigold and Myrtle had walked to the beach each morning after Marigold expressed the desire to run along the sand barefoot again. Myrtle agreed that a change of scenery would do her sister good.

As they reached Beach Lane, the smell of the sea drifted across the fields, and Myrtle took a moment to appreciate her environment. Once past the pebbles on the shore, Marigold raced the waves along the sand, whooping and cheering at the seagulls, while Myrtle collected sea glass.

Suddenly, she stopped in her tracks and looked at her sister. The birds screeched and screamed before flying out to sea. Waves rolled and crashed towards the shoreline in large grey mounds, and the wind blew dry sand across the fields in a spiral. Marigold swung around and looked at Myrtle with a wild stare.

'It's time. Gaia – he has come to take her!' she yelled with what appeared to be great excitement.

Marigold snatched up her socks and boots.

'I said it's time. Run!' she shouted as she made for the entrance to the lane and village.

Startled, Myrtle registered what her sister had said and ran to join her, then found the energy to race ahead. She had to find a way to stop Marigold and the Longe family.

They arrived at the Hensons' house, and before Marigold could rush through the garden to the front door, Myrtle blocked her way.

'You cannot go shouting and ranting around their home. You will get yourself locked away – as a trespasser or a batshit crazy woman. Think about this, Marigold. The spirit you call Dad is out for Gaia, but it is not your place to give her to him. She's my child, I will do it – go home and do not do anything that will get you arrested – or worse.' Myrtle spoke fast, pretending she would give up Gaia to the Longe spirits, but was not certain Marigold fell for the lie.

Marigold stared at her through narrowed eyes, but Myrtle was not in the mood for a stare-down; she had to get to her daughter.

'Go. Home,' she said. 'If you don't, I will have you sectioned. I will tell them you were intent on harming Gaia; you are jealous of her.'

Marigold intensified her stare, and Myrtle pulled her wand from her pocket. She rarely carried it with her but recently took to picking it up whenever she was with Marigold. She had bound a black obsidian stone to the handle. A stone with powerful protection properties, she had also rubbed the wooden wand with cedarwood oil, which was also used to ward off negative energy. Her anger rose the harder Marigold stared at her; her sister had unwittingly helped Myrtle gain enough spiritual energy to cast a bounding spell.

'May your mouth dry and be silenced. I banish your intent and increase mine. I am Myrtle, the mother of Gaia, and you will relinquish your hold. My fury and flame will bind you to Plumtree Cottage until I return. A thirst will overcome you. Home, Marigold, home!'

Marigold finally dropped her gaze and turned to face the trees at the bottom of the road.

'Yes, go home. Take the woodland path, and do not stop. Walk to your home and stay indoors. Go home, Marigold, quench your thirst. As I command it, so it will be done!'

Myrtle raised her wand and brought it down behind her sister, and it glowed. Glancing swiftly around the house, hoping no one had noticed, Myrtle was relieved that none of the net curtains had moved.

'Keep walking, Marigold. Go!' Another flash of light stemmed from the wand, and Myrtle's body temperature rose.

Anger, keep the anger, Myrtle.

She needed to keep the momentum going. Marigold did not look back, and Myrtle was confident her spell would uphold.

From inside the house, she heard a scream and ran to the front door, pushing her wand back into the inner pocket of her jacket. She beat on the front door with the palm of her hand.

'Gaia— Lucy!' she called out, quickly correcting herself, then rang the bell. 'Richard! Sheila!'

A noise on the other side of the door brought relief, and it was barely open before she rushed inside.

'I heard a scream,' she said to Gaia, who was standing in front of her trembling with tears rolling down her face.

'What is it, my love?' Myrtle took her daughter's hands.

'Mum, it's Mum. There was a strange noise, and she was screaming about dark shadows and ghosts. I ran downstairs and … I just found her on the floor in the kitchen. I, I think she's dead.' Gaia started sobbing.

Myrtle pulled her daughter to her and held her tight.

'I take it your dad's not here,' Myrtle said.

'He's at his surgery,' Gaia replied.

'I am going to ring him, stay with me,' Myrtle said.

She went to the telephone in the hall and dialled the doctor's surgery. She left a message stating that there was an emergency at the Henson residence, Sheila had fallen, and that Richard was to return home as soon as possible. She then rang Eve and asked her to tell the women working at her unit to pack up and go home, and no one was to disturb Marigold.

Myrtle closed her eyes briefly; she just hoped Marigold was still bound under her spell.

'Sit here on the stairs and hold my bag for me. I am just

going to check on your mum, Lucy. Don't be afraid; I will be back when I've seen her,' Myrtle said, before walking into into the kitchen.

Sheila was lying face down and Myrtle bent to check for a pulse, but there was no beat against her fingertips.

'Oh, Sheila, I am so sorry. Thank you for caring for my child. Blessings on your soul and spirit.'

Not sure whether to cover her up, Myrtle left her as she was and gently closed the door. A dark shadow formed outside the front door window as she did, and Myrtle stopped and held her breath, but she felt no fear, no sense of a presence in the home, and she released it when she heard the thrum of Richard's car engine – the cause of the shadow passing by the house.

'Is everything okay, Aunty Myrt?' Gaia's soft voice asked.

Myrtle turned to her and drew her into her arms. 'It is now that your dad is home, sweetheart.'

After comforting both Gaia and Richard, Myrtle headed home.

Back at the cottage, she noticed Marigold sleeping in her armchair. A jug of water and glass sat on the coffee table beside her. The thirst spell had worked. Myrtle guessed that Marigold's anxiety and anger had been a heat of the moment thing – literally.

Not wanting to lose the opportunity of gaining increased powers, Myrtle went outside and lit a lamp and stood facing the moon, whispering her plea to the Moon Mother and Mother Earth.

> *'Mother, Maiden, Crone,*
> *I am worthy of receiving a greater power,*
> *Yet dark forces overwhelm me,*
> *Goddess Gaia, strengthen my divination, allow*
>   *freedom to my manifestation,*
> *Allow my witch light to shine.*
> *I call on you to increase my ability to reduce fear,*
> *And grant me the fire of Theda, the energy of the*
>   *sky, the pull of the moon, the ferocity of the*
>   *wind and the nourishment of the rain.*
> *I am your servant my Mother Earth.'*

Once inside she blessed the home and lay on her bed listening out for Marigold to disturb the night, but when she woke in the morning, to her relief her sister was working in the barn as if nothing had happened.

Richard approached Myrtle after Sheila's funeral.

'Sheila has no family, nor do I, and Lucy needs a woman to help her through life. Will you continue to be that woman for her, please?' Richard asked.

'Always. The time is not right for her to know the truth, so we must be careful,' Myrtle replied.

Richard looked thoughtful.

'Or we never tell her. Losing Sheila and being told that who she thought was a family friend is really her biological mother might be too much for her to handle,' he said, his eyes boring into hers. Since Sheila's death he had become overprotective with Gaia, to the point that the girl complained about his suffocating ways.

Myrtle felt the impact like a punch to her gut and inhaled to calm herself. He could not call the shots over whether Gaia found out the truth or not, so she chose to not rise to what appeared to be a command rather than a general thought.

'It is out of our hands. We can keep quiet now, but I think time will decide when she learns the truth. Until then, we will keep things as they are for her sake,' she said and left Richard to mourn his wife.

Chapter Twenty-Three

1999

'That's a stunning piece of work, Myrtle. Gaia will be thrilled,' Eve said as she stared at the dress hanging on the back of a door draped in a sheet to protect the lace.

'I hope so,' Myrtle muttered, 'I still can't believe she asked me to make it for her.'

Eve placed a comforting arm around her shoulders. 'Myrt, she has seen enough of your embroidery and sewing skills over the years to know you were the one who could create her dream dress. Even Sheila must be looking down and smiling; it's exquisite.'

'It's a bit more than a child's pinafore dress, though,' Myrtle said, her nerves tingling. For the many years she had been Gaia's 'aunt', she had sown outfits and made school-play costumes and party dresses, but to make her a wedding dress meant so much more than handing over a gift or doing Sheila a favour.

With each stitch, she wove a blessing and spell for health, wealth and happiness. She threaded her needles with love and stitched her heart into the gown. Gaia's dress symbolised Myrtle's connection to her as a mother.

The slam of a car door took their attention away from the dress, and Myrtle could see Gaia and her friend giggling their way up to the front door.

Pulling open the door, Myrtle greeted them with a wide smile.

'Merry meet, come in!' she said, inviting them both through the door.

'I'm so excited, Auntie Myrt. I can't wait to see the dress,' Gaia said, kissing her cheek.

'Well, don't get too excited. You might not like the end result. You've not seen it since the last fitting. The overlay was hard work, but your wish is my command,' Myrtle said with a laugh.

'Lucy, Jane. It's lovely to see you again.' Eve smiled at both girls. I hope you are ready for the most amazing surprise, Lucy.'

Once Myrtle and Eve had pulled off the outer shroud, Myrtle stood back and waited for a response, watching Gaia's every move. Her daughter's eyes welled up with tears, and she clamped her hands over her mouth.

'I don't know what to say, it's incredible – amazing, stunning. Mum would have loved it, and I think Dad is going to be a bit emotional – I mean, he's not used to seeing me in anything but denim,' Gaia said, looking down at her jeans and laughing.

'I'm so glad you like it, Lucy. It was an honour to make it for you, more than you'll ever know,' Myrtle said, holding back the extent of her emotion. She felt Eve's hand, her forever supportive friend, on the small of her back.

Watching her daughter exclaim over a wedding dress was something Myrtle had never thought she would see, and an enormous moment of gratitude overcame her.

When Gaia had announced she was marrying Simon Grisham – an estate agent from Holt – Richard had not welcomed the news. But Myrtle had assured him that twenty was old enough for Gaia to decide about her future, and he had gradually come to terms with it.

What he did not know was that with a month to go till the wedding, Gaia had recently confided in Myrtle that she was pregnant, warning Myrtle that her dress might need gentle adjustments and forcing a promise to say nothing to her father.

Not wanting to come between them both, Myrtle tried to persuade Gaia her father would not be upset and would give her the best of care, but Gaia was adamant, and Myrtle honoured her wishes.

'Honestly, I don't know how you do it; look at the little bows and pearls around the neckline!' Gaia exclaimed. 'It must have taken you hours, and they are such a lovely touch; I wouldn't have dared ask you to do that.'

'You did right with the simple A-line, but it needed something around the neckline to finish it off. The bustle bow is something I think you might like; it can be removed as a keepsake,' Myrtle said, turning the gown around. Again, Gaia gasped with joy.

Carefully, Myrtle lifted the bow off the dress to show off the embroidered initials of Sheila on one side.

'Your mother will be with you on your day, if in name only,' she said.

After contemplating whether to carry out this idea, Myrtle had honoured the woman who had raised her daughter.

'That's so sweet of you, how lovely. Thank you,' Gaia said.

'Forget face creams; you should make wedding dresses.' Jane smiled at Myrtle.

Lucy stroked her gown. 'You are so right, Jane. Can I try it on now? Is it pin-free?' she said, looking eagerly at Myrtle.

'Eve and I will help you. There are just a few pins for the last-minute alterations.'

After the fitting and when everyone had left the house, Myrtle took a moment at the altar.

She lit candles and rolled a small piece of cloth in rose oil, and added tiny pieces of clear quartz and green aventurine, the perfect combination for a balanced marriage, luck and abundance. She placed it into a dry piece and laid it out in front of her. She touched her wand to the fabric and concentrated upon happiness.

'Bless the wedding dress, the groom, the day. Bless my

daughter as she seals happiness and love through marriage.'

She sat quietly sewing the small cloth into a tiny poppet and stitched it into the back hem of the dress. All she could do now was hope she had blessed and protected enough. She wrote down her thoughts and cast her happiness intention into the fire.

———

On the day of Gaia's wedding that June, a slight breeze touched the tops of the flowers in the Henson garden, and they bobbed their heads in unison. Myrtle took time to contain her emotions, then went inside to help her daughter with her wedding dress. She was struggling to keep her tears of happiness at bay. Gaia was a vision in white – she looked every part a princess or film star.

'Have you eaten?' Myrtle asked.

Gaia nodded. 'Yes … though I felt a little sick this morning.'

'Okay then, we had better let your dad see you – oh, wait, your flowers,' Myrtle said and went to the box to pick out Gaia's bouquet, an eye-catching collection of tiny pale pink rose buds, deep pink peonies, blue cornflowers, lilac alliums, white stocks, sweet peas, various shades of green foliage and herbs. The fragrance added to the beauty of it all. Myrtle tied a strand of mixed crystals for happiness and unity to the pink-dyed twine, which shone against the green stems.

'There, all done. Marigold chose these and she chose well – she wants a large slice of wedding cake in return for her efforts,' Myrtle said.

'Dear Marigold, she's an odd one, but I bet you wouldn't change her for the world,' Gaia said.

Myrtle smiled, and tried not to think about her sister's parting words to her that morning as she'd ventured out of the door.

'She will look beautiful when she meets her grandfather today. He is excited. They all are.'

Shaking off the brief moment of worry for Gaia's safety, Myrtle reminded herself of every spell and intention she had cast to protect Gaia over the past twenty-four hours and returned her focus to her daughter.

'Lucy, I just wanted to say, with Sheila not here today in physical form, you must always know that your mum is by your side,' Myrtle said and kissed her daughter on her cheek.

'I feel something is close to me, so I think you are right, Auntie Myrt.'

Opening the door to the main area where Richard stood, Myrtle stepped to one side and allowed Gaia through to greet her father. He looked to Gaia and then Myrtle with wide, moist eyes.

'Beautiful. Truly beautiful,' he said.

'Her mother would have been so proud today,' Myrtle whispered as Gaia twirled round to show Richard the bow.

'I think she is; I definitely know she is by her side,' Richard said, offering his daughter a gentle smile.

'Eve and I will leave you and head off to our seats. Have the most wonderful day, Lucy, soon-to-be Mrs Grisham,' Myrtle said before her resolve not to cry left her.

'Oh, what a beautiful bride,' a man's voice whispered to Myrtle's right-hand side. She turned but no one was there, she looked to her left, but again, no male sat close.

'Soon she will be mine. Your spells and witchcraft won't work on me. Her grandfather is watching with you…'

Myrtle's blood ran cold. Her father was nearby!

Unable to cry out to banish him, nor wanting anger and rage to encroach on her happiness, she slipped a pouch of black salt from her handbag and discreetly flicked it across the aisle beside her just before Gaia passed by.

'I banish you from our presence and call on my ancestors to help me,' she whispered into a handkerchief pretending to dab away a tear.

A movement caught her eye at the end of the garden where the official side of the ceremony was to take place. A fox walked along the edge of the boundary then disappeared. Willow was watching too. Suddenly, Gaia stumbled slightly and Richard supported her, just as a shadow registered against the brick wall, and Myrtle turned to get a better look. On top of the wall sat a dove, it fluttered its wings and cooed, and everyone turned to look.

Gaia smiled and looked up at her father before proceeding towards her waiting fiancé.

As they walked, the dove hovered near and then flew into the trees, just as the shadow disappeared. Ragnis flew onto the brick wall and dipped his head at Myrtle. All was well, again, the Longe family were unable to break through the protective energy created by the sisterhood; all invisible guests gathered to watch the ceremony.

After the ceremony and reception, when Gaia and Simon had left for their honeymoon, Richard approached Myrtle.

'Thank you for everything, Myrtle. It can't have been easy for you,' he said.

Touching his arm, Myrtle took a breath. 'It was easy because you involved me and allowed me to be part of her day. So the thanks go to you.'

'Now, if you will forgive me, I must go and collect Marigold's extra-large slice of cake and take it home to her. She earned it for those beautiful flowers. Even I was surprised; she'd never made anything as delicate before. I did have a back-up plan in mind when she offered, but I should have had more faith in my sister.'

Richard surprised her when he leaned forward and kissed her cheek.

'You are both incredible women, and it is a privilege to call you a friend. We've had our moments over the years but only declared what we thought was in Lucy's best interests. We should have trusted her instincts much more; she has a strong spirit,' he said.

'She certainly does, and it will get stronger over the years. Despite being married to Simon, she will always be an independent woman. It's in her genes,' Myrtle said with a gentle smile.

Chapter Twenty-Four

2004

Gaia gave birth during a January night, and Richard dropped by Plumtree Cottage to announce the news. Myrtle listened to him chatter excitedly about the sandy-haired baby, and all she could think of was that she was now a grandmother to baby Summer June.

'Lucy's asking for you. I said I would drive you over this afternoon if that's okay with you.' Richard asked.

'I'd love that, thank you,' Myrtle replied, 'I have a few baby clothes I've made, so this morning I can trim them in pink!' She didn't let on that they were already finished because Myrtle had never doubted her daughter would produce a girl.

'She'd better not bring it round here,' Marigold muttered, almost growling out her words. 'I won't see them. I won't.'

'But Marigold, this is Lucy's baby. I thought you liked Lucy,' Richard said, frowning.

'Her real name is Gaia, and you both know babies are not safe near me. I don't like babies. Keep it away!'

Myrtle looked at her sister, she saw the anger etched across her brow. Richard needed to tread carefully; Marigold was allowing her powers through. But Marigold should show more respect, threatening their grandchild was not something Richard nor Myrtle would tolerate.

'Lucy will be with her and you can stay clear when they visit, but I will not have them threatened. You will not frighten Lucy, Marigold. You will not!' Myrtle said her anger brewing. Yet again her twin was spoiling a special moment in Myrtle's life.

In response, Marigold stomped away and with a sigh Myrtle turned to Richard.

He shook his head.

'I thought she had improved, but her threats worry me, Myrtle. How many more years of this will you put up with. Our granddaughter's safety is my concern, and I am not happy for Lucy to visit Plumtree Cottage with Summer.'

'It is not your place to tell her what to do. She's a married woman and a mother now, and must live her own life,' Myrtle said, annoyed and suddenly surprised by a warm tingling sensation inside her chest.

'She will know Marigold intends to harm her baby if she comes around here. There are some things which have to be told,' Richard said and left Myrtle standing alone in the kitchen.

She walked to the walls of the cottage and touched the bricks, feeling the warmth and reassurance that the spirits still protected her home. Marigold's powers had not disturbed them, Myrtle relaxed and took a healing stroll through the woods.

The Tree of Life

Today, a shimmer of hope rippled amongst the sisterhood. Gaia Mystia Netherwell has given birth to the daughter who will weaken the Longe family bloodline. Myrtle has made a vow to encourage Gaia and her child into connecting with their ancestors when Gaia learns of her parentage.

I felt the whispers of the spirits tingle through my bough and trunk, there is great excitement for the Netherwell future.

Myrtle still has a sword to yield against the dark demon testing her soul and threatening her daughter and granddaughter, but her witchcraft grows stronger, and her protection powers respond to her inner energy.

Chapter Twenty-Five

2008

Gaia turned to Myrtle for advice on several occasions on how to encourage Summer to eat vegetables, but no amount of cajoling got Summer to eat what she considered yukky foods.

During a tantrum in the garden, Marigold yelled at the four-year-old and chased her from the area near the barn.

'You will frighten the animals!'

Summer, being a bold child, opted to speak back and Marigold's temper heightened until Harry stepped in and encouraged Summer away.

'Both of you go away. Go away!' Marigold shouted and threw clods of soil at them followed by curses and mutterings.

Myrtle arrived at Summer's side to hear her sob out her story of Auntie Marigold shouting at her. Harry nodded.

'She did, but she was also right, you were scaring the animals,' he said.

Dabbing away Summer's tears with a handkerchief, Myrtle tutted.

'All this over not wanting to eat vegetables,' she said.

'Vegetables?' Harry asked as he walked through the gate.

'They are yukky!' Summer said and sulked.

'Not if you grow them yourself,' Harry replied. 'I never ate them until I grew my own. I'm sure Auntie Myrtle will let you grow some on a patch, and then you can wash them, cook them or eat them raw. They'll have your magic in them,' he said giving Myrtle a wink over Summer's head.

By the time Marigold had returned to the garden, Harry and Summer were already halfway to preparing a patch of ground and by the end of the day seeds of various kinds had been planted.

Marigold remained moody through to the next day, and Myrtle kept her distance.

Harry arrived and pointed to crows and pigeons pecking at the patch, feasting on the seeds.

When he had left for home Myrtle turned on her sister.

'You did this! You called the birds down. Why?'

Marigold said nothing as she walked away laughing.

'Leave them alone!' Myrtle called after her sister.

The next day Harry replanted the seeds and built bird scarers. When he called Myrtle to see his wigwam works of art, sporting silver milk bottle tops on string, she knew her sister would see this as a challenge.

Day after day Harry's patience was put to the test. Myrtle suspected that Marigold and not the birds or rabbits were the culprits. It was her sister's way of driving him and Summer away. When they found the bamboo sticks lying on the ground, Myrtle challenged her sister over breakfast.

'I asked you to leave Summer and Harry alone. They are doing no harm. What you are doing is wrong, Marigold.'

'I don't want them here. There are too many people, he doesn't like it, he cannot reach her,' Marigold said.

'Who can't reach who?' Myrtle asked.

'Ingulf, he wants the child. Dad said she is bad blood – weak blood, but there is too much energy around her. I can't get through to her and he's angry,' Marigold replied, shovelling spoonfuls of scrambled egg into her mouth.

'Slow down, eat properly,' Myrtle demanded, 'and there is no bad blood here. Put him out of your mind, Marigold. Don't listen to him! Harry and Summer will be in the garden this morning, so find something to do which won't upset us all.'

Brushing her arm across the table and sending the crockery crashing to the floor, Marigold strode out of the door muttering curses at Myrtle.

When Summer arrived, the first thing she did was run to see Myrtle. Harry had not arrived.

'Where's Harry?' she demanded, with a foot stomp and pout.

'He is probably helping his mummy with chores,' Myrtle told a disappointed Summer.

When Harry didn't turn up again on his regular day,

Myrtle began to think he was avoiding them – and another thought occurred to her.

'Did you cast a spell to keep him away?' she challenged Marigold.

'What if I did, the place is quieter now with one of them gone,' Marigold replied.

'You're cruel, spiteful. You had better leave Summer and Gaia alone,' Myrtle said.

'Little Lucy and her squealing child. Time is not on their side.' Marigold chanted her words much like a child singing a nursery rhyme.

Myrtle walked away. Marigold had light and dark days, and today was a day when she could not get through to her.

Myrtle took herself down to the beach where the gentle breeze carried the salty scent of the sea, calming her with the soft sounds of waves trickling across the pebbled shoreline.

She licked her lips and tasted the briny air settling on her skin; a reminder of the day years ago, when she and Harry had enjoyed candy floss together. The seagulls dipped between the water and the sky, and she watched them, reminded of children at play, squealing with delight. In the distance sailboats drifted across the horizon on a sea reflecting shades of blue and silver. Myrtle wondered what it must be like to have the freedom to sail away into the distance, and leave all your troubles behind. A sense of déjà vu overcame her, as if she was someone else looking out at the sea. Had Theda, Brigid and Willow stood where she had and marvelled at the view – easing their troubled minds and wondering what lay ahead.

Rays of sunshine danced across the tips of the waves, a tranquil moment of calm unravelling the knots of anxiety inside her chest. Then, with a sigh, Myrtle turned around and walked home ready to face new challenges once again.

Chapter Twenty-Six

2016

'Oh, look at this lovely picture of us all together. I love sitting beneath the Tree of Life; it keeps me calm. Makes my body tingle. Everyone should hug trees,' Gaia said laughing, showing her mobile phone to Myrtle.

'I agree about hugging trees. The Tree of Life is a lifelong friend once you show it respect. I wonder what makes you tingle when you are there, Lucy. Be careful, maybe some of me and Marigold is rubbing off on you,' Myrtle said with a light laugh.

Gaia shrugged. 'Oh, I don't know, it's just I feel connected to it somehow. Silly, as you've told me its history and the connection to only your family, but it gives me comfort.'

Inwardly, Myrtle smiled. The ancestors had found their way to Gaia. She might not have found her full energy to communicate with them, but they had found a pathway to get through to let her know she was not alone.

Introducing both Gaia and Summer to the tree had been the right move. They had spent many years picnicking around it, sitting beneath it during a full moon, while Myrtle told them stories of when she and Marigold were young, and of how they watched the adults enjoy the various Sabbats over the years. In a quiet way she'd told them of her past so when time released the truth, they would understand more about her background.

'It is a calming area and your open mind to relaxation and our ways will bring about a connection of sorts. Who knows, maybe my ancestors hear more than even I realised. If you feel it is helping, keep going and enjoy the time spent there,' Myrtle said.

Waving to Summer, Gaia spoke with a soft voice. 'It got me thinking about her connecting to her dad, but I'm not sure I want him in her life. He's a bully,' she said.

The skin on Myrtle's arms chilled. They'd all experienced shock when Richard caught Simon hitting out at Summer, and when questioned, Gaia showed him her own bruises. Richard insisted they moved back to his home after giving Simon a choice, stay and be held accountable or leave and never make contact. Simon took off and never returned. He made no effort to communicate with either Gaia or Summer and they were happier without him in their lives.

'If he is truly interested in her, he will make contact

when she is older. She doesn't ask about him, he frightened her. I'd leave well alone,' Myrtle said.

A few weeks later Myrtle heard a scream from the garden. Marigold ran out of the barn to join her on the pathway.

'Who was that?' Marigold asked, her eyes searching their land.

'It came from the woods, I think. You stay here and look around. I'll go to the tree. I'll shout if I need you.'

She ran towards the tree. 'Gaia!' She called, before again correcting herself, 'Lucy!'

Her daughter lay huddled in a heap against the tree, and as Myrtle approached Gaia lifted her head.

'Who am I?' she asked, her voice trembling and weak.

Kneeling beside her, Myrtle took her into her arms.

'You are Lucy, Lucy Henson,' she said.

Gaia shook her head. 'No, who am I really? I came here to think and I heard voices. A woman told me I am a Netherwell, but I couldn't see her and then something which looked snake-like crawled along my arm, and a crow attacked me! What is going on Myrtle?'

Pulling Gaia close, Myrtle cradled her and kissed the top of her head as she had done when Gaia was a child.

'You've had a scare, but you are safe now. Let's get you to the cottage to rest,' Myrtle said easing Gaia to her feet. 'No talking, save your energy.'

Out of Gaia's view, she touched the tree trunk. It was

warm and there was a slight vibration. Something from inside had been disturbed when Gaia was in danger from the Longe attack.

Once back at the cottage, Myrtle settled Gaia on the couch and made her a soothing drink.

'I wonder if you are a bit run down and working too hard, Lucy? I should never have told you about my family and how I feel connected to them through the tree. It's stimulated something in your imagination. Maybe a need to connect with Sheila? A cold breeze on your arm and the sound of a startled crow is bound to have added an atmosphere.'

'It was real. The crow attacked me,' Gaia insisted with a slight sob.

'Well, you are safe now, and you need to rest and clear your head. What made you go to the tree today? Why are you not at work?' Myrtle rushed her words, trying desperately to throw Gaia off from asking who she was for a second time.

Easing herself into a sitting position, Gaia looked at Myrtle, her eyes circled by dark rings which Myrtle had not noticed the previous week when she had seen her daughter.

'Dad. He's not well. The board have asked him to retire,' Gaia replied.

'Richard? What's wrong with him, is it serious?' Myrtle said.

Gaia shook, then nodded her head. 'I shouldn't tell you, I promised not to, but he has dementia. I had to call his colleague for advice. It all happened so quickly after that, and he is angry with me.'

Sitting down beside Gaia, Myrtle took in her words.

'He's angry with himself and frightened. He adores you and it is important you – we, help him. Don't mention today, Lucy, just focus on your dad, and you must both tell Summer.' She took her daughter's hand. 'And don't forget, our door is always open to you both. Now drink your tea and relax, I'll get one of the girls to run you home so you can rest up before Summer gets back from school.'

As she spoke Marigold entered the room looking every bit the wild creature. Her eyes were wide, her hair in disarray and she fidgeted from foot to foot. Myrtle inwardly berated herself, she had forgotten Marigold was also out looking for the screaming someone.

'Did you find who screamed?' she demanded.

'I did. It was Lucy. Something frightened her in the woods, and she was attacked by a crow,' Myrtle said.

Marigold looked at Myrtle with a strange stare. Her face twisted into a puzzled frown.

'Is she still here?' she asked, her voice low and cold.

Myrtle's neck hair stood on end and she rubbed away the feeling that Marigold knew about the attack.

'She's fine now and heading home,' Myrtle said quickly.

She knew Marigold could not be too close to a weak Gaia if Ingulf or Edmunde's power had increased.

'Wash your hands. There's fresh scones on the table. I'll take Lucy home.'

The distraction of the scones worked as Myrtle knew

they would, and before Marigold came back into the room she had ushered Gaia outside to Gaia's car.

'I'll keep you company and then walk home,' she said to Gaia when she fussed about Myrtle going with her. 'I won't speak with your dad if that's what you are worried about. He will reach out when time decides.'

Willow

I saw the dark one staring down at Gaia from the treetop.

He sensed she is troubled, weak, and he tried to claim her with a strand of evil intent. I watched as he draped his way down the trunk and touched the top of her head, feeding on her energy. In my form as a crow, along with Ragnis, I attacked. She is safe for now, but for how long we do not know.

Danger is close.

Chapter Twenty-Seven

Seeing Richard sitting in the chair staring out of the window was heart wrenching. He looked tired, frail and bewildered.

'Hello, Richard,' Myrtle said softly so as not to disturb the other residents in the home. Richard's condition had gone beyond the kind of care she and Gaia had managed for a year. He rarely recognised them and thought Summer was a nurse he used to work with when he was a junior doctor. All three of them visited regularly, but today Myrtle wanted time alone with him.

Richard lifted his head; he studied her face intently then touched her cheek. His hands were cold.

'I know you,' he said, his words slurred with tiredness.

Myrtle smiled at him. 'You do. You delivered my baby in a storm, in the woods. Sheila was there, your wife. Remember? I am Myrtle.'

Turning his head to look out of the window, he sat a while, still and peaceful before turning back to her.

'Lucy's mother,' he said.

'Sheila, yes that's right,' Myrtle said.

Richard's hand flapped and he twisted them together in an agitated state.

'No. You. Gaia. Lucy's mother,' he replied.

Reaching out, Myrtle touched his arm. 'Yes, I am Gaia's mother. Her birth mother.'

'Take her back. Keep her safe for me,' Richard said, then closed his eyes.

A clock chimed in the corridor nearby and someone jumped in their seat. The carer in the room rushed from the room and returned shaking her head.

'Well, that's the first time in ten years I've ever heard that clock chime. It ticks, but never chimes. Oh well, something else to wake them up for lunch,' the woman said to Myrtle with a laugh.

'Time,' Richard said.

The word sat in the air between them. Myrtle pondered the moment.

'Yes, it is time. You are right, Richard.'

After leaving the nursing home, she went and sat on a bench to take stock of what had happened inside. Was the clock chime a signal for her to tell Gaia the truth, or should she wait until Richard had died?

Not finding the answers in the roses growing in the garden or the clouds above her head, Myrtle decided to wait for the next sign or happening. As she rose to her feet a woman called out to her.

'Miss Netherwell?'

It was the nurse who had commented about the clock.

'Richard said this is your daughter's,' she said handing over a blue book.

Myrtle took the book and looked at the cover. It was engraved with the words, Gaia Mystia Netherwell.

'Thank you,' Myrtle said and slid the book into her bag.

'I saw your name in the visitor's book,' Gaia said on her next visit to Plumtree Cottage. 'Thank you, Auntie Myrt, you are a good friend to Dad.'

Myrtle smiled at her. 'He has been a good friend to me over the years. He never judged us or pressured me to put Marigold in a home when our mum died. He kept the authorities at bay. It saddens me to see him there, but he was awake this time and mentioned you. It was a good day.'

Gaia filled the kettle and placed it on the Aga.

'I don't think he has many of them left if I am honest. As old as I am, I am not sure I'm prepared to be an orphan quite yet. I expected longer with him. Thank goodness for you.' She smiled over at Myrtle, who was wrestling with her conscience. She had chosen to put the book away and for the past five days it had called for her to read it, but she refrained, it was private from Richard to his daughter.

Whatever was written inside Myrtle had to trust Richard had done the right thing.

Months drifted by with life revolving around Marigold, Richard, Gaia and Summer, and Myrtle's business orders increased. Life was busy but she coped, despite Eve's and Harry's concerns she was doing too much.

Myrtle did not tell them that keeping busy was her way of not facing the inevitable. Richard was not far from death, and she would be left alone to tell Gaia the truth, a day she was not looking forward to because it carried so many complications.

Myrtle was sat at her desk finishing off her tax return when she heard Gaia's car pull up outside the cottage. She set down her pen and as she did so, a strange sensation raced through her arms and chest. Standing for a moment, she realised it was an external sensation, one channelled via someone else's energy and not anything related to her own body.

Rushing out from her office into the packing area and main workspace, she checked on her staff, now six in number, but all reassured her there was nothing wrong and resumed their particular tasks.

From the doorway she could see Marigold berating a goat who'd managed to escape and eat an empty hessian sack, and Gaia still sitting in her car looking down at what Myrtle assumed was her mobile phone. She glanced up at Myrtle and immediately Myrtle knew time had moved things forward. Richard was dead. Gaia's grief had channelled the energy that Myrtle had received.

Gaia eased herself out of the small fiat and ran into Myrtle's arms. No words were needed as Myrtle guided her daughter into the cottage.

'I'll just go and tell Marigold and the staff to leave us alone for a while,' she said as she eased the sobbing Gaia onto the sofa.

Once she had instructed her staff to finish early and lock up the unit, she found Marigold.

'Hey there, did you get your sack back?' she asked with a light laugh.

Marigold huffed. 'He'd already had the bottom of my dungarees, look!' Marigold said lifting her right leg to show off a tattered trouser leg.

Myrtle gave her a grin, then entered a more serious mood.

'Listen, Gaia's here and she's upset. Richard died today. Summer is with friends. If you need a drink or something to eat, go to the unit. Understand, Marigold? Give me and Gaia a bit of time together,' Myrtle said.

'Gaia's here. Okay,' Marigold said and walked away.

Apprehensive, and worried, Myrtle returned to the cottage. She had to trust Marigold would not be calling on the dark side to interfere when Gaia was so vulnerable.

Telling Gaia the truth about her adoption had been put off for too long and Myrtle had always struggled with when might be the right time. When Richard had gone into the home, he'd arranged for the house to be sold and bought Gaia an apartment in Holt with some of the proceeds, as well as setting aside a fund for Summer. All of his private papers were in a suitcase, which Myrtle had stored at his request, in her secure office. Once she had given Gaia the suitcase, she would give her the book he had asked her to keep safe.

But first they had to respect Richard and lay him to rest.

Chapter Twenty-Eight

A few weeks after Richard's funeral, Myrtle arranged to meet with Gaia to tell her the truth about her birth. The previous day had been Gaia's thirty-seventh birthday and they had enjoyed a meal together, along with Summer, in Holt. But for Myrtle, the urge to share her story with Gaia became stronger every day, and she'd decided she could not wait any longer.

At last, Gaia pulled up in her car and waved. Myrtle waved back and picked up the food basket.

'I thought we could sit in the shade beneath the Tree of Life today, Lucy. I have a picnic treat for you.'

Gaia slipped her arm through Myrtle's, and a shimmer of fear ran through Myrtle's body. Telling her story could be the last time they were together, and the thought was unbearable.

'Let's go,' Gaia said, 'it's a glorious day for a walk and picnic.'

Once settled at the tree, Myrtle performed a series of blessings and cleansed the area. Gaia looked on. 'I love your ability to bring calm to a space and share your respect for nature,' she said.

Shaking out a blanket, Myrtle sat down and patted a space in front of her.

'It's part of being a priestess; nature deserves respect. This area has played a big part in my life,' she said.

Pulling out goblets, she poured elderflower cordial into them both.

'Let's toast your parents, Lucy. This place featured in their lives, too. I'll tell you why if you will hear me out without comment until I've finished. Promise me?' she implored Gaia.

'You're very serious, Auntie Myrt, but I want to hear the story. Did Dad propose to Mum here?' Gaia asked.

Taking a large gulp of her drink, Myrtle pulled out the file and book, placed them on her lap and took a deep breath.

Her trembling hands were clenched together in her lap, and her chest pained her as she tried to control her voice and breathing. She could not stop blinking to clear the tears and focus on Gaia sitting opposite her, waiting patiently for what she had to tell her.

'When I was young, I dated a boy named Dan. By the time I was seventeen, though, he had left England to live in Spain with his parents. I thought we would be together for life, but the night before he left, he – well, he abused me. He was very aggressive and he frightened me. He left for Spain and he never made contact with me again. So I … I couldn't trace him when I found out I was pregnant, but I'd decided that he didn't deserve to know my child, anyway.

'Early on in my pregnancy, my mother died, and I had to care for Marigold alone. As you know, she hates babies, they trigger something dark inside her, and she feels the need to harm them. Marigold was extremely vocal about what she would do if I brought my child up at Plumtree Cottage, so I knew, to keep my baby safe, I couldn't keep her. Your father … he was my GP, offered to help.'

Gaia opened her mouth to speak, but Myrtle lifted her hand. 'Please, hear me out, my love,' she said, and Gaia nodded. 'I came here under the tree to think one day,' Myrtle continued, 'and I went into labour, during which a dreadful storm brewed and I struggled with the delivery. Your parents found me in the woods. They heard my cries and your father delivered my baby.' She took a deep breath. 'What I need you to do now is have an open mind. What your parents did not know was that they had protected me from a dark soul determined to kill both me and my child.'

Gaia took a sip of her drink and stared at Myrtle, her eyes wide and her attention fully focused on her.

'Carry on,' she said, her voice calm and low. Myrtle knew she had guessed what was coming next, and her chest tightened.

'I had already made an adoption agreement with your parents, and they took you home. I named you Gaia Mystia – which became your middle names.' Myrtle watched as Gaia took in the story.

'So, my real name is Gaia Mystia Netherwell, and you are my biological mother?' Gaia asked, her voice dipping and cracking with emotion.

Myrtle dropped her head to her chin.

'I'm so sorry.' Her apology choked her, and she dared not look up at Gaia. Then she remembered the files from the suitcase and the book. She reached into her bag and took them out. Eventually, she found the courage to look at her daughter.

'Your dad gave me this file and left this book for you. Inside the file is the agreement we made between us, allowing me to be a part of your life, and your birth certificate. It names me as your mother and the father as unknown. It's all a mess, but I had to protect you. Marigold allowed our own father's dark demon into our lives, and it is linked to the past. It sounds unbelievable, with true stories of the burning of woodland, the execution of a witch named Brigid ... and more. To you it will seem far-fetched, totally unbelievable, but for me it is my every breathing moment – a real-life battle with the unseen.'

Myrtle stopped talking and drank her goblet dry. Her daughter sat staring at her, and Myrtle could see she was working out whether Myrtle was mad or telling the truth.

'Lucy, I am truly sorry, but I have no regrets in keeping you safe. You and Summer are the centre of my world, and I've tried so hard to keep my secret.'

The woodlands rustled to a hush and the only tree to shimmy out a sound from its leaves was the Tree of Life.

They looked up at its tip, then Gaia reached out to touch the trunk.

'I feel something,' she said quietly, then picked up the book Richard had left for her and turned the pages. Myrtle sat watching, and waited for Gaia to shout at her and leave, but her daughter sat calmly, lifting out her birth certificate. She studied it and stroked her hand against the paper.

'Sheila was a pious cow,' Gaia said quietly. 'She never had a nice word to say about you.'

Myrtle looked at Gaia in shock. 'She was a good mother, and I trusted her with you. She loved you.'

'She loved the idea of me. Dad did all the hard work. Don't be fooled by what you were shown when you visited. I played the role of a loving daughter, but the truth is, I felt more love from you than Sheila. Once I even prayed you could be my mother.'

A silence fell between them. Myrtle's heart went out to Gaia.

'What does your dad say in the book?' Myrtle asked eventually, breaking the silence.

Gaia looked down at the items on the rug. 'Who cares? It's a fairy story. It's a book of lies. The only real thing about it is the name on the front. The true story? My mother gets pregnant by a bully – a rapist?' She looked at Myrtle and Myrtle nodded then watched Gaia shudder.

'Her mother dies and she's left looking after a sister with anger issues. She cares for both the daughter and granddaughter with so much love and holds the secret in her heart for nearly all of her life. It must have hurt like hell, but not once did she break the promise made to a couple who took advantage of her to gain what they wanted. That's the true story.'

'Lucy, don't be bitter,' Myrtle said softly.

'Bitter? I'm not bitter, I'm relieved. You've been my only mother figure and shown me what sort of mother I needed to be while coping with divorcing a bully of my own. You *are* my mother, you gave me life and never walked away, and all the while you guided me here, to the tree – to a point of safety for me and my child. You have just explained my dreams, my fainting spells and why I have always loved you with such fierceness over Sheila. You saved me the day I was attacked here. I assume you will tell me more about whatever is going on in your life – your witch life?'

Myrtle stood and held open her arms. 'Oh, Lucy, how can you forgive me for giving you up?' she asked.

'There's no forgiveness to be given, you did the right thing.' Gaia smiled. 'To think, my friends used to whisper about you being a witch, and I used to tell them off, saying you were just a kind lady who was a friend. If they'd known the truth...'

'I still can't believe you are so positive about the whole situation. Aside from Summer, can you please not say anything. Eve knows, but Harry doesn't, and well...'

'You want to tell him yourself. I understand. We will explain it all to Summer and tell her to keep it to herself. She'll be thrilled that you are her grandmother, she adores you.'

Myrtle felt the bloom of happiness inside her, but she

kept her voice steady. 'Gaia, too much talk about it will trigger something in Marigold, too. We must think about her reactions. I will tell her when the time is right,' Myrtle said.

She and Gaia spent the rest of the afternoon talking about the future, and the support they could both offer one another.

Myrtle's life story had turned another page and formed a fresh chapter, she was ready to fight the dark shadows. She would share the news to Gaia that she and Summer might harbour inherited powers another day.

Chapter Twenty-Nine

2023

Myrtle's life became less mundane with Gaia and Summer visiting more often, both with fresh ideas for Naturally Netherwell.

Her staff no longer needed her watching their every move, as both Gaia and Summer had forged new roles in her business, with her blessing. Most days she was left to please herself and began taking the opportunity to visit Harry and Mel at the garden centre. Occasionally helping out when they were busy.

One morning, she arrived as planned to work a full day while they coped with a large Christmas tree delivery. She did her usual walkabout, casting blessings on her friend's business, when raised voices caught her attention as she entered the indoor area, and she saw the couple squaring up to one another in a heated argument. It was an upsetting scene, and Mel was shouting the kind of abuse that no other person should be hearing. Her unhappiness in the bedroom was not for public consumption and Myrtle could see a few customers arriving in the car park.

'Hello? Anyone around?' she called out as she backtracked to the main doors. To her relief the shouting stopped.

'Be right with you, Myrtle!' Harry replied, as a door slammed at the far end of the building. Myrtle knew it led to the back of the garden centre and guessed Mel had taken herself home.

'Morning,' Harry said as he appeared at the checkout, where Myrtle was pulling on her pinafore and preparing for the day ahead.

'Morning. Ready for the rush?' she asked hoping her voice did not appear too false and chirpy. She felt for Harry, he had dark circles beneath his eyes, and a sadness around his mouth.

'Just me today,' he said. 'Mel's under the weather, she—' Harry made Myrtle jump when he slammed his hand onto the counter. 'No, darn it, she is leaving me, Myrtle. I found out last night she's been having an affair with one of the delivery guys – I'm not surprised, I've never been enough for her.'

'Oh. Oh,' Myrtle floundered as two customers walked through the door. 'I'm so sad for you. Let me ring Lucy and Summer, they'll come down and help. You go home and save your marriage,' she encouraged.

Harry shook his head. 'I can't save it, Mel is not worth it, if I am honest. I would be grateful for the help, though, and maybe time with you this evening – she's moving out and I don't want to sit at Mum's listening to a lecture on being a weak man for two hours,' he said.

'You are welcome in my home any time, Harry. Marigold will behave, I'll make sure of it,' Myrtle responded swiftly, as two of Harry's customers approached. 'And you are not a weak man, far from it.'

She looked him in the eyes, secretly pleased that Mel had removed herself from Harry's life. Helping him heal would not be easy but it was not a task she would walk away from – Harry was too important to her.

Time was kind to Myrtle, it brought family and friends together around the table on more than one occasion. Both Gaia and Summer kept their promise, and even Marigold never let on to Harry that Gaia was Myrtle's daughter. In fact, Marigold had mellowed, and another Yuletide came and went with no drama.

Myrtle helped Harry move back to his mother's house, and supported him throughout the divorce proceedings. In the end, Mel accepted a payment to step away from Harry's Garden Centre, and left town.

But January dropped a life-changing bombshell for Myrtle, just as the Wolf Moon shone.

Chapter Thirty

M yrtle smiled as she pulled back the curtains and allowed the moonlight to fill the bedroom.

'Blessings, new moon,' she said and snuggled beneath her covers.

Nightshade sat in the moon's glow on the windowsill, and the night sounds silenced.

A groan from Marigold's room disturbed the peace, and Myrtle lay listening, waiting to see if anything was wrong. After a few moments she felt her eyelids grow heavy and gave into a deep sleep.

The dawn chorus rang out and Nightshade nudged Myrtle awake.

'Morning already? I suppose you are hungry,' she said stroking Nightshade's head.

She shivered and dressed quickly, then glanced out of the window. Winter had set in overnight; snow had fallen and iced the countryside with its beautiful flakes.

She rushed downstairs and pushed her feet into her boots, pulling on her parka, then stepped outside to tend to the animals.

'Merry Meet, Ragnis,' she called out and smiled when she heard his call.

She pulled open the door of the barn expecting to see Marigold tending the goats, but there was no sign of her sister.

She broke the ice on water buckets and threw down handfuls of grain for the goats.

The pigs snuffled in their stye, and she threw buckets of scraps over the gate, puzzled to see there was still no sign of her sister in the pens or the chicken coop.

Trudging back into the cottage, Myrtle stomped the snow away from her boots and scooped up a handful of fresh snow, placing it on a cleared patch of ground by the door, and watched it melt into the soil, taking her wish with it – a wish for life to continue peacefully and without drama.

Shutting the door against the cold and embracing the warmth of the fire filling the room, she noticed Marigold sitting in her chair. Myrtle took a moment to look around the kitchen and noted Marigold had not eaten breakfast – the only reason she would delay heading outside – and Myrtle frowned.

'Morning blessings, Marigold. Wasn't it a wonderful full moon last night? Our crystals will be brimming with energy. I remembered to put them out to bathe in the light.' Myrtle went to the cauldron, noticing that the porridge pot was still full.

'Aren't you hungry today?' she asked.

Marigold rose from her seat and walked over to the saucepan of porridge, peering into it, then stirred the porridge before returning to her seat.

'What is it, what's wrong with the porridge?' Myrtle asked Marigold, looking her sister in the face. Vacant eyes stared back at her, and Myrtle instantly understood what was happening in her sister's head.

'Marigold. Where are you?' Myrtle asked anxiously.

Closing her eyes, Marigold remained seated and quiet.

'Marigold? Don't let them take you travelling. Eat, wake up and eat your breakfast,' she said patting her sister's cheeks. She got no response.

Myrtle busied herself upstairs making the beds, when she heard a noise in the kitchen. She went downstairs to check on her sister, but the back door clicked shut before she had a chance to speak with her. Guessing Marigold was tending to her animals, Myrtle sat eating breakfast alone.

The Tree of Life

The words of the Netherwell ancestors came through as one today. A clambering of voices all with the need to be heard.

Their prediction was loud and clear as they prepared Marigold Netherwell for her journey beyond Earth.

They spoke of how she must allow her always tightly-bound mind to settle and be calm. This was not a time to allow the confusion she had lived with all her life cloud reality. She must not let the Longe family take hold of her before death.

The sisterhood are fearful and unnerved by a darkness waiting in the soil beneath my roots. It has not weakened me, but they feel its threatening force taunting in readiness to overwhelm them. I sensed a heightened tremor when Marigold's name was mentioned as the next matriarch. A witch with such dark association was a breach in the recent barrier they had built.

Marigold's death will become Myrtle's final battle, and she will need all her powers to support her, but if the demon is released, they are a doomed family and Myrtle, Gaia and Summer will not live to see another year.

Marigold returned. Her clothes were wet through, and her face was pinched with the biting chill outside. Myrtle ushered her to the fire, and filled a pan with water, ginger, cinnamon and black pepper, and placed it on the flames to warm through.

'Why on earth didn't you wear your coat and boots. Get your slippers and socks off, we'll soak your feet. Warm them through. You don't want chilblains,' she said, shocked as Marigold did what she was asked. Once the water was warmed through, she poured it into the washing-up bowl and gently lifted Marigold's feet into the aromatic, warming remedy.

Marigold pulled the blanket Myrtle offered around her and gave the same groan as Myrtle had heard in the night.

'What is it Mari, tell me. What's worrying you?' she asked, not truly sure she wanted to hear the answer. Marigold's face looked troubled.

'Marigold, you are scaring me. Speak to me. You shouldn't have gone out if you are unwell, it is too cold.'

To her surprise, Marigold patted Myrtle's head.

'Don't fuss. I'm going to die soon,' she said, in a matter-of-fact voice, and Myrtle stood upright, stunned by the news.

The wind outside the window blew a small branch back and forth, creating a heartbeat rhythm on the glass and both looked its way.

'I'll trim that back,' Marigold said and went to get out of her seat.

'Stay where you are. What's all this talk about dying? Who put that idea into your head?' Myrtle demanded in a tone that shocked even her.

Marigold did as asked and gave an annoyed flick of her head.

'I am only telling you what I know. I feel my body dying. Can't you feel me dying?' Marigold gave her a hard stare, defying Myrtle not to cry.

'Is it the Longe family, are they sucking life from you? You can fight them you know,' she said. 'Come to the altar, let's work on getting you released from their grip on you.'

Silence filled the room, and the heaviness of Marigold's words lingered in the air. Her life was ebbing away, and it was out of their control. No spell could alter what was meant to be, but Myrtle was not prepared to let her sister die without a fight. With the suddenness of the illness, it had to be an attack by their father's family. Marigold needed protecting, and while she was weak, Myrtle also had the opportunity to influence her – weakening the Longe hold.

'I'll be back in a minute. I must put the heating on in the unit to stop the pipes freezing over,' she said, using the only excuse she could think of for going back outside.

Inside the unit, Myrtle made a small healing spell bottle for Marigold to wear around her neck.

'Give strength and healing powers to this charm,
May it absorb the pain and bring relief.
I anoint it with water bathed in the presence of the
*   moon goddess,*
And bless it with the blood from my veins.'

As she spoke Myrtle pricked her finger and squeezed three drops of blood into the file. Once mixed, she sealed the cork with candlewax.

Returning inside, Myrtle looked at her sleeping sister. Her skin was dull and her breath rasping. She placed the healing bottle beside Marigold and worked out a plan of how to persuade Marigold to see a doctor. Each time she looked at her sister, she seemed to be getting paler.

Chapter Thirty-One

A t sunset, a knock at the back door distracted Myrtle from staring at her sister, willing her awake.

She heard the back door click open.

'Myrtle?' Harry's voice called out.

She jumped to her feet. 'Come in Harry,' she greeted him as he entered the kitchen. He waggled a bottle of Malbec at her.

'Get the glasses out, we'll stave off the cold. It's stopped snowing at last,' he said, his voice happy, and Myrtle welcomed his jovial spirit.

'Marigold's not well at all, so we'll go into the sitting room,' she whispered, giving him a soft smile. 'Thanks for the wine. A glass will be a treat. I'll light the candles, and we'll relax until madam wakes up. I want her to see a doctor. I've never known her so ill.'

As they went into the sitting room, Nightshade suddenly bounded passed them. He arched his back and hissed at a corner of the room. His hair stood on end and his ears were pinned back.

'What can you see?' Myrtle asked him, but before she could reach him, a candle flickered a wide shadow across the room and Nightshade ran from one side of the room to the other, hissing and mewling loudly.

'What the heck is going on, Myrt?' Harry said, rising to his feet in an attempt to help her catch Nightshade. When Nightshade ran from the room into the kitchen, a row of candle flames flickered out, and the darkened room grew cold, despite the log fire burning fiercely in the grate. A bright yellow light flashed from a corner point in the ceiling, followed by red and blue sparks, and Myrtle relit candles as fast as she could, but as she did they went out.

'Go and check Marigold for me, check she's not awake and wandered off anywhere,' she said, turning to Harry.

She heard Ragnis screech outside of the window, and Myrtle turned to see another shadow in the room and Ragnis frantically pecking against the window.

'Harry, check on my sister, please!' Myrtle insisted as she ran to the window and let Ragnis inside. His screeching grew louder, and joined Nightshade's hisses when he returned and prowled the room again.

Myrtle's throat tightened, and her chest ached.

A dark force had entered the cottage. Her brain throbbed with the thought that it might be Harry, but she dismissed it as fear over rational thinking. Harry would have shown his hand as belonging to the Longe bloodline years ago.

She shuddered as the temperature dropped again and

Ragnis screeched. This was a dangerous entity, growing by the second. Something was feeding it power and when Myrtle rushed to touch the walls, they were ice cold. The ancestors had been blocked. She was alone.

'Begone! I do not invite you to enter. I banish all negative energy. Dark spirit begone!' she murmured as she threw handfuls of camomile, bay leaves, thyme and angelica into the fire, protecting the chimney from another entity entering. In a metal dish she placed the same herbs and set fire to them, wafting the smoke around the room, keeping only the area near the open window free from smoke.

'Leave my home. I banish you from Plumtree Cottage. This is my sacred place! Exit, evil.'

Despite the chill in the room, Myrtle's inner core felt red hot.

'How dare you come here when my sister is unwell. You do not frighten me. You are not welcome to cross my threshold. Go! Leave!'

Myrtle snatched up her mother's wand, which lay on the altar – the place she had always kept it.

A heat stung Myrtle's hand, and to her amazement, light glowed from the wand. Moving quickly around the room, she raised it high and low.

'With my mother's fire I seal this room. Feed on my hexes, eat my contempt for your weakness. There is no great power for you to feed upon in my home. I protect the energy force named Marigold Netherwell. I banish you from this place!'

A force of air drew the smoke towards the window and Myrtle watched as two dark shadows slithered across the windowsill. Once gone, she ran and closed the window, wafting the smoke around the room once more.

'Seal this room. Keep us safe! Ancestors, return and protect our home!' she cried.

'I think Marigold's unconscious!' Harry called out.

Myrtle threw the remainder of the burning herbs onto the fire and ran to the kitchen.

Marigold's chest barely moved, and her facial features were slack.

'She's alive, but I can't feel any connection – like twins can sometimes,' Myrtle said kneeling to listen to her sister's chest. She shook her head. 'She's weak.'

'I'll get her to bed,' said Harry. 'You call the doctor. Here, use my mobile, don't go out to the office phone. I've never seen Marigold like this, ill – and all the weird stuff, what's wrong, Myrt?' Harry gently lifted Marigold into his arms.

'I don't know,' Myrtle said and lifted her address book from the desk drawer. 'I'll call Richard's old colleague. He told me to ring if ever Lucy needed help. He'll help us.'

Harry walked by with Marigold in his arms.

'But the weird stuff, Nightshade and flashing lights. What was that all about?' he asked.

Myrtle gave her sister a swift glance, then looked at Harry.

'The cottage is old, there's bound to be weird stuff to spook a cat. Thank you, Harry. I'll get her some help.'

The doctor broke the news that Marigold was at the end stage of life with cancer in her stomach and must have hidden her symptoms and pain well from Myrtle.

Having been reassured that a care team would come to the home when they were able, Myrtle thanked him as Harry hovered downstairs to let the doctor out.

Myrtle joined him and looked around the room. Nightshade was no longer rampaging around the furniture and Ragnis had flown from the window ledge. The atmosphere was now one of sadness and not aggression.

'What did the doc say, something she's eaten?' Harry asked, his voice full of concern.

Myrtle shook her head and sat at the kitchen table.

'I can't take it in, Harry. He said she is dying of cancer. Last stages – can you believe it? Harry, I'd have noticed, surely? Marigold, well, she would have told me if something was not right, she hated feeling unwell – she's been digging the garden this week, for goodness' sake!'

She put her head in her hands and sighed heavily.

'No wonder the Longes were sniffing around tonight, she's weak and they are draining her power to increase their own. She'll reach the sisterhood and then they will feed her their darkness to bring us down. I have to find…' Myrtle stopped speaking, realising she was rambling her thoughts out loud, and that Harry was oblivious to their struggle.

'I'm hearing you, but haven't got a bloody clue what

you are talking about, Myrt. You are in shock. Let's step back. From what you are saying, Marigold hasn't long to live, right?' His face transfixed on hers and Myrtle nodded.

'He said her body has been shutting down for a while now, and she's either disguised it, or has an incredible pain threshold. It's too late for me to help her,' Myrtle said; the sadness lay heavy in her chest and the shock made her feel sick.

In one stride Harry was kneeling beside her with his arm around her shoulders.

'I'm here for you, Myrt. For Marigold, too. All that witchy stuff going on earlier was the cottage warning you. Old places, old souls. We'll help Marigold. The carers and chemo, they will get her back to her grumpy self, you'll see.' Harry kissed her forehead and Myrtle leaned her head on his shoulder.

'No carers. The coven, Gaia and Summer will help me. Marigold's not able to have chemo – I asked. He said she may not wake up again,' she said softly.

Harry rose to his feet. 'I'll stay down here tonight, you look after your sister. Tomorrow, I'll do whatever you need me to do, but first I want you to get sleep. You've had a terrible shock and it's going to be a tough road ahead for a while. I'll be here, Myrt. Always.'

Uncurling herself from the makeshift bed beside Marigold's, Myrtle checked on her sister. Marigold was still sleeping soundly. Downstairs, she heard Harry talking to Nightshade, and shaking out kibble into a dish.

'May you find peace in my home, Harry Tye,' she whispered, and took a moment to collect her thoughts and sense the mood of the cottage. With Nightshade content, and no shadows lurking at the foot of the stairs, Myrtle was ready to face what lay ahead.

Three days later, as the afternoon bled into a winter's evening, Myrtle rose to stretch her body and look outside to watch the stars appear. A carpet of lights bloomed like flowers on a spring day. White for a wedding. White for Peace, for acceptance.

'I wonder where yours will shine, Marigold?' she said softly. 'It will be bright, and if stars have sound, loud. Will I know if it is thunder or you who will be moving above me, Mari?' Myrtle gave a sisterly giggle. 'I shouldn't tease, not now, but we both know it's true.'

The stars moved into their set places within the deep navy sky and Myrtle continued to stare at them calling out each constellation or lone star she recognised.

'Ah, Cassiopeia the Queen, she has come out to escort you home. She's marked the sky with an upside-down M. M for Marigold,' Myrtle said and wiped the fog of her breath from the windowpane.

'Listen to me, wittering on about silly things. Maybe I should read to you instead. Or sit quietly – I know, I'll put your favourite songs on.' She rummaged through Marigold's stack of tapes, slotting one into the old tape recorder her mother had purchased years ago, the only piece of technology Moonstone had accepted. Even when CD players were invented, her mother had refused to move away from tape recordings.

Soon the soothing sounds of Enya and 'May it Be' rippled around the room.

After listening to Marigold's breath change, Myrtle moved to the window and lifted the sash window an inch or so in preparation for Marigold's spirit to fly free. She gave a soft smile when she heard the soft drums and harmonious Celtic chant songs from their friends forming their protective circle around the cottage.

'Our friends are with us, Marigold. Listen they sing for you. Dear friends, with hearts of gold. Warrior women who love and protect us. I'll light the way for you my dear, dear sister,' she said as she lit the last of four candles. Each one representing North, South, East and West. 'I anoint your hands with the oils of the garden you tended.' Myrtle stroked the fragrance oil into Marigold's hands and the aroma of rose, lavender, lemon thyme and rosemary filled the room.

She gently lifted Marigold's hands and turned them palm upwards, placing an aquamarine crystal in one and an amethyst in another.

'May the crystals of courage take you beyond the veil, into the arms of our mother once again. Go and find peace, my dear.'

Within the semi-darkness of the room, Myrtle stood back to witness the gradual manifestation of a wispy, aqua-green aura encircling Marigold's head as her spirit prepared itself to leave her body.

The air hung heavy with an unsettling silence, broken only by the relentless sound from the antiquated timepiece Marigold had repaired when they were ten years old.

It now sat on the dressing table like a metronome counting down the moments with an eerie precision. For Myrtle it was a silent requiem, an inescapable soundtrack to the unwanted scene unfolding, where time continued its relentless march forward and Myrtle wanted to throw it to the floor – to stop time.

Lighting candles Myrtle pushed back the curtains to allow more moonlight into the room.

Clouds parted as if they heard her silent request and casting a silver glow upon the bedspread, the moon's gentle radiance encouraged shadows to slip away, and the room became draped in a celestial elegance. A peace settled around them and the ticking clock stopped.

'Don't be afraid Mari, it is time.'

Stroking her sister's cooling hand in her own, Myrtle fought back the tears. Marigold needed to hear her strength not her sorrow.

'It's okay to go, Mari. I can't say I'll be fine without you, but I promise I'll find a way to cope. I love you and all of your quirky ways. Have a safe journey and we'll meet again at the Tree of Life.' She leaned over to kiss her sibling, 'Go to sleep, brave sister.'

No sooner had she stood upright than Myrtle felt a tremble and a tightening within her chest. Her heart skipped several beats before taking on a slower pace. Her breath hitched in her throat; no matter how hard she tried to control her breathing, it became erratic and raspy. Not daring to move, Myrtle stood with one hand cupped against her throat. Were they meant to go together? Was this her time to leave, too?

A cool wind whispered through the gap in the window, and the candle dedicated to the West flickered. The gripping ache in her chest eased, and her heart rate settled into a steady rhythm.

Myrtle took in the silence from beneath the bed covers.

The setting of the sun had been announced.

White lights flashed around the room, and rose petals danced in the breeze, drifting from the window behind Marigold's spirit.

'So mote it be,' Myrtle whispered as she pushed the sash window higher. 'May the world survive without you, Marigold Netherwell. Fly high.'

Chapter Thirty-Two

After a day of pottering around Plumtree Cottage, wondering what would become of her without Marigold to fuss and fret over, it was time to lay her sister to rest.

Proudly dressing in her purple robes which she trimmed with a deep green ribbon – Marigold's favourite colour – Myrtle walked into the woods carrying her sister's casket of ashes on the cusp of sunset.

Taking a moment to compose herself, she gazed at the dark silhouette of the Tree of Life's branches stretching towards the sky, like gnarled fingers reaching up to snatch at the clouds. As she listened to the haunting melody created by the wind passing through the empty, leafless arms, she felt the tree's song reverberating through her. The howling wind showcased the tree's strength and reminded all who shared the planet that it too had a place and a right to be heard.

Myrtle took comfort in the sound and decided it was Marigold's voice shouting out her last goodbyes and found it reassuring her that her sister's spirit was still nearby. Moving further into the small group of people ahead of her, Myrtle took a moment to appreciate the coven standing alongside her that evening. Seeing their faces, she clung tightly to her grief, afraid that if she let go, it would never end. But then, she felt an arm slip around her shoulders, and Summer leaned her head into Myrtle's shoulder. At the same time, Gaia took Myrtle's hand, offering her a reassuring squeeze of support.

Summer's voice was heavy with grief as she spoke. 'May she run the woodlands and hug the trees, just like she always wanted, Myrtle.'

Ragnis gave out a rasping call and took flight, circling above them. The coven lifted their heads to the sky and watched in silence. As the sun receded, illuminating the tips of the bird's wings, the moon took watch over the earth and a red seam divided the horizon. Slowly, it faded into a haze of peach and eventually a magnificent star-speckled navy.

'I think her journey has begun,' Myrtle whispered, sensing a strange tingling through her body.

'May we all be blessed with her strength and courage, and may Marigold take your love and worries to your elders,' Gaia said. 'It is fitting she passed on the dawn of Imbolc, and joins your mother on a full moon.'

Myrtle agreed. Marigold would have approved her passing on the rising sun of the spring equinox and joining their mother on the eve of the full Snow Moon. The moon struggled through the clouds, but it made a positive effort to spread shards of soft light across the forest. The flames of the candles surrounding them sent shadows scuttling between shrubs and trees. Myrtle shivered, not from cold or fear, but from the weight of her grief.

She closed her eyes to focus and then opened her arms skyward. A hush settled over the coven.

> *'Oh, mighty wind take my word,*
> *Let my verbal sorrow reach beyond; let it be heard.*
> *Our sister leaves this earth – may her spirit remain*
> *   tethered in our hearts,*
> *Yet free to fly amongst the stars – as I speak, so*
> *   mote it be.*
> *Take her Mother Earth, this woman who showed*
> *   you respect and love. Our beloved sister*
> *   Marigold Netherwell whose teachings were*
> *   focused upon your well-being. Use her as she*
> *   would wish and feed the tree she loved. Her*
> *   spirit is risen, and she will watch over us,*
> *   guide us and will forever have our love. Blessed*
> *   be...'*

After the public farewell, Myrtle moved slowly towards the altar where the group gathered around her. Summer rang the altar bell three times and once again the coven members settled into a quiet state watching as Myrtle and Eve lifted their offerings from a wicker basket.

'I offer dandelion for luck on her travels to beyond,

lavender and holly tips for protection, with rose for love. Safe journey to our sister, my beloved Marigold.'

Myrtle placed the items in a bowl, while Eve poured moon-blessed water from a silver chalice. Together they returned to the Tree of Life and Myrtle poured its contents around at the base of the trunk.

'May your roots grow strong, and your wisdom show us the way,' she called out.

'As we speak so mote it be,' the members of the coven called out in unison.

From within the group, the soft murmur of a sound bowl rang out, and slowly the beat of a Samhain drum joined it, the softness of the sound bowl grew louder and stronger until several other bowls were offering up their tune to the universe. Myrtle laid down a circle of crystals chosen for love, peace and connection around the base as the music and chanting increased. Eventually, she put her arms to the sky and silence fell.

'We gather today to celebrate the life of my beloved sister – the other half of me – who peacefully departed from this world. In honour of Marigold's memory and the renewal of springtime, I invite you to join me in our home under the gentle light of the new moon. Let us come together to share our stories, laughter and love. May this evening fill us with the energy and hope we need to embrace life challenges ahead and cherish the beauty of life.'

As the evening moved into night at Plumtree Cottage, the comings and goings of friends and family breathed fresh vitality into the home. Myrtle graciously received their condolences and expressions of love, inviting each visitor to cross the threshold and share in the warmth of the cottage.

But even amidst the swirl of activity, Myrtle couldn't shake the sense of unease gnawing at her.

The Tree of Life

As the mists of time rose above the ferns and glistened on the gorse flowers, I have received the lifeblood of the beloved sister Marigold into the world of the dead. Her life was troubled, but her belief and loyalty to Mother Nature were bold and fierce.

Now, the battle begins. The revenge sought by the Longe family is at its most powerful, the daughter, Marigold, adds another power to her father's bloodline – a devious and unruly one.

The living must find a way to survive.

Chapter Thirty-Three

Myrtle rubbed the sleep from her eyes and listened to the silence of the cottage. Despite trying remedies like lavender oil and Valerian tea, she had not been able to sleep.

Without Marigold, even night-time felt abnormal. Myrtle sensed a deep absence inside her as if a part of her was missing.

The bedroom walls were no longer vibrating with Marigold's deep snores, and Myrtle missed hearing her sister's heavy footsteps echo around the cottage.

Myrtle lay outstretched, listening for a new sound, but only heard the distant hum of the refrigerator downstairs.

She forced herself to get up, feeling unusually exhausted. She guessed it was the weight of grief that she still carried with her.

She sat looking at the new journal on her desk.

Myrtle stroked the brown leather-covered journal, which had an image of the Tree of Life etched on the front.

On the inside left of the cover, Gaia had written:

To my dearest mum, much love, Gaia Mystia Netherwell x

In March of 2023, Myrtle picked up her pen and wrote in her journal.

Blessed be this day dear journal.

A sense of calm has entered Plumtree Cottage but strangely, I miss Marigold's mess and muddle. Today, I closed the original Netherwell Book of Voices and intend to create a new one – a fresh start for future generations.

My daughter and granddaughter will be part of the new book, and it makes me happy they are no longer a secret. They give me the strength to carry on.

I am also ready to create a fresh book of spells and work on a new project close to my heart. Dear journal, a fresh path awaits me. Although I am still mourning my twin, it's the start of a new chapter, and I'm prepared to live again for as long as time allows.

Summer is in love. She and Eve's grandson, Tim, are a couple and both Eve and I are delighted.

Harry is proving to be the dearest of companions. I am content to accept him as that, but there are days when I have

the urge to express more, and to tell him of my love for him.
But for now, I will take the happiness he offers me, and the
comfort he gives on sad days. I cast for his protection each
day, and set my intention as his protector every morning.
I end this entry with a full heart.

Myrtle laid down her pen and, lost in thought, looked out the window, half-expecting to see her sister working in the garden. Ragnis hopped from tree to tree; a robin pecked at the suet ball Summer made; pigeons, doves, squirrels and the odd blackbird all brought activity into the main garden. Spikes of fresh green forced their way through the last of winter's harsh soil, and two tabby kittens jumped and leaped amongst the bushes. Myrtle adjusted her cardigan and stepped outside for a breath of fresh air. Ready to re-immerse herself in nature, clearing her mind from the fog of grief.

While wandering through the garden, Myrtle picked herb and flower tips and breathed in their fragrances. Inspired by the bed prepared and labelled marigolds, inspiration struck, and she hurried back inside.

Later in the morning, the sound of Harry's van pulling up beside the barn distracted her from her recipe book. Her heart gave a flutter. Harry had checked on her every day since Marigold's death.

'Merry Meet. How is business? Busy, I hope?' she asked.

Harry removed his baseball cap and rummaged in his pocket.

'Yes, we've had a busy week. I've closed for an hour. I

wanted to check on you. I've brought you a little something which I hope will make you smile and not cry,' he said.

'Oh, Harry, bless you. A present – that's so kind of you,' Myrtle replied and took the gift bag.

Inside, she lifted out a small flat box, lifted the lid and stared at a silver necklace nestling on the velvet pad.

'It's a marigold flower,' Harry said.

'So I see, and a really pretty one,' she whispered, choked with gratitude for such a precious gift. 'Thank you, it is beautiful.'

'Here, let me put it on,' Harry said and moved behind her, clasping the chain in place. Myrtle reached out and touched his hand, which was resting on her shoulder.

'It means so much. Thank you, Harry,' she said.

Harry kissed the top of her head. 'You are welcome. I see a new project is underway,' he said, sitting opposite her and nodding at her notepads, drawings and colourful pens on the kitchen table.

'I've had an idea, and your necklace is certainly a sign. I've designed Naturally Marigold. A whole range of products made from the flower in Marigold's memory.'

Harry stood up and smiled at her. 'I think it's a cracking way to remember your sister. Now, instead of standing around here, I'd better get back and sort out more marigold plants and seeds, I've a feeling you'll need more flowers than ever,' he said and headed for the garden.

Marigold touched her necklace, and an outpouring of love for Harry hit her. Having a companion in her life like

Harry was the biggest blessing, aside from her small secret family.

Chapter Thirty-Four

Naturally Marigold stimulated great excitement with Gaia and Summer, and Myrtle's staff threw themselves into its production. Myrtle's dream was realised by the end of March, and Ostara was celebrated by the giving out of samples.

Summer organised fundraising events for cancer charities in Marigold's name, and Myrtle joined Summer, Tim and Eve for a trip to a town called Diss to promote the product at a fayre.

After raising impressive funds for a local charity, and with an hour to spare before they needed to leave for home, the four of them chose to go shopping in town. Although Myrtle disliked shopping outside of Sheringham and Holt, she was not prepared to sit in the car for hours.

Summer and Tim went in search of a cake shop. So Eve and Myrtle strolled arm in arm, chatting about how much they had enjoyed their first day out together for years.

When Eve found a wool shop and began talking with the woman behind the counter, about knitting patterns, Myrtle chose to stroll further down the road. She took herself off towards what looked like a lake near a tourist advice centre and stood a while watching the birds on the water and children playing in the park.

When she returned to join Eve, she couldn't resist peeping into the window of a charming book and gift shop named the Diss Publishing Bookshop.

To her surprise, the smiling face of what she assumed was a member of staff peered back at her, and they both laughed. The bright colours inside and the tempting array of books on the shelves called to Myrtle, and she had the unexpected urge to browse.

She stood outside for a moment, although she was used to her business meetings, shopping in town still made her nervous. As Myrtle entered, a warm sense of welcome washed over her.

It had been far too long since she had the luxury of sitting down with a good book. As a result, her pile of romance and crime novels grew rapidly the more she wandered around the shop.

When she met with Eve again outside the wool shop, she waggled her bags.

'Essential purchases. Books to keep me company when the nights draw in,' she said.

'Look at you, shopping alone, Myrtle Netherwell. Changes are upon us,' Eve quipped. Both giggled their way to Tim's van, and they set off on the road home. Myrtle was happy and content.

The approach to Norwich was busy with traffic, and the sky darkened. Rain fell as clouds raced across the sky, and an exceptionally strong wind set in, making driving conditions tough.

The wind rocked the van, scattering unsecured items onto the streets as they drove out of the city and through village after village.

Myrtle sat quietly in the back. Her insides churned, and her head pounded. Something was not right. She felt so unwell. Travel sickness was not usually a problem for her.

A crash to their right made everyone jump and gasp with shock.

'You okay, Tim?' Summer asked.

Myrtle noticed the white across Tim's knuckles as he gripped the steering wheel.

'Another few minutes, and I'll have you home. I'll drop Nan off and then head over to Weybourne,' he said.

'No, Tim. Get these two home first. Gaia will be worried sick,' Eve said.

More debris hit the side of the van. Myrtle watched a flock of seagulls struggle to fly against the wind, now wild and swirling around them.

'Did you hear of a storm coming?' Eve said to anyone who was listening.

'No. I didn't,' Myrtle said, still feeling strange and only partially awake, something was draining her body and no matter how hard she tried to fight it, she failed. A pain leeched across her brow, and her left eye ached. She wondered if she was having a stroke.

'If Marigold had been here, she would have known. She would have predicted it and laughed at us going out expecting it to be all sunshine and daylight. I bet my last penny on it,' Eve said, and Myrtle appreciated her attempt at lightening the worried atmosphere.

A trampoline crash-landed on a bus stop, and Tim had to swerve around them both.

'Bloody hell, where the fudge cakes did that come from!' he shouted. 'Sorry, Nan, sorry, Myrtle.'

'Swear away, lad, I'm coming up with a few new ones myself,' Eve replied. 'You okay, Myrtle. You're awfully quiet.'

Myrtle gave a nod.

'Nearly there, Gran,' Summer said as they drove past the corner café and The Ship Inn.

Once they pulled up outside the cottage, Myrtle offered Eve and Tim a bed for the night, but they insisted on leaving for their own home. Summer grabbed their belongings from the back of the van just as lightning illuminated the woods, silhouetting their orchard.

'Get home before the storm gets worse,' Myrtle instructed, 'and thank you for today.'

Without warning, a sharp pain surged through Myrtle's abdomen, and she doubled up with pain. She groaned.

'I'll carry the bags, you get to the door,' Summer instructed. 'Tim, get home. Text me later.' She kissed him. 'Love you.'

Myrtle struggled in pain along the pathway.

A flash of lightning accompanied a fresh crash of thunder as Gaia rushed out from the cottage to help them inside.

'What a night! Oh, you look pale as a ghost, Mum. Are you in pain?' she asked when Myrtle bent over and put her hand to her mid-abdomen. 'Get your coat off. It's soaked through. I'll get the kettle on. This storm is a shocker. We'll stay here the night, we can't travel in this – if that's okay with you.' She looked at her mother.

With a nod, Myrtle agreed. 'Of course, your beds are always made up for you to stay,' she said.

An extra loud clap of thunder made them all jump.

'I think the eye of the storm is above us,' Summer said.

Leaving the others in the kitchen, Myrtle made her way into the sitting room and stretched out on the couch in the hope it would ease the ache in her abdomen. She struggled to her feet just as Gaia entered the room.

'The chickens,' Myrtle said with a sense of urgency, trying to ignore the sudden wave of nausea which hit her.

'Summer checked. They are fine. I've got logs for the fire, and soon we'll be cosier than the fox outside. I wouldn't want to wander around in this!' Gaia turned her attention to drawing the curtains.

'The fox?' Myrtle asked.

Gaia nodded. 'It's been sitting by the apple tree since just before the storm. It's funny how it never worries the chickens,' she said.

Myrtle shivered. This was not a natural storm. The vixen

had come to warn her of danger. Ancestor Willow was nearby watching over them.

'Leave the curtains open,' she said, as she pointed to the window opposite the sofa. 'I like to see a storm. It reminds me of how vulnerable we are, and the power of Mother Nature.'

As Myrtle watched the lightning flash across the sky, a new sense of dread and anxiety alternated with the nausea. She had felt it once before when she'd had her first contraction with Gaia. She went to the kitchen and snatched down a jar of dried nettles from the shelf and poured some into a dish. She placed it on the table, picked up her besom and swept some into each corner, then sprinkled them onto the windowsills.

'What are they for?' Gaia asked.

'Nettles, ash and charcoal to fend off the lightning from striking the cottage,' Myrtle said as she walked back into the sitting room. Without warning, her pained body shuddered, and she broke out into an uncomfortable sweat.

'I think I'll head to my bed,' she said.

'Are you sure you're okay?'

'Tired. It's been a busy day,' Myrtle replied, dismissing Gaia's concerns.

Across the room, she heard Summer whispering to Tim on her phone and called out goodnight.

Worn out, she climbed into bed and relaxed into the mattress. Despite the constant tap of the raindrops on the window and her discomfort, she drifted off to sleep.

She woke pain-free in the early hours of the morning

and was relieved to find the storm had subsided. Quietly, she climbed from her bed, pushed her feet into her sandals and tiptoed downstairs. The cottage was silent, and she stepped out into the garden where the air cooled her skin. Suddenly, her skin prickled, and her body itched. The pain in her abdomen returned. She looked for the vixen but could not see her.

A flash of lightning zigzagged across the horizon and another wave of dread washed over her. The storm turned and headed back – this was certainly no ordinary storm.

Instead of going back inside, Myrtle walked towards the Tree of Life, the drive to get to the tree became more urgent with each flash across the sky, and she increased her speed, stumbling against fallen branches on the way.

Night sounds had never worried her in the past, but tonight each rustle and fox scream made Myrtle twitch and jump. Her nerves were on fire.

As she approached the clearing, even the Tree of Life appeared ominous, as if it had taken on a new persona – never had she been scared of approaching the tree, but in that split second she hesitated, ready to return home. The faint voices returned, a muddle of hisses and misheard words and Myrtle struggled forward, not prepared to bend to whatever attempted to control her body and mind.

A feeling of someone watching her halted her next step. Breathless and surrounded by fresh woodland chaos, she became more convinced it was an entity.

It was tall with its outstretched arms as if it were impersonating a tree's upward-reaching branches. With a flapping frenzy, Ragnis flew to sit on a large moss-covered concrete pillar beside Myrtle, startling her. It was too late for him to be active, especially in the height of the storm.

'Go home, Ragnis. Watch over the cottage,' she whispered, and Ragnis cocked his head.

'You are in danger, Myrtle!' The voice of her mother rang out around her. Ragnis channelled the warning.

'Go, watch over Gaia and Summer!' she said, and with his familiar call, Ragnis did as asked.

Myrtle touched the tree's trunk and felt nothing. No warmth or vibration greeted her or reassured her that all was well. At speed she called out the names of the Netherwell women, but only one replied – a male voice.

'Your time has come!'

The words resonated around Myrtle in a continuous echo and sent uncomfortable vibrations inside her head. She clamped her hands over her ears and dropped to her knees.

The voice continued to yell out around her, and Myrtle only lifted her head when a shadow crossed her feet. She hoped someone had arrived to save her.

Instead, her twin's dark outlined image stood over her, and it swayed with the wind. Behind Marigold, Myrtle saw another shadow, larger and darker. Their father had made his move and trapped Marigold into his cold dark world. Together they were battling against the sisterhood and Myrtle.

Chapter Thirty-Five

'I control the Tree of Life now, and you will hear only my voice. Only one Netherwell woman will speak to you again, and my words will bring you to stand on the side of justice.' Marigold's voice rang out.

'Justice? Marigold – Mari – don't listen to them. Stop this war between us!' Myrtle cried out.

Suddenly, the other shadow stepped away from the tree, showing its full form. Myrtle watched in horror as the shadow widened and grew in height. The Longe males were one entity and were using Marigold's powers to reinforce their own.

'Sisters, I call to you. Draw on your powers, take back your energy. Use me as your vessel, give me your anger, your fire!' she shouted at the top of her voice.

More thunder roared and lightning struck a tree to the right of Myrtle. Her own anger rose, and the abdominal pains were back, draining her strength, but she knew she must not let Marigold take control of the genetic flow within her body that they obviously still shared.

'Leave me alone, Mari. Don't let them destroy us,' Myrtle pleaded.

Marigold's form spun around, drawing up a mound of rotting leaves and twigs into a funnel before expelling them out into the wind.

'We are one!'

Marigold's voice screamed into the night.

Her words echoed as the storm she had unleashed continued to swirl around them, angry and dangerous. The forest glowed with crackled lights of energy, bouncing from tree to tree. Lightning streaked across the sky, sending fiery bolts like arrows from a bow.

The fear of losing control overwhelmed Myrtle, prompting her to unleash all her powers as she cried out to the sisterhood, desperately seeking their support.

Still, she heard nothing but the destruction of her precious woodlands. Great mounds of leaves and twigs fell to the floor, before a thick branch from the Tree of Life snapped and fell at Myrtle's feet.

She looked down and took in how close death was and of how weak she was against her sibling and the Longe family.

'I did everything for you, Mari. Find a way of setting yourself free from their hold,' she whispered. Her senses were sent into overload by the musty smell of the woods, unidentifiable sounds, sharp and piercing, filled her ears.

Myrtle dragged herself through the clearing, the

challenging pain inside her was slowing her down. Behind her, Marigold's temper heightened, and inside her head, Myrtle could hear nothing but insults, curses and calls for her to join her sister on the other side. The dark power was sapping her own, and Myrtle feared for her life – and that of Gaia and Summer still asleep. She needed to get back to the cottage, to protect them before it was too late.

Once home, she grabbed a thick skirt and jumper from the airer in the kitchen and pulled on her parka. Drying her feet, dabbing at the blood from snags and scratches, Myrtle pulled on a pair of Summer's bright woollen socks and her wellington boots. She then concentrated on gathering the items she needed to battle with Marigold and defend the Tree of Life.

She filled her pockets with protective herbs and crystals. If she could weaken her sister's magick and hexes, then the storm might dissipate, and the ancestors regain control enough to draw Marigold back into their care.

Once she had filled a large hessian bag with everything she needed, she tied a ready-prepared spell bag for her personal protection over her wrist and once satisfied she could continue alone, Myrtle headed back outside and scattered the contents of her pockets at the door entrance of the woods, blessing the various crystals and herbs with her wand, and salts. Before leaving the garden, she gave the bedroom windows a quick glance and was relieved to see she had not disturbed Gaia or Summer.

I call back my powers.
Protect my home and loved ones.
May the light overcome the dark,
And they live in peace,
So mote it be.

Back in the clearing, Myrtle went to the large stone altar several feet away from the Tree of Life. The storm still raged, though she saw no sign of Marigold. She knew, however, that if the ancestors could not hold her back, she would reappear now that Myrtle had returned.

Unloading her basket, Myrtle pulled out a storm lantern to protect her chosen candle. All items were prepared and cleansed beneath the sun or moonlight, and using the light from the deep purple candle dressed and set for banishment, Myrtle worked quickly.

The time had come to cast spells she'd never dreamed she would have to use against her sibling. She removed her coat and lifted out her priestesses cape, and spent a few frustrating moments wrestling it from the grip of the wind before tying the cord around her neck and waist. She lit a sage stick, and with one hand drew the smoke over her body.

'Beloved Earth Mother and Father Sky. I bring my respect and seek your protection this night. My enemy is of my blood and is part of my spirit. A spirit with evil intent. I ask for peace, understanding, and the strength to release her from my weakening body. I draw on your strength and trust in your healing ways, as I wish it so might it be...' Myrtle chanted her request three times.

Once finished, she moved towards the Tree of Life, blessing her besom as she walked around the trunk.

'Protect the protector. Remove the canker and destroyer of life,' she said, as she swept away an area three times around the base as best she could against the raging wind. She felt the air grow colder and a fresh growl of thunder rumbled in the distance.

Once she had cleared and blessed the tree's roots, Myrtle went to the altar and laid out the crystals she'd brought with her. She held a large, uncut amethyst in her hands and called for love and understanding. Her hands burned hot with each crystal as she held them and asked them to give her all the energy they could offer towards her battle with Marigold.

She sprinkled black salt, crushed with rosemary, and her own blessed cascarilla and eggshell powder into a circle, framing a collection of the dried crushed herbs and plants also used for protection. She mixed angelica, and birch, with dried marigold and milk thistle seeds. Anything she could think of for protection and banishment, and blended them with eucalyptus oil.

The fragrance stirred a determination inside her and Myrtle selected a large bay leaf from her collection and a pen from the basket. With an unsteady hand and poor vision beneath the flame, she wrote the words which broke her heart.

The spell to change her life forever.

Banish Marigold Netherwell from my heart.

Then on parchment she wrote more.

> *Break our blood ties.*
> *Release me, Myrtle Netherwell, daughter of*
> *Moonstone Netherwell, from the bindings of*
> *my sister, Marigold Netherwell.*

Determined not to cry in the knowledge one stray teardrop would give Marigold more power over her, Myrtle laid the leaf in the centre of the circle of herbs. With a cupped hand, she shielded it and set it alight. In a loud voice, she repeated the words on the leaf and paper.

From her bag, she lifted the gold chalice and poured moon-blessed water into it, before chanting the words again. She added mint, rose petals and a carnelian crystal to the water.

With her mind focused on the task, she stirred the mixture three times towards her, then closed her book of spells. Task done, Myrtle clasped the chalice in both hands and held it out to the tree.

'I drink for peace, love and protection. What energies I have, I give to you and my ancestors. May they find courage and banish the negative soul of my twin Marigold Netherwell, who has chosen to follow the dark side of my blood. Banish her from the Tree of Life, from the pain that rages within her heart. So mote it be,' Myrtle chanted.

She kept her voice loud and steady as the storm brewed into something more than grey skies and lightning.

'By the strength given to me by my mother and the women who uphold me, I send you to a world beyond the confines of the veil. I condemn your soul, Marigold Netherwell, to walk alone. For the Longe power inside of you to seep into the depths of a black hole and be starved of the ability to move amongst the stars. You will never see the light of day again. As I wish it, it will be done!'

She sipped the drink, walked to the Tree of Life, and poured the rest around the roots. Her last act was to prick her finger and drip her blood onto the soil. Myrtle had done all she could to protect herself, her child and granddaughter.

Unsure what would happen next, Myrtle settled onto a stone beside the altar.

Trust was now with the unseen.

> *Banish the negative,*
> *Bring me calm,*
> *Sooth my soul with joy,*
> *And keep my heart from harm,*
> *Blessed be…*

Chapter Thirty-Six

The Tree of Life

Marigold Netherwell was cast out into the void. The air crackled with an unsettling scream as she fell through the veil, spiralling into a dimension where time stands still. The demonic forces of the Longe family, who had given over their power to her, no longer exist, their energies drained in the desperate throes of her final battle.

My roots will know peace and stability from this day forward. I feel my power restored each day. No dark shadows wind their way through my branches weakening my connection with the Netherwell women.

As dawn rose across the top of Weybourne village, Myrtle

stretched her arms above her head and looked around at the after-storm mess around the altar.

A branch had fallen across the top, and her offerings were scattered far and wide. Slowly a tip of a sunrise hinted at a better day and Myrtle took a moment to give thanks. Birds sang, and a hare dashed across the meadow opposite. A moment of peace after the battle of wits she had encountered during the night.

After Myrtle had banished Marigold, her sister had whipped up lightning bursts and thunderous rainstorms; she had ranted curses, too. Her anger summoned winds of such incredible speed that Myrtle feared it would uproot the Tree of Life – she guessed that was the ultimate aim of the dark side.

Myrtle's throat was sore from shouting out her protection and banishment spells. She had chanted for over five hours.

Marigold had not held back, cursing Myrtle for many things in their past.

At times Myrtle faltered with her banishment spells, but she knew that in order to survive, something inside her needed to be expelled. Her weakness was the love she had for her sister, but she knew if she held onto that love, then she also held onto Marigold's and the Longes' need for revenge.

Marigold's final scream still echoed in Myrtle's ears, a haunting reminder of the darkness they had faced. But she knew that other sounds – the whispering of ancient spells, the song of the wind through the trees – would soon drown out that memory. As Marigold's energy flickered like a dying flame, Myrtle had felt a surge of triumph pulse through her veins. The air crackled with tension, and then, with a deafening roar, the Longe shadows erupted, a torrent of writhing darkness spiralling towards the black hole behind her twin.

In that moment, the world seemed to pause, then a blinding flash lit the night, illuminating the twisted branches of the surrounding woods and the shadows dissolved like mist under the sun, their guttural wails fading into silence.

Myrtle had stood firm, her heart racing as the remnants of their battle swirled around her, eventually leaving only a charged stillness – a moment of tension.

'There you are!' Summer's voice cut into the softer sounds of the woods now emerging from the previous night.

Myrtle rubbed her hands down her skirt and slipped off her cloak.

'I said to Mum, I wondered if you had got up early to check on the tree and the altar,' Summer said.

With a nod and a smile, Myrtle held out her arms. 'You're a welcome sight. Come here and give me a hug.'

Summer's hair smelled of summer flowers, and Myrtle inhaled the sweet perfume as they embraced.

'How do you feel this morning? Pain gone?' Summer asked.

'I'm tired but feeling better. It's been a restless night. A long one,' Myrtle said.

Marigold Netherwell
Born 1962 – Died 2023

Myrtle looked down at the plaque bearing her sister's name. She stood alone and in silence. Marigold had left her. Her spell had worked, and she no longer felt any attachment to her twin. Two weeks had passed since she endured the worst night of her life.

That morning, she commemorated her sister on the edge of the circle with the plaque facing outwards towards the woods, well away from the Tree of Life, out of respect for the tree and her ancestors.

She closed her eyes against the sunlight, and as she delighted in its warmth, she smelled the gentle, soap-like fragrance of lily of the valley.

'Who's there?' she whispered.

A soft rustle nearby disturbed the silence, but Myrtle dared not open her eyes. Something brushed across her face but did not frighten her, and she remained still, waiting for the next connection.

They came one by one, each whispering their name. Her ancestors had overcome the trauma. Then came her mother's tender voice with its familiar Norfolk twang – a comfort blanket woven with love.

'Myrtle. I only have a short time. Listen carefully. The Tree of Life granted us passage for a short time. The tree is recovering, and we survived. Marigold tormented me from the day she was born. She suffered a tortured soul, as did your father. She is with him now, in a place you will never see, my child. His ancestors were the persecutors of those brave Netherwell women of our past; his blood was tainted with a lust for a side of life I never understood. Be brave, my darling girl. Trust in the good. Embrace the love of those around you. Go tell your story.'

Chapter Thirty-Seven

Calling on the coven members the following day, many hours were spent clearing the woods.

Myrtle noted that the Naturally Netherwell unit was thankfully unscathed, but the barn had lost a piece of felt roofing. On their arrival, Harry and Tim set out to repair any damage they encountered.

As the sun dipped lower in the sky, casting a warm golden glow across the garden, Myrtle settled into a comfortable chair beneath the arching branches of the apple tree. The table before her was laden with treats.

Despite the exhaustion from the physical nightmare of the previous night and the hours of baking and preparation that afternoon, a sense of joy, of renewal, bubbled within her. She took a moment to breathe in the sweet air and listened as people laughed around her.

This impromptu gathering wasn't just a feast, it was a celebration of her journey into this new role, the mantle of becoming the new living matriarch of the Netherwell family resting comfortably on her shoulders. She embraced the moment, feeling the weight of her responsibilities transform into something beautiful, a legacy of love and togetherness.

With a gentle smile, Myrtle stood and began to arrange the flowers from her garden into a centrepiece. She could hardly wait for the evening to unfold, knowing that every bite shared and every story told would weave them all closer together, creating a tapestry of memories that would last for years to come.

After Gaia, Summer and Tim had left to spend the night at Eve's, Harry remained to help with the last of the washing up.

'Lucy told me you were up early checking on the animals and the woods. You should be more careful, it could have been dangerous for you,' he said as they worked together.

Myrtle suppressed a giggle. If only he knew.

'Oh, I was careful, but it's kind of you to care so much, Harry,' she replied. 'Let's leave these to soak. Fancy a nightcap?' she asked.

'Now you're talking,' Harry said with a smile.

Seated in the sitting room lit only by candles, Myrtle felt calm. Something had changed in her unseen surroundings. Inside the cottage, there appeared to be a shift in atmosphere, and she frowned to herself. She walked to the walls of the room and touched them; they were still warm, and the vibrations of the cottage still shimmied through her hands, but there was a sensation of excitement.

Harry sat himself down on the sofa and poured a bottle of stout into two glasses.

'Are they falling?' he said and held out Myrtle's glass.

She laughed.

'No, they appear to be stronger than ever. Warm and inviting,' she said, accepting the glass.

Harry leaned back in the seat and crossed one leg over the other.

'There's a lighter atmosphere here than the one I experienced when I last visited you. Even old Nightshade here is snoozing. The cottage and woods attract freak weather and vibes,' he said.

'And strange men,' Myrtle said, laughing and raising her glass of stout. 'Cheers.'

'There's definitely a calmer atmosphere. Maybe it's just because we are both more relaxed around one another again,' Harry said.

Myrtle shifted closer to him on the sofa.

'Maybe, but it's okay to say it's because Marigold is not here; she filled the place with her mess and bad moods,' she said.

'And did her best to push us apart,' Harry said, and Myrtle noticed his cheeks flush.

'Whatever bound me to Marigold left my body after the storm, but I still have something to offload. I'm not sure when it will happen, but it will, and then I can truly move on with my life,' she said and took a large sip of her drink.

Harry yawned. 'Right, well, I'm off, it's been a long day, and I don't want to be around when the indoor fireworks start,' he said and let out a belly laugh.

His laugh filled the room, and Myrtle felt its vibrations bounce from the walls and into her chest. The cottage had never had residential male voices or laughter inside. She looked at Harry and she could not have loved him more.

'Come tomorrow and help eat the leftovers?' she asked.

Harry kissed her cheek. 'You bet,' he said, and when the door closed behind him Myrtle let out deep sigh.

Nightshade stretched and gave a mew.

'I know, I know. I have to work on my chat-up lines,' she said, laughing, and as she climbed the stairs to bed, she knew her challenges were not over, she had one more hurdle to jump.

The following morning, after a good night's sleep, Myrtle woke up to a glorious spring day and realised she had nothing to do except clear her breakfast things away.

For Myrtle, today was a big day, and she had plans.

Looking through her crystal collection, she selected several to recharge in moon water, after which she dressed a yellow candle designed for communication and unity.

When she lifted out various items from her box of craft stash to make good luck charms, her hand brushed over the piece of twine Marigold had once rescued from a tree in the garden. She lifted it out and held it in her hands.

It felt cold and had nothing to offer her, but like

anything linked to Marigold she came across, it unnerved her and needed removing for good. Lifting out her small cauldron used for ceremonial burning, she placed the twine inside along with a bird feather. She placed a sage leaf and wrote on a bay leaf the words *expel negativity* and set fire to them all. Standing on the back step, she watched the smoke swirl away from the home and disappear down the front lane towards the coastal path. Satisfied the task was complete, she went back inside to finish her preparations.

A cheerful whistle filtered through the window and drowned out the moan of the mild breeze blowing through the slight opening, which was used to air the room. Harry had arrived early.

'Just come to help with the animals, I'll start with the goats,' he called out through the back door.

Myrtle hurried to the door and pulled it back open before he disappeared into the barn.

'Morning, Harry!' she called out and gave him a wide smile.

Harry gave her a wave. 'Morning. You are a cheery one today. Won the lottery?' he asked with a laugh.

Myrtle grinned. 'After you've fed that lot, do you have five minutes? I need to speak with you,' she said.

'Does it come with a cup of your honey and ginger tea?' Harry asked.

'And a slice of my lemon cake,' Myrtle replied.

'Then I'll give you ten minutes of my time, boss,' Harry said and laughed loudly.

As Myrtle told Harry the story of her past, she watched him nibble and pick at his generous-sized slice of cake. Not once did he frown. His expressions were of concern and compassion. His soft, encouraging smiles touched her, and at no point did he make her feel cheap, foolish or crazy.

During her preparation for the room-cleansing ritual that morning, Myrtle had decided she wanted a stronger relationship with Harry, and the only way it could happen was if she told him her secret.

Before he could comment on her first story, she launched into the nightmare of the Longe family, banishing Marigold and what that had entailed.

'As you can imagine, it's been exhausting keeping my secret, but it's out there now, the most important people in my life know everything,' Myrtle said.

Washing down his cake with the last of his tea, Harry licked his lips with satisfaction and wiped them dry with his napkin before speaking.

'If I am honest, I don't know what to say to you other than I will always be your friend and listen. Your life has been tied to the past for too long,' he said and stood up.

Myrtle looked up at him, and he gave a gentle smile that gave her courage.

'I'd like us to be more than just friends, Harry. To spend time together and—'

Harry leaned down and kissed her – not a kiss on the cheek, but a firm, loving one on her lips.

When they broke apart, both breathless and warm, Myrtle looked up at him.

'I fell in love with you the first time I met you, and when Mel captured your heart, mine broke,' she said, surprised she had found her voice at last.

'Mel was because I couldn't have you,' he said, gazing at her. 'I needed a distraction. She knew I loved you – I even told her that once.'

'Can you forgive me for not telling you about Dan and my baby?' Myrtle asked, her heart thumping in her chest.

'What is there to forgive? It is private to you. You had good reasons to protect yourself. I don't profess to understand your witchy ways, and I am grateful for your friendship over the years. What I want now is for us to work out what we want for the future. We'll never forget the past; it is part of who we are, but we can put the sadness in a box and release the happiness we both deserve.'

'Where do we begin?' Myrtle asked.

Harry looked around the room.

'I hope those walls can't see,' he said, kissing her again. Myrtle felt the deep passion in his kiss and held him tight, making up for wasted years. She relaxed into his kiss, then led him by the hand to the foot of the stairs.

'Let's turn back the clock and enjoy candy-floss kisses upstairs,' she whispered.

Chapter Thirty-Eight

2023

'I'll never forget your birthday. What a party we had, and typical of you to turn it into an engagement celebration for Summer and Tim. Selfless, that's what you are, gal,' Harry said as he turned over soil ready to plant new vegetables.

'I don't need birthday parties, and besides, Summer and Tim deserve to be celebrated. I'm an excited grandmother now that the wedding is nearly here. May Day and the party seem ages ago.'

'I thought you didn't like weddings – you didn't like mine,' Harry teased her, with a grin.

'I do, Harry. You know I do,' Myrtle said, laughing.

Harry stabbed his fork into the ground and stood with one hand on his hip and his foot on the base of the fork.

'Hold your horses, gal, I've not asked you yet,' he said, laughing.

From the top of her breastbone to her brow, Myrtle could feel the flush of embarrassment rise.

'You daft brush. You know what I meant. Get back to work, then come indoors; I've been baking,' she replied, squeezing his hand.

Harry comically doffed his baseball cap and winked at her.

'I'll not be long,' he said.

His gesture took her back to their college days, and she thought how true love really did stand the test of time.

'Summer looks beautiful. You and Eve did an incredible job with her gown. Thank you, Mum,' Gaia said, as they admired Summer in her wedding dress.

She had opted for a cream satin gown with a long lace waistcoat embroidered with forest animals, trees and flowers. The colours stood out, and Eve and Myrtle were proud of their hard work. Summer's long hair sparkled with crystal accessories, and she wore a fresh floral crown made by her mother.

Her bouquet was formed of flowers and greenery from Plumtree Cottage, and a silver tree bearing a heart with her new name inscribed on it, hung down from it – also made by Gaia. Summer had told Gaia she wanted to remove June from her name as it was a connection to her father, who had chosen it, while her mother had picked Summer. She asked Myrtle if she could use a family name and had this registered by deed poll before she married Tim.

As high priestess, Myrtle was performing the handfast and hoped her tears of joy would be held at bay. Watching Summer walk down the pathway on Gaia's arm brought a scrabble for a handkerchief.

'I bind thee, Summer Moonstone Netherwell, to Timothy Barry Green. Your hands are bound fast to represent the strength of your love for one another,' she said. Then, she invited Gaia and Eve to tie a knot into the ribbons to fasten the couple's hands together.

'May you lead long and happy lives as one; this is my desire, and it is done.'

As they repeated the final cheer for the newlyweds, Mr and Mrs Netherwell-Green, Myrtle's heart swelled with pride and looked forward to spending the evening around the Tree of Life. A tree which now wore handmade rag pompoms, fairy lights and large cut-out leaves, each bearing the name of a Netherwell woman from the past through to Summer. Bunting fluttered amongst the fairy lights and lanterns, and by the time the evening light faded into a navy sky, the clearing looked magical and romantic. Seats were draped with hessian bows and greenery with flowers and petals decorating the base of the Tree of Life and altar. Summer had planned everything; it was all about their family, and a new one was created the second she married Tim. Even the light rain shower at seven o'clock never dampened the atmosphere or the dancing.

As the evening wore on, Myrtle found two seats beneath the tree and beckoned Harry over to sit with her.

'My feet ache,' she said with a giggle.

'I don't dance, so it's my jaw for me. Everyone and his son wanted gardening tips,' Harry said and laughed.

Turning her head towards Harry, Myrtle smiled.

'So here we are, as it is meant to be,' she said.

They leaned back in their seats and held hands as they watched the stars ping their way into position, and the moon, in its waxing crescent stage, sat pretty in the sky.

Myrtle put her nightmares to bed and trusted Harry to keep her safe. She no longer had to be the protector; he had promised to be hers.

Chapter Thirty-Nine

I n December of that year, the air was crisp and biting as Myrtle stepped out into the garden.

'Brrr, it's a chilly one for sure,' Summer said, and Gaia agreed.

'The walk will do us good, warm us up,' Myrtle said. 'Come on.'

Frosted grass crunched beneath their feet, and their breath vapours skipped around them. Once they had reached the Tree of Life, Myrtle busied herself at the altar, clearing and cleaning, refreshing crystals, pinecones, holly, and ivy, and then sprinkling dried rose petals around a large candle burning bright.

Summer and Gaia helped her clear and sweep the tree's base and lay out the new greenery and crystals.

Once satisfied she had achieved all she wanted, Myrtle stood back and checked to ensure everything was ready for the ceremony.

'Perfect,' she said and placing her arms across Gaia and Summer's shoulders, she drew them to her.

'May the day be peaceful and filled with courage and love; I will it so,' she said.

'Blessed be,' whispered Summer.

'So mote it be,' came Gaia's response.

The clearing looked glorious – with winter foliage, encased candles, and hessian and lace bunting hanging from the branches of the Tree of Life.

Holly and Ivy posies were laid out in a circle where the bride and groom would make their vows.

When it was time, Myrtle stepped inside the circle and waited patiently, watching candles flicker amongst the pretty foliage.

Slowly, a procession of excited guests arrived and sat on the white chairs adorned with red or green ribbon, and she greeted each one with a smile. Four large cauldrons filled with logs and pinecones burned around them, and the warmth filtered amongst the grateful family and friends. Myrtle listened to their chatter filter over low harp and flute music played by women of the coven.

Gaia and Summer stood outside the circle, looking towards the lane leading to the area where Ragnis sat on a mossy fence post.

Holding up her hand, Summer gave her grandmother a wave and nod.

Myrtle checked that everything was in place for the ceremony about to take place and removed her priestess cloak.

She smiled at the waiting guests as they commented on her heavily embroidered green velvet dress. The triple moon goddess symbol along the front hem had taken Myrtle a month to sew, but it was a tribute to her mother and had to be perfect. Hidden inside was a tiny marigold flower stitched in a circle of words; what once glowed is now dimmed but never forgotten.

Myrtle had found it easier to forgive Marigold than to remain focused on what her sister had tried to do. Life was short and too precious to waste.

Gaia stepped inside, picked up the cloak, and draped it around her shoulders. Also wearing a green velvet dress, Summer stepped into the circle, placed a large crown of fresh flowers onto Myrtle's head, and fussed around her gown and hair. She kissed Myrtle's cheek and stood to one side. Eve, also dressed in green velvet, stood by the altar holding the ribbons for the handfasting of her two dearest friends.

Even Nightshade played his part and sat on a berry-red velvet cushion beside the wedding rings, enjoying the fuss and attention of the guests.

Soft drumbeats began to play, and Myrtle watched as Harry, looking smart in his green tweed suit, walked towards her. He smiled and held her gaze. Neither of them wanting to miss one moment of their wedding day.

Gaia was now the coven's official registrar and was delighted to accept the honour of marrying and handfasting them. Summer's role was to be the bridesmaid and read a marriage blessing.

As he stepped into the circle, Harry held her hand. Myrtle felt it shake, but she also felt its warmth. He kissed her cheek.

Gaia and Summer carried out their duties and stood back to listen to Myrtle and Harry pledge themselves to one another for the rest of their lives.

'I, Myrtle Netherwell, join my heart with yours, Harry Arthur Tye. May we be blessed with a life worthy of our love for one another. As I, Myrtle Netherwell-Tye, wish it, so it will be done.' She gave Harry an encouraging smile to say his vows and heard the leaves on the tree shimmy, and the ground beneath her feet gave off a gentle vibration. The ancestors had blessed them.

'I promise my intentions are good, my love is true, and we will watch our united families thrive together. I'm a proud man to take on the Netherwell name, for I know the sacrifices made, the strength of the love that binds it and the woman who fought to defend it.

'I, Harry Arthur Tye, take thee Myrtle Netherwell as the woman at my side forever and a day. This is my desire,' Harry said loud and clear.

Myrtle smiled up at him, squeezing his hand, and ensured that her voice was as loud and confident as his.

'As it is mine. You have my heart and soul for all eternity. Blessed be…'

Chapter Forty

Reaching for the new book of voices, Myrtle sat at her desk and took a moment to gather her thoughts. She lifted her pen and began writing.

Merry Meet, and blessings to a fresh page of *The Netherwell Book of Voices* volume II.

My name is Mrs Myrtle Netherwell-Tye, wife of Harry Arthur Netherwell-Tye. Yesterday, we were married beneath the bough of the great oak tree, the Tree of Life, in the village of Weybourne.

Last night, he whispered the word 'wife' into my ear. I have earned another title, making my heart sing loud and clear. I do not need love spells to encourage his embrace, nor do I need to seek out his attention. Harry gives all of himself to me, and I give all of myself to him.

I also write to share news about my granddaughter, Mrs Summer Moonstone Netherwell-Green, and her husband, Timothy Barry Netherwell-Green.

They have expressed a desire to train as a High Priestess and Priest respectively, and create a coven for all sexes. They have purchased a piece of land near Horsford Woods, the original home of our ancestor, Theda, and intend to build a cottage where they can support Mother Nature and enjoy the company of a like-minded community.

They have also shared that they are to be parents, and the scan shows they are to have a son! The curse of Brigid has been lifted. Netherwell women are no longer tied to only giving birth to daughters. A new bloodline free from the clutches of the Longe family fills my heart with joy.

Gaia is content with running Naturally Netherwell, and I am officially retired.

Life has been overwhelming and filled with more drama than most families have to deal with, but it has made me a stronger woman. I no longer doubt my powers or hide my spiritual beliefs. I mourn the loss of my youth but have my twilight years to enjoy.

I will sit back and watch the family flourish until my light no longer shines and I find my place within the roots of the Tree of Life, but until then, I will travel with Harry on our honeymoon; our first trip is to pay homage to the witches executed around Britain and watch the sunset together in gratitude for our fresh start in life.

If my memoir in *The Book of Voices* volume I reads as if I am cold towards the death of my sister, I am not. I light a candle for her every day, but what I cannot do is allow my past to suffocate my present.

I have opened my heart to Harry and received compassion, trust, understanding and love like I have never known.

I live in the light with him at my side.

As I wish it, so mote it be…

The Amber Raven Success and Positivity Spell Pouch

You will need
A small hessian pouch and label.
Blended dried herbs and flowers.
Lemon balm – assists with easing anxiety.
Wood betony – to aid with dispelling negativity.
Holy thistle – Hex breaking – gain blessings.
Dandelion leaf – Helps positivity and inspiration.
Rose petals – for self-love.
Sunflower – for confidence and fertility of the mind.
Mixed with
Black salt (or salt of preference) – for protection.

Stir all in a clockwise direction to encourage the energy to flow your way.
Place inside the pouch with a
Red Jasper stone for creativity and willpower.

Wording for the label

Grant me the joy of success and self-love
As I wish it so
May positivity flow
So Mote it be...

You can keep the pouch with you or hang it in an area where you feel the combination will benefit you.

Blessings and love,

Amber Raven

The Netherwell Book of Voices

(A short extract)

Brigid Netherwell

My mother, Willow Netherwell, gave birth to me in the woodlands surrounding our cottage. I marvelled at her shapeshifting magic and her ability to heal those who sought help at our door.

As I lay giving birth to my child – conceived during the days of Lammas with a kindly farm hand with whom I foolishly lay during harvest – I weakened and heard my mother's voice urging me to fight the darkness surrounding me. I must find my strength and future path to continue our bloodline.

Warmth flooded my veins when I stared, seeking comfort in the moon. The clouds parted, and the stars shone their light so brightly that my beautiful Celeste arrived. We hid in our cottage, away from the threatening world and the men who tainted our souls.

Celeste Netherwell

My mother trusted her neighbour, but I did not; he seduced me beneath the Tree of Life, and then he had me sent away in the dead of night to the other side of Norfolk.

When I returned with my belly full, my feet bleeding and my mind in need of help, my sisters of Weybourne cut my hair and gave me a new name, Star.

He never knew my true identity, or his daughter, Luna, but he knew the sharp end of a knife when he came sniffing at our cottage door in lust when she was but a woman. The blade ensured he could no longer father another, and the banishing spell saw him take his shame to another county.

Luna Netherwell

My mother told me the truth of my conception. She also told me I am the child of Mother Earth and have no need of anyone but her to guide me through the mysteries of life. I failed her after her death and fell for the charms of a cowhand. Like my father, he declared I had cast an evil eye over him. The sister circle hid my shame and taught me the lessons of self-respect and to help heal others. My child Allegra will learn from my mistakes.

Allegra Netherwell

My child is born, but her father will never see her face. Before our hands were bound with the ties of marriage, he was taken to fight a war against our American cousins and never survived. His mother mourned her son and cared for me.

When his child entered the world, she asked me to name her Thomasina, for the father who never returned. I accepted her wishes, and together, we grieved. My mother doted upon us both, and our lives in Weybourne were free from persecution. Her death was a sorrow for me, but I continued to do good in her name and remain content in our ancestorial home, Plumtree Cottage – a poor woman's mansion built with love.

Thomasina Netherwell

My life in Weybourne is a solitary one. I live that way by choice.

There is a tree my mother shared with me. A raven speaks to me of the past and my future. The Tree of Life knows my secrets, and I live by its word.

Beneath its branches, I followed the path of my ancestors and conceived a child out of wedlock. I knew what I was doing, for I cast the spell for a child but not the bindings of a man. Some men can be ignorant of the true witch, and I am not prepared to tread a path where I have to hide my true self.

My daughter, Mystia is a gift, not a secret. She will learn to live and love the woodlands of Weybourne as I do. The cottage is still my home and houses the spirits of learned women – some call them dark witches or evil, but they are pure. I will ensure my child lives graciously and with kindness. I will show her that she can survive with or without a man, but she must choose her partner wisely, or she will lose herself to the dark side of our bloodline. I will protect, but I cannot see the evil; it lurks and waits…

Daisy Netherwell

My mother spoke to me today.

She told me of my gift, of how I am a strong woman, and that I must not allow the disappointment of a broken promise to prevent me from overcoming the shock we both have experienced. There is a baby – a girl – lying swaddled in a wooden crate.

She is sleeping the sleep of a newborn. I am innocent in thought of how she became, and my body trembles. I shake in shock and fear. I cry for my sin. My mother is not angry and says it is the way of the Netherwell witches that we endure and overcome when it comes to nurturing a child without a father. She reassures me I will be the last of those women, that the new century will bring about more acceptance, and men will not be afraid to complete their marriage promises without taking women to their beds before handfasting has come around.

We cast a spell to manifest a good life for the girl we named Rowan and one to grant the ancestors access to her strengths. So, mote it be...

Bibliography

Everyday Folklore by Liza Frank

Wicca by Harmony Nice

The Witches Familiars – Corvids by Rachael Coates

Acknowledgments

Writing this book and getting it to publication has been a challenge of the heart and soul, but it is a thrill to share Myrtle Netherwell's life with you.

Huge thanks to my publisher, Charlotte Ledger, and the editing team for their input, guidance, and patience. I also want to thank everyone who has worked on this book, from cover to sales – you are all superstars!

My thanks to my children for sharing their amazing souls with the world. It is a better place with you and your families in it – I have nothing but love in my heart for you all.

To my family and friends, thank you for always cheering me on.

Thanks to my sisterhood, you are incredible women who have stood beside me for years (you know who you are).

I would like to thank The Wymondham Emporium for housing such inspirational pieces and for making me feel welcome whenever I visit. It is incredible how my credit card appears to come alive each time I visit your magical shop!

To Melanie, The Celtic Witch, thank you for inspiring me and many others daily with your Facebook page.

To Raggy (Ragnis), the raven who visited me with your funny wing and sat watching me through the office window for several years. I miss your call for food. I like to think that the hooded crows who have taken your space on the rooftops are watching over me as you did.

To Mother Nature, thank you for the beauty you show me daily.

The author and One More Chapter would like to thank everyone who contributed to the publication of this story...

Analytics
James Brackin
Abigail Fryer

Audio
Fionnuala Barrett
Ciara Briggs

Contracts
Laura Amos
Laura Evans

Design
Lucy Bennett
Fiona Greenway
Liane Payne
Dean Russell

Digital Sales
Lydia Grainge
Hannah Lismore
Emily Scorer

Editorial
Janet Marie Adkins
Kara Daniel
Charlotte Ledger
Laura Mccallen
Ajebowale Roberts
Jennie Rothwell
Caroline Scott-Bowden
Emily Thomas

Harper360
Emily Gerbner
Jean Marie Kelly
emma sullivan
Sophia Wilhelm

International Sales
Peter Borcsok
Ruth Burrow
Colleen Simpson

Inventory
Sarah Callaghan
Kirsty Norman

Marketing & Publicity
Chloe Cummings
Grace Edwards
Emma Petfield

Operations
Melissa Okusanya
Hannah Stamp

Production
Denis Manson
Simon Moore
Francesca Tuzzeo

Rights
Helena Font Brillas
Ashton Mucha
Zoe Shine
Aisling Smythe

Trade Marketing
Ben Hurd
Eleanor Slater

The HarperCollins Distribution Team

The HarperCollins Finance & Royalties Team

The HarperCollins Legal Team

The HarperCollins Technology Team

UK Sales
Isabel Coburn
Jay Cochrane
Sabina Lewis
Holly Martin
Harriet Williams
Leah Woods

eCommerce
Laura Carpenter
Madeline ODonovan
Charlotte Stevens
Christina Storey
Jo Surman
Rachel Ward

And every other essential link in the chain from delivery drivers to booksellers to librarians and beyond!

YOUR NUMBER ONE STOP

ONE MORE CHAPTER

FOR PAGETURNING BOOKS

One More Chapter is an
award-winning global
division of HarperCollins.

Subscribe to our newsletter to get our
latest eBook deals and stay up to date
with all our new releases!

signup.harpercollins.co.uk/
join/signup-omc

Meet the team at
www.onemorechapter.com

Follow us!
 @OneMoreChapter_
 @OneMoreChapter
 @onemorechapterhc
 @onemorechapterhc

Do you write unputdownable fiction?
We love to hear from new voices.
Find out how to submit your novel at
www.onemorechapter.com/submissions